"I think something has happened to my wife."

A slight shift in the tone of the 911 operator's voice went unnoticed as Clay tried to stay calm.

"Is she there with you now, sir?"

"No. She's not. I just got home from work and found the front door unlocked. There's some stuff spilled and broken in the kitchen, and blood in the bathroom."

"Have you been injured too, sir?"

"No," Clay muttered. "I told you…I just got home."

"Yes, sir. I'm dispatching a unit."

"Okay, thanks," Clay said numbly.

Three police units and a pair of detectives later, Clay was beginning to realize that they were disinclined to look further than him as to a reason for his wife's disappearance. And if they thought he was responsible, then they might quit looking further. They had to find her. There was no life for him without her.

Sharon Sala has a "rare ability to bring powerful and emotionally wrenching stories to life."
—*Romantic Times Magazine*

Also available from MIRA Books and
SHARON SALA

SWEET BABY
REUNION

And watch for Sharon Sala's newest blockbuster
coming November 2000
only from MIRA Books

SHARON SALA

remember me

MIRA

ISBN 1-55166-535-2

REMEMBER ME

Copyright © 1999 by Sharon Sala.

Visit us at www.mirabooks.com

Printed in U.S.A.

Memory is a strange thing. It can often be selective, even deceitful, but I would rather have bad memories than no memories at all.

And so my readers, as you begin this book, think back to your childhood, to the bully who taunted you, or to the best friend you lost, and know that, for whatever reason, their journey through your life is what made you who you are. And if who you are is not who you expected to be, then remember this:

> If you can see colors
> and hear laughter,
> if you can cry tears
> and know joys as well as sorrow,
> then it is enough.
> Forget the past. Turn it loose. Let it go.
> As long as there is a tomorrow, there is hope.

One

"Francesca...come here to me, baby."

Frankie LeGrand was beginning to worry about the darkening clouds, but as her husband's voice wrapped around her, her thoughts shifted. She pivoted, turning her back on the window at which she'd been standing, as well as the view of the storm about to hit their Denver home.

"I think it's going to rain," she said.

"I think I don't give a damn."

Frankie smiled. Clay LeGrand had been her husband for exactly a year and one day—all six feet four inches of him. On most days, he was a law unto himself. It would seem this day was one of those times—and it was part of why she loved him. Clay liked what he liked, and laughed when something struck him as funny, and didn't give a good goddamn what anyone else thought.

She gave him the once-over as he leaned against the doorway, her wifely instincts kicking in to make sure that when he left, he would be prepared for a wet day ahead.

He was ready for work. Blue jeans, a long-sleeved shirt, and, of course, a flannel-lined denim jacket and work boots. His hard hat would be in the truck. As foreman of his father's construction company, it was something he never left home without.

Thunder rumbled overhead, rattling the window behind her. Although the weather was not unusual for an October morning, she shivered suddenly, hugging herself in reflex. Before long it would be winter, and she hated the cold.

"Hey," Clay said. "If you need a hug, let me do that."

"Then hug," she said, and opened her arms.

When his arms wrapped around her, she closed her eyes, savoring the safety of his love. The fabric of his shirt was soft against her cheek as she inhaled slowly, cupping his backside as she pulled him closer.

"You smell good," she whispered.

His voice lowered to a growl. "Francesca..."

"Clay, am I in trouble?"

He grinned. "Why?"

"Because the only time you growl at me is when you're angry."

He frowned. "I am never angry with you and you know it."

She arched an eyebrow. "Well...maybe disturbed is a better word. And don't deny it, because I know you were *disturbed* when you caught the bag boy at the grocery store winking at me last week."

"Damn right," he growled, then scooped her into his arms, kissing her hard all the way to the bed.

"You're going to be late."

Ignoring her warning, he yanked her shirt over her head.

"Clay, what will your dad say?"

"Probably something like, 'Where the hell are my doughnuts?'"

Her laughter shattered about him, causing him to flinch. He loved her so much it scared him. She made him weak, and Clay LeGrand had never been a weak man.

As he wrapped her in his arms, she knew that she was blessed. Clay was diligent to a fault, but a few minutes late would put him in no danger of losing his job, especially if he showed up with a dozen of his dad's favorite chocolate-covered doughnuts.

She savored his kisses, feeling the warmth of his lips against her skin. When the tip of his tongue laved her nipple, she sighed and closed her eyes. For Frankie, Clay was her joy, her reason for living. Raised in an orphanage, she'd been alone in this world—until him. He wasn't just her husband, he was her everything. She cupped his face with her hands, momentarily stopping his excursion.

"Clay?"

He raised himself up on one an elbow. "What, sweetheart?"

"When I was standing at the window..."

He gazed down at her, wondering how something as simple as black hair and brown eyes could be so enchanting in one woman's face.

"What about the window?" he muttered.

"You started to say something to me. What were you going to say?"

"That you looked sexy as hell in my shirt." Then his eyes darkened as he looked at her there beneath him, hair tousled, sleepy-eyed and naked. "But you look even better in nothing."

She arched toward his touch as he stroked the length of her body. His eyes glittered as she grabbed his hand, stilling its journey.

"What?" he growled.

"Take off your clothes and make love to me now, before I die from pure want."

He grinned. That was a request he could easily fill.

Minutes passed. Outside, the storm made good on the promise of rain. Now and then, a hard gust of wind would shatter the rhythm of the raindrops against the windows, but nothing could stop the rhythm of the lovers as they rode out a storm of their own.

The day dragged from one hour to the next. Even though most of the construction on the site was being done indoors, the rain still hampered deliveries. It was too wet to haul Sheetrock, and too wet to finish the roof on the north end of the complex. Clay's dad had gone home at noon, leaving only a skeleton crew, with Clay in charge. By four o'clock, Clay called a halt and sent them home, as well. The delay wasn't crucial. They were several weeks ahead of schedule as it was, and going home early would be good. Maybe he and Frankie would order in a pizza. If the temperature kept dropping, they might even build a fire in the fireplace. Frankie would like that. She hated the cold.

Clay's mind was spinning as he stopped off at the supermarket. He made a dash for the door, splashing through the puddles as he ran, then stopped at a pay phone just inside to see if there was anything she needed in the way of groceries before he went home.

Shivering slightly from the chill, he dropped the coins into the slots, then counted the rings, each time expecting Frankie to pick up. She didn't. He hung up, absently pocketing the coins that the phone had returned as he started toward the back of the store. She was probably taking a shower. You couldn't hear the phone if the shower was running. A few minutes later, he headed back to his truck, a half gallon of Rocky Road ice cream richer than he'd been before he'd gone inside.

It was forty-five minutes after four when Clay pulled into the driveway and parked. The rain was coming down in sheets, almost obliterating his view of their little house. In fact, as he began to gather his things, it almost looked as if there was a wall between him and home. He shuddered, wondering where the thought had come from. Normally, he wasn't the fanciful type. He tucked the sack of ice cream beneath his jacket as he got out of the truck, then made a run for the house. The childish feeling of trying to outrun the rain had him laughing at himself as he loped in the front door.

"Frankie…I'm home!" he shouted, still laughing as he shrugged off his jacket and took off his boots. "Hey, honey! It's me! I brought you a surprise!"

He picked up the ice cream and started toward the kitchen, expecting her to step out of a room—

any room—at any minute. Halfway across the living room, he stopped and turned around, looking back the way he'd just come. The hair rose on the back of his neck as the quiet of the house suddenly wrapped itself around him.

The front door.

It hadn't been locked.

He turned slowly, suddenly aware of the silence. He heard nothing familiar. Not a radio. Not a TV. Not even the sound of running water. Only the downpour on the roof. He clutched the ice cream a little tighter.

"Frankie... Francesca... Are you home?"

No one answered.

As he stood, the cold of the ice cream began soaking through his clothes. He looked down, as if surprised to find that he still held it, and started toward the kitchen.

A clap of thunder rocked the house as he stepped across the threshold, rattling cups in the cupboard across the room. He jumped as if he'd been shot.

"Damn," he muttered, and then headed for the refrigerator. Halfway across the kitchen floor, he stopped again, but not because of the storm. It was the broken coffee cup and the puddle of coffee in which it was lying that brought him up short. Spilling coffee wasn't a big deal. But spilling it and leaving it was. Panic hit, knotting his belly and shortening his breath, until he caught himself gasping for air.

He pivoted sharply and started running, shouting Frankie's name as he went.

Back through the living room.

Down the hall.

Into their bedroom.

The bed was unmade, just as it had been right before he left. He stared at it, remembering the passion of the morning, and trying to reconcile it with the panic he was feeling right now.

The shirt she'd been wearing was on the floor near the closet, as if she'd stood there and changed into something else. None of this was like Frankie. She was neat to the point of aggravation. He shook his head like a man who'd been blindsided and moved toward the bathroom. The smear of blood on the sink stopped his heart.

''Jesus,'' he whispered, and would have gone to the floor had he not backed into the wall instead. ''Oh, Jesus, Jesus, please, no.''

His legs were shaking as he walked back through the house. His fingers were so cold he could hardly feel them, and it took him a moment to realize he was still holding that damned half gallon of Rocky Road.

He started for the freezer when something—call

it instinct, call it a foreboding—told him not to touch a thing other than the phone.

He set the ice cream down on the table, then reached for the cordless phone on the cabinet nearby. He kept telling himself that he was making a big deal out of nothing. That things like this didn't happen to people like them. It wasn't Frankie's day to work, but maybe someone had called in sick at the library. Maybe she'd just left in a hurry.

He punched in the numbers, then closed his eyes and took a slow, deep breath.

"Hello, Denver Public Library, Mary Albright speaking."

He pictured the middle-aged woman with her bright copper hair. "Mary, this is Clay. Is Frankie there?"

"Why, no, dear. She isn't scheduled to work until day after tomorrow."

His hopes slipped a notch. "Yeah, I know," he said. "I just thought...well, that someone might have gotten sick."

"No, dear, I'm sorry. Is everything all right?"

He shuddered. "I don't know."

He hung up in her ear.

Focusing on the next set of numbers, he made the next call, taking comfort in the familiarity of his mother's voice.

"LeGrand residence."

"Hey, Mom, it's me, Clay. Frankie isn't there, by any chance, is she?"

Betty LeGrand frowned. She knew her son too well not to recognize the anxiety in his voice.

"No, she's not. In fact, I haven't talked to her since early yesterday morning."

"What about Dad?"

"Oh, I'm sure he hasn't, either," Betty said. "If he had, he would have—"

"Ask him."

"But Clay, I'm—"

"Dammit, Mom, ask him, okay?"

Betty's heart skipped a beat. "Sure, Clay. Just a minute."

He waited, praying, hoping, telling himself that this was nothing but a bad dream.

"Clay?"

"Yeah, Mom, I'm still here."

"He hasn't talked to her, either."

Clay's legs buckled. It was all he could do to stay upright.

"Okay, thanks, Mom."

"You're welcome," Betty said. "Is there anything we can do?"

"No...at least, I don't think so. Oh, and, Mom..."

"Yes?"

"I'm sorry I snapped."

"That's all right. Should we go looking for her? Do you think she had a breakdown in the truck or something?"

He closed his eyes. He had their only vehicle. "No. I had the truck. Look, I've got to go. I'll call you."

He disconnected once more, then hit the power button again, waiting patiently for the dial tone to come on in his ear. As soon as it began to hum, he made his last call.

"911, what is your emergency?"

"I think something has happened to my wife."

A slight shift in the tone of the woman's voice went unnoticed as Clay tried to stay calm.

"Is she there with you now, sir?"

"No. She's not. I just got home from work and found the front door unlocked. There's some stuff spilled and broken in the kitchen, and blood in the bathroom."

"Are you Clay LeGrand, at 1943 Denver Avenue?"

"Yes."

"Have you been injured, too, sir?"

"No," Clay muttered. "I told you...I just got home."

"Yes, sir. I'm dispatching a unit."

"Okay, thanks," Clay said numbly, unable to believe he'd just made the call.

The 911 operator's voice rose a notch. "Sir, I need you to stay at the address until the officers arrive."

A chill of foreboding swept over him. Without Frankie, where the hell else would he go?

Three police units and a pair of detectives later, Clay was beginning to realize that they were disinclined to look further than him as to a reason for her disappearance. Not only did it make him angry, he was beginning to get scared. If they thought he was responsible, then they might quit looking for her. They had to find her. There was no life for him without her.

"So, Mr. LeGrand, you say the last time you saw your wife was around eight o'clock this morning?"

Clay took a deep breath, willing himself to a calm he didn't feel. The smell of wet clothing and warm bodies was beginning to turn his stomach, and the thought of Frankie somewhere out in this storm was making him crazy. He didn't know where she was, but wherever she'd gone, he knew it was not of her own free will.

"No, that's not what I said, and you know it. I

told you, I didn't leave the house until almost nine."

Detective Avery Dawson glanced at his notebook. "Oh, yes, that's right." Then he looked back at Clay. "But you did say that you normally report to work at eight o'clock."

Clay suddenly snapped. "That's right," he said, and stood up, moving until he was face-to-face with the heavyset detective.

"Look, you son of a bitch. I'll repeat this one more time, and then I'm not going to say it again. I love my wife. Last night was our first wedding anniversary. We spent it in bed. I was late for work because I took her back to bed this morning." Then his voice broke, but his composure did not shatter. "When I left, she was wearing my shirt...and a smile. Do you get my drift?"

One of the assisting officers chuckled beneath his breath. Avery Dawson glared at him, then returned his attention to Clay.

"Yes, Mr. LeGrand. I get your drift. But asking these questions is the only way I can get the answers I need. Do you get mine?"

Clay was so angry he was shaking. "The message I'm getting from you is that you think I'm responsible for Frankie's disappearance, which is real convenient for you. If you decide to pin this on me, your job is over. But that won't find my wife.'' Then he doubled his fists and slammed them on the table between them. ''Don't you understand? Hell yes, I'm mad, and I'm scared to death. If you blame me, you'll quit looking for her.''

Dawson's mind was racing. LeGrand was aggressive. Most times it took several interviews with a spouse before they would get this defensive. Adrenaline surged. He was certain they were on the right track with this man.

''You have quite a temper, LeGrand.''

Clay's voice was suddenly thick with tears. ''I have quite a wife. I want her back.''

At that moment, a crack began to form in Avery Dawson's opinion. There was always the possibility that the man was telling the truth. But damn it, the story was too pat. LeGrand had to know something he wasn't telling. No woman just up and disappeared without someone seeing something. His eyes narrowed thoughtfully. The man was either one hell of an actor, or…he could be telling the truth.

The moment he accepted that fact, the thought crossed Dawson's mind that it was time to think about retiring. There'd been a time in his life when he had not been so jaded about the crimes he investigated. He had to admit that when he'd arrived on the scene, his first instinct had been to suspect the husband. Even after an hour of questioning, his opinion hadn't changed—until now. He'd been looking for reasons to blame LeGrand, rather than looking for clues. Disgusted with himself, and for the job that had hardened him to this degree, Dawson flipped his notebook shut and slipped his pen in his pocket.

"I suppose that's all for now," he said. "We'll be in touch."

Clay threw up his hands in disgust and then reached for the phone and phone book.

"What are you doing?" Dawson asked.

"I'm going to hire a private investigator. I want my wife back."

"If she's been kidnapped, as you seem to believe, you should wait until someone asks for ransom. Getting private security involved in this could screw everything up for your wife."

Clay snorted beneath his breath. "There's not going to be a request for ransom."

Dawson eyes widened. Why would the man know that, unless...

"How do you know that?" he asked.

Clay leaned forward. "You still don't get it, do you? My take-home pay is less than two thousand dollars a month. My wife works part-time at the library. My parents aren't wealthy, and Frankie is an orphan. We don't even own this house. What are they going to ask for? The keys to my eight-year-old truck?''

A flush spread up Dawson's neck. The man was making him feel like a fool. He didn't like the feeling.

''I don't suppose you have any life insurance on your wife?''

At that moment Clay could willingly have decked him. He gritted his teeth, making himself focus on the question instead of the man who'd asked it.

''Actually, the only life insurance in this family is on me. If I die, Frankie would get a half-million dollars. If she dies, I get a broken heart. Now, if you people are through, I've got some calls to make.''

Without waiting for permission, Clay grabbed the phone and stalked out of the room. A couple of the uniformed officers standing nearby gave Dawson a curious look. Dawson glared back.

''Has my partner come back?'' he snapped.

One of them shook his head. ''No, sir. Someone said Ramsey's still canvasing the neighborhood.''

Dawson stalked toward the front door. This whole investigation left a bad taste in his mouth. He was tired of this day and of everyone in it.

As he opened the front door and stepped out onto the porch, a gust of wind blew rain against his pant legs. He was also damned tired of this rain. He stepped back, huddling beneath the small roof as he scanned the block for his partner's car. Finally he saw it at the end of the street. A few minutes later, he saw Ramsey coming out of the house at the end of the block. Dawson waved at him, indicating he was ready to go. Moments later, Ramsey pulled up in front of the house, and Avery Dawson bolted off the porch and into the rain.

"Damnation," Dawson grumbled as he tumbled into the seat, slamming the door shut behind him.

Paul Ramsey grinned. "You won't melt. You're too damned old and tough."

Dawson leaned back in the seat and sighed. "Yeah, I think you might be right."

Ramsey frowned as he pulled away from the curb. "Defeat? At this time of the day? Hell, pardner, we've only been on the job a little over ten hours. The day's still young."

Dawson sighed. "Maybe so, but I'm not."

"What do you mean?"

"I walked into that investigation with prejudice. I'm not proud of that," Dawson said.

"So you think the husband is telling the truth?"

Dawson shrugged. "Maybe...maybe not. Did you get anything?"

"The woman at the end of the block said that, as she was coming home from shopping, a black car with dark windows nearly sideswiped her at the stop sign. She said she thought it had just pulled away from the curb across the street, but she couldn't be sure.''

"I don't suppose she got a tag number?''
Ramsey shook his head.

Dawson sighed. "And why doesn't that surprise me?''

"So what's on the agenda?'' Ramsey asked.

Dawson sighed again. "Verifying LeGrand's statements and praying for leads...and while we're at it, praying that this damned rain lets up. I'm sick and tired of going home with wet feet.''

Clay sat in a corner of the living room, staring out the window into the dark. The house was quiet now. The police had been gone for hours, as had his mother and father, who had arrived soon after the police had left. Their confusion had only added to his panic. Frankie had been his anchor, and her disappearance left him feeling disconnected from reality.

He flinched as wind splattered rain against the windows. It was getting colder by the hour. They were even predicting the possibility of snow.

The squall of a siren suddenly broke into his thoughts, and he pushed himself up from the chair in which he'd been sitting and strode to the door.

A fresh gust of wind blew rain in his face as he stood in the opening, staring into the night. Beneath the streetlights, raindrops glittered like crystal tears, puddling, then flowing swiftly into the gutters. He stepped onto the porch, peering into the shadows as if Frankie might miraculously appear. Except for the rain, the silence was devastating.

He started to shake. This couldn't be real. There had to be some stupid answer to this horrible situation that he hadn't remembered. What if she was lost? What if she was out there—somewhere—trying to find her way home?

He stepped off the porch and into the rain, drawn by the need to find the woman he loved. He'd promised to love her and keep her, in sickness and in health. He'd promised to protect her. A sob crept up the back of his throat. Sweet Jesus. How could he protect her when he didn't even know where she was?

The cold wind blew more rain against his face, stinging his skin and blurring his vision as he walked into the middle of the street. His heart was hammering against his chest; his belly was in knots. It hurt to breathe. It even hurt to think past her name.

Rain plastered his hair to his head like a black skullcap. His clothes were soaked to his skin. He stopped in the middle of the street, staring to his left, then his right. There was nothing between him and oblivion but the goddamn rain. Pain boiled from his belly upward as he threw back his head and screamed out her name.

"Francesca!"

Then he held his breath, praying for the sound of her voice. It never came.

Two

Denver, Colorado: Two years later

The October rain hammered on the top of Clay LeGrand's hard hat as he tossed his tool belt in the front seat of his truck.

"That's it for the day, men. Pack it in. We can't do anything further until this rain lets up."

The men grumbled as they headed for their trucks, but they knew their boss was right. Working in weather like this upped the risk of on-the-job accidents, and none of them wanted to be on the downside of a hospital bed.

Clay glanced back at the building site one last time, then got in his truck. Being the boss was a lot different than being foreman. Different set of headaches. Different set of rules. But buying out his dad had also been the saving of his sanity.

He started the engine and then backed up, pausing one last time to give the work site a final once-over. Everything seemed to be in place. With a sigh, he put the truck in gear and drove out of the area toward the nearby freeway.

The last twenty-four months had been months of rehabilitation, both for him and the company. But, during that time, he'd also been hounded by the police, vilified by the press and pretty much branded a killer by society in general, even though there had been no proof to back up the facts.

A woman had gone missing, and someone had to be blamed. The husband—in this case, Clay— was the obvious choice. The fact that the light had gone out in his world didn't seem to matter to any- one except him, and, of course, his parents. Public opinion had branded him a man who'd gotten away with murder. He'd become bitter and, for the most part, hardened to it all. Only now and then did something happen that got under his skin, and when it did, he was always surprised by the onset of fresh grief. As hard as he had tried to get on with his life, until he had some sort of closure, it would never happen.

Now that his mind was forced to consider some- thing other than work, he dreaded going home. Truth was, it wasn't much of a home anymore, just the place where he slept. His parents had been try- ing to get him to move for months now, but he couldn't bring himself to do it. That little frame house was the last place he'd been happy. It was the last place he'd seen Francesca. He wasn't at the point in his life of being able to give up the connection.

In the last two years, he'd spent more hours viewing unidentified bodies in morgues across the country than he cared to remember. After the third time he'd been called to make an identification, something inside him had died. He continued to make the journeys when the calls came in, but with less and less vigor. It was almost as if Francesca LeGrand had never existed. And except for a small album of wedding pictures and the hole her absence had left in Clay's heart, even he would have believed it was so.

Up ahead, a fire truck sped through an intersection, sirens going full blast. Clay watched until it was nothing but a streak of color disappearing through the gray downpour. He frowned. It seemed odd to think of things burning in this deluge, but he knew stranger things had happened. Like people disappearing without a trace.

A short while later, he turned down his street. The moment his gaze fell on the small frame house, his belly started to knot. It was always the same. And it didn't help that last week, which would have been their third wedding anniversary, had been marked by a local television station as the two-year anniversary of Francesca LeGrand's disappearance. Some small-minded producer who seemed better suited to tabloid journalism than responsible reporting had seen fit to dredge up the old story, along with an update on Clay LeGrand's life. The impression that young and handsome Clay LeGrand was happy and prospering with his up-and-coming company, while his wife's disappearance had gone unpunished, had been impossible to miss. They still blamed him. So what else was new?

He pulled into the driveway of his house and parked. For a while, he just sat, listening to the rain hammering against the roof. Maybe they were right. She'd been his wife. He hadn't been able to protect her. If someone had to take the blame, it might as well be him.

"Hell," he muttered, and got out on the run.

By the time he got to the porch, he was soaked. He unlocked the door, still dreading that first moment of entry.

The house.

It was always so damned silent.

And then he was inside, turning on lights, as well as the television, adding a pretense of normalcy to his existence. He tossed his keys on the hall table and then looked around on the floor for the mail that was usually there, compliments of the mail slot in the front door.

It was missing.

Frowning, he turned to see it stacked in a neat pile on the end of the couch, then shrugged. Even though he had a cleaning service, Betty LeGrand often felt the need to oversee their work.

After giving the stack of letters a quick glance, he headed for the kitchen. A hot cup of coffee sounded good, and it would take some of the chill from his bones.

As he began to fill the carafe with water, he noticed a dirty plate and fork in the sink and grinned to himself. His mother had eaten that last piece of cherry pie. Damn. He'd been thinking about that off and on all afternoon.

Then he shrugged off the thought and finished making the coffee. A piece of pie was the least of his troubles. With the coffee in progress, he headed for the bedroom. Maybe a hot shower and some dry clothes would change his attitude. The television was blaring as he walked back through the living room. He picked up the remote just as the broadcast of the local news began.

"Repercussions from the earthquake that struck southern California at noon yesterday are still being felt. Transportation is difficult, both in and out of the state. Some airlines have resumed service, but travel into the area is being discouraged at this time. At this hour, the death count is rising, with many still unaccounted for.''

Clay frowned, then hit the down arrow on the remote. When an old rerun of *I Love Lucy* appeared on the screen, he upped the volume and tossed the remote on a nearby chair as he headed for his room.

In the act of unbuttoning his shirt, he noticed mud on his boots and paused, hoping he hadn't left a trail of it behind him. The floors were clean. Just to make sure they stayed that way, he leaned against the wall and took off the boots, first one, then the other, carrying them with him as he entered the bedroom.

He automatically glanced toward the bed, and he frowned as he noticed the jumble of covers. He could have sworn he'd made it before he left. But as he continued to look, the covers suddenly moved, revealing a dark head and a long, slender arm. He took a sudden step back. His belly lurched, and he closed his eyes.

''Sweet Jesus...I don't need this.'' He took a deep breath.

He looked again, certain the ghost he'd just seen would be gone. He was wrong. It—*she*—was still there.

Completely shaken by the image of Francesca asleep in his bed, he let the boots he'd been holding slip from his fingers to hit the floor with a thump.

At the sound, the ghost rolled over slowly, opening her dark eyes and smiling at him with that sleep-sexy grin he knew so well.

"Hi, honey," Frankie said, and then glanced toward the window. "My goodness, is it still raining?"

Staggering backward, he grabbed at a wall for support. He'd known for months that he was operating on guts alone, but he'd never thought he would lose his sanity. Not this completely.

"Francesca?"

His soft whisper barely stirred the air. He couldn't bring himself to say her name again for fear she would disappear. Then something clicked, and his heart started pounding. What if she was real? As soon as he thought it, he discarded the notion. It was impossible.

He watched her roll over to the side of the bed, then sit up. As she did, she turned pale, reaching toward the side of her head and frowning.

"Oooh, that hurts," she said.

"Frankie?"

She shook her head, as if trying to clear her thoughts.

"Clay, sweetheart, you're soaked. Why don't you get a hot shower while I start dinner?"

Clay walked across the room like a man in a trance. When she stood, he felt an overwhelming urge to turn and run. And then she suddenly swayed on her feet and sat back down on the bed with a thump.

"I don't feel so good," she said. "My head is swimming."

But Clay wasn't listening. He was in shock. Tentatively, he reached forward, expecting to feel nothing but air. Instead, his fingers curled around her wrist, absorbing the warmth of her skin.

"Sweet Jesus," he whispered again, and grabbed her by the shoulders.

"Frankie... Frankie...my God, you're real."

She frowned. "Have you been drinking?"

He couldn't answer. Instead, he slid onto the bed beside her and pulled her close, rocking her in his arms where they sat.

And then reality hit, and as suddenly as he'd held her, he thrust her away. His voice was low and shaking as he focused on her face.

"Where the *hell* have you been?"

She stared. "You *have* been drinking."

Clay stood abruptly. "I want answers, Francesca."

Frankie frowned. "Answers to what?"

He stared at her as if she'd lost her mind. "For

starters, answers as to where you've been for the past two years."

Something skittered through her mind. Something dark—something frightening. But it was gone before it became solid thought. Before she could answer, Clay suddenly grabbed her arms. Pain shot up her elbows as he yanked her close. She gasped. Stunned by his behavior, she missed the shock spreading across his face.

Clay felt numb. The needle tracks on her arms were impossible to miss.

"Drugs? You've been doing drugs?"

She looked at him as if he'd gone mad. "What are you talking about?"

"This!" he yelled, and turned her arms so that her hands were palms up.

She looked down, frowning at the faint bruises still evident on her skin. Again something pulled at her memory, and again it was gone before she could focus. She rubbed her fingers across the tracks, stunned by their presence. When she looked up, there were tears in her eyes.

"I don't do drugs. You know I don't," she muttered, and then closed her eyes as the room began to spin.

"Then explain these," he growled, yanking both arms toward the bedside lamp.

She groaned. The pain in her head was increasing, as was the nausea. She pulled away from his grasp, clutching her head with both hands.

"I don't feel good, Clay."

He was shaking so hard he couldn't think.

"Hell, Francesca, neither do I. You disappear out of my life for two goddamn years, and then you waltz back into it, talking about wet clothes and cooking dinner as if you'd never been gone. Have you lost your mind?"

She couldn't do anything but stare. He wasn't making sense. Two years? Why did he keep harping about two years? He'd only been gone a few hours. But before she could pursue the issue, the room started to spin.

Clay saw her lose focus. He was grabbing for her as she started to slump. Within seconds, he had her back on the bed and was dialing 911.

"What is your emergency?" the dispatcher asked.

For a second Clay didn't know how to answer. A wife had come home. A missing woman had been found. And then reality surfaced, and he blurted it out.

"My wife just passed out. I don't know what's wrong, but I think it might be an overdose of drugs. Please...I need help."

"Sir...is she breathing?" the dispatcher asked.

Clay leaned down, feeling the soft ebb and flow

of her breath against his cheek. As he did, tears sprang to his eyes.

"Yes, yes, what do I do?"

His hands were shaking as he followed her instructions.

Ah God, don't let her die. Not here. Not now. Don't give her back just so I can watch this happen.

A few minutes later, he became aware of sirens.

"I hear the ambulance," he told the dispatcher. "I need to go let them in."

The dispatcher hung up, and the moment the connection was broken, he began to panic. He bolted to his feet and dashed toward the front door, waving frantically as the paramedics came running toward the house in the rain.

His panic increased as he watched them taking her vitals, listening to a jargon he only half understood. When they loaded her onto a stretcher and started out of the house, all he knew was that he couldn't let her disappear. Not again.

"Please, let me go with her," he begged.

"Sir, there's just not room."

"Where are you taking her?"

"Mercy Hospital. You can follow us there."

Clay ran back in the house and grabbed his coat and keys. He was halfway out the door when it dawned on him he wasn't wearing shoes.

"No," he groaned, and headed back to the bedroom. His hands were shaking as he sat down to put sneakers on. And then it occurred to him that he was going to need backup.

He grabbed the phone and dialed. He was so shaken that when his father answered the phone, he wasn't sure he could even make sense.

"LeGrand residence."

"Dad, it's me, Clay."

"Oh, hi, son. Shut 'er down early, did you? Say...why don't you come over for dinner. Your mom made pot roast. Your favorite."

"Dad, I need you and Mom to get to Mercy Hospital as soon as possible."

Winston's heart skipped a beat. "What's wrong?"

"Francesca...she came back. She was asleep in my bed when I got home. Something's wrong with her. The ambulance is already gone. I'm on my way to Mercy now."

There was a moment of stunned silence. "Holy mother of... We'll be right there," Winston said.

Clay started to hang up when another thought came. He got another dial tone and made another call. He knew the number by heart. Only this time it was out of self-defense, rather than consideration. He glanced nervously at his watch as he waited for someone to answer. Already four minutes had passed since the ambulance had left. He was starting to hang up when a man's voice came on the line.

"Third precinct, Dawson speaking."

Clay gripped the phone a little tighter. "Detective Dawson, this is Clay LeGrand. If you're interested in closing the file on my wife's case, then I suggest you get to Mercy Hospital right away."

Avery Dawson pulled himself up from a slouch. "What are you implying?" he asked.

Suddenly, the years of anger boiled over. "And while you're at it," Clay snapped, "why don't you call the television stations and the newspapers and every other goddamn member of the media who's been trying to hang me for the last two years."

"Is this a confession?" Avery snapped.

"You could call it that," he said.

"Be there in ten," Avery said.

The line went dead in Clay's ear. He dropped the receiver back into the cradle and headed for the door.

"Did he really say he was going to confess?" Ramsey asked.

Dawson glanced at his partner and then back at the road. Driving this fast in this kind of weather was risky, but he couldn't get over the notion that if he delayed, Clay LeGrand would change his mind about the call he'd just made.

"He said I could call it a confession," Dawson muttered, and then quickly braked as the car ahead of him suddenly hydroplaned and spun out into the center median.

"Shoot, that was close," Ramsey muttered, and tightened his seat belt.

Dawson glanced in the rearview mirror. "Looks like they'll be needing a tow. Call it in."

Ramsey nodded and proceeded to notify dispatch. The flashing blue light on the dash of Dawson's car illuminated the strain on his face. The disappearance of Francesca LeGrand had eaten at him in a way few of his cases ever had. From the start, he'd felt frustration at their lack of clues. And, in spite of months of dogged investigation, he still had not been able to uncover enough to convince the district attorney to take Clay LeGrand to trial. Just thinking about LeGrand's call made him jumpy. He didn't trust the offer. He'd gotten away with the crime. Why confess to it now?

"There's the hospital," Ramsey said, pointing to the stoplight up ahead.

"Yeah, I see it," Dawson muttered, and took the turn on a yellow light. As he did, Clay LeGrand's company truck suddenly appeared in front of them.

"Hey, there he is!" Ramsey said, pointing.

"I see him, " Dawson said.

They pulled into the emergency-room parking lot almost in tandem. Clay was out of the truck and running toward the doors before Dawson could unbuckle his seat belt.

"He's in an awful big hurry for something," Ramsey muttered.

They followed, running through the rain and splashing water up over their shoes. By the time they got inside, they were soaked.

To their surprise, Clay LeGrand's father was waiting for them by the door.

"Detectives. Follow me."

Both men looked startled. What was LeGrand playing at?

"Look, Mr. LeGrand, we came to talk to your son, and we'd rather talk to him out here."

Winston shrugged. "Suit yourself. But if you want to know the truth, follow me."

He turned and started down a hall toward a cluster of chairs, where his wife was waiting for him to return.

"Hey, there's LeGrand," Ramsey said, pointing past Winston to a man leaning against the wall.

Moments later, the two old adversaries were once again face-to-face.

"So, LeGrand, what do you have to say?"

Clay's expression was blank as he pointed into the doorway. "Gentlemen, I'd like to introduce my wife, Francesca LeGrand. Sometime today, she showed up at the house, a little the worse for wear. She passed out while we were talking. The doctor is still examining her, but the needle tracks on her arms are a pretty good sign of what's wrong."

Ramsey pushed past Dawson, who was staring in shock at the woman stretched out on the examining table.

"Is this a joke?" Dawson snapped.

Clay stared at the detective as if he'd just lost his mind. "Do you see me laughing?"

Dawson and Ramsey moved past the trauma team for a closer look at the woman on whom the doctors were working.

Pain was roaring through the tunnel in Frankie's mind. From a distance, she thought she could hear Clay's voice, but she couldn't focus on the words long enough to understand what he was saying. She turned her head in his direction, giving the detectives a clear view of her face.

"Holy mother of God," Ramsey muttered, and made the sign of the cross, while Dawson just stared.

Betty LeGrand stood up from where she was sitting.

"Yes, this is a miracle, isn't it?"

"Looks like," Dawson said, and moved away.

Betty put her arms around Clay. He looked stunned, almost as if he didn't know what to do next. She took him by the hand.

"Clay, sweetheart, come sit down by me," she said softly.

At the sound of her voice, he blinked and then focused.

"Thanks, Mom, but I don't think I could sit still."

She patted his arm and then sat down by Winston, taking comfort in his presence, as she'd done so many times over the years. In spite of what was happening, there was something about Frankie's condition that didn't add up. She'd never seen anyone who'd overdosed before, but she'd read about it, and some of these symptoms didn't fit.

Meanwhile, Dawson turned to Clay, still suspicious of this miraculous reappearance.

"Where the hell has she been?" Dawson asked.

Clay's eyes darkened angrily as he pointed back into the room.

"You tell me," he said. "She wasn't wearing those on her arms when she left."

Dawson looked again, this time focusing on the bruises and needle marks on Frankie's arms.

"Well, I'll be damned," he muttered.

Ramsey glanced at his partner, then shoved his

hands in his pockets. "Look, Mr. LeGrand, I'm sorry we were so tough on you, but you know how things looked."

Clay stood. "Yeah, I know how things looked from my side of the fence, too."

Dawson had the grace to flush. He extended his hand. "For what it's worth, I'm sorry."

In the examining room, Frankie suddenly moaned and then screamed, as if she was in terrible pain.

Clay's heart skipped a beat. He was inside the room before they could stop him.

"What's happening?"

"Sir, please wait outside," a nurse said, and started pushing him out of the room when Frankie suddenly jerked.

"Look out for that bus!" she moaned.

An alarm began to beep. Clay looked frantically at Frankie, and at the machines surrounding where she lay. Before he could focus on which one had gone off, they had pushed him out of the room.

Three

The hospital room was quiet, unlike the busy corridor outside Frankie's door. Clay stood with his back to the window, staring down at his wife. She had yet to regain consciousness. Any anger he'd felt at what he viewed as betrayal had long since turned to worry. No matter what she had done, he could never wish her ill. He loved her. Would always love her. Even if that love hadn't been enough to make her to stay.

He sighed, letting his gaze rake her features. Her heart-shaped face, the straight, perfect nose, that wide, sensuous mouth. All of them made up the woman who was his wife. Yet, standing there, it hit him how little he really knew of her past, and that, only what she'd told him.

Orphaned at four, she'd spent the next fourteen years of her life at Gladys Kitteridge House, an orphanage in Albuquerque, New Mexico. After that, college in Denver, sandwiching studies in library science between two part-time jobs. Clay remembered walking into the steak house where she had been working. Slender almost to the point of skinny, she had been balancing a huge silver tray loaded with four steaming orders of steak. And she was laughing. He could still remember the knot that had formed in the pit of his stomach. He'd wanted her then—even before he'd known her name. He sighed. But that was a lifetime ago, before she'd walked out on him—before the bottom had fallen out of his world.

A muscle in her left cheek kept twitching, and her eyelids were fluttering. He wondered if she even knew where she was. Her breathing was slow and shallow. The tumble of dark hair spilling across her pillow only accentuated the pallor of her skin. He frowned. She was too damned still. From what he'd read, her symptoms did not fit addiction withdrawal. Yet what other explanation could there be for the tracks on her arms? And there was that strange outburst just before she'd passed out. Something about a bus. What the hell did that mean?

He thrust his fingers through his hair, momentarily separating the short dark strands. They fell back into place as he began to massage the muscles in his neck. He didn't know what hurt worse, his head or his heart. He still couldn't believe this was happening. On the one hand, Frankie's reappearance was like a dream come true. But why had she left him in the first place? For most people, getting high didn't require going into hiding.

Unconsciously, he leaned closer, wishing he could penetrate her mind. He needed explanations, not more mysteries. But there were no obvious answers, only more questions.

A lump began forming in the back of his throat. Overwhelmed that she was really here, he took a deep breath, willing himself to touch her. Careful not to disturb the IV in the back of her hand, he reached out, his fingers shaking as he traced the length of her arm. He'd spent the last two years refusing to bury her memory, yet now that she was here, he was afraid to let himself hope. When she got well—*if* she got well—would she stay?

He was still struggling with questions when Frankie suddenly inhaled, almost gasping for air. Clay jerked, watching as her eyes flew open. For a moment he could have sworn they were filled with terror. Then cognizance faded, her eyes glazed over and her lids drooped. Seconds later, she was out again.

He bent down until his mouth was only inches away from her ear.

"What is it, Frankie? Why did you run?"

She sighed.

He watched, his heart breaking as a single tear

suddenly slipped from beneath her lashes and ran down the side of her face and into her hair. Then he moved his mouth just a bit to the right, and for the first time in more than two years, he kissed the woman who was his wife.

Hours passed. Hours in which Clay's thoughts had gone from one scenario to another, trying to make sense of all this. But no matter how many ways he tried to explain her absence and her dramatic return, it was impossible.

Suddenly the door to Frankie's room swung open. Clay turned. It was Carl Willis, the doctor who'd examined her.

"There you are, Mr. LeGrand. I've been looking for you."

Clay's heart skipped a beat. "Do you have the results of my wife's tests?"

"Most of them."

Unaware he was clenching his fists, Clay took a step forward. "The drugs?"

Dr. Willis shrugged. "I don't know what she's been injecting into herself, but it wasn't the kind of drugs you're implying. Added to that, her symptoms do not coincide with any drug withdrawal I've ever seen. There were no traces of any illegal substances in her body. The only things out of the ordinary were traces of sedatives. Did she have trouble sleeping?"

Clay was stunned. No drugs? He turned and stared down at Frankie, trying to assimilate this new information. If not drugs, then what?

"Mr. LeGrand?"

Clay jumped. "I'm sorry, you were saying?"

"I asked if she suffered from any form of insomnia."

"No...no, not to my knowledge." He touched the side of her face again, cradling her cheek in his hand. He wanted her to wake up. He needed to tell her he was sorry. He needed her to tell him where the hell she had been. "What's wrong with her?"

"Right now she's suffering from a pretty severe concussion. And she has some faint bruising on one side of her back and shoulder that would coincide with injuries from a wreck."

Clay flinched, remembering what she'd said before she'd passed out. *Look out for that bus!* "Can you tell how long ago it might have happened?"

Dr. Willis had been briefed on this couple's history by the detectives when she'd been processed. He remembered reading about Clay LeGrand. To his shame, he'd believed the man guilty of murder. Now that he knew better, he was even more curious to help solve the mystery of where this woman had gone, as well as what had brought her back.

"The cut on her head is still seeping, so I'd guess within the last three or four hours."

Clay paled, remembering how angry he'd been. His voice shook.

"Is she going to be all right?"

Dr. Willis hesitated.

It was enough to make Clay's belly roll. "What?" he asked.

Willis sighed. "Barring any unforseen complications, I expect her to make a full physical recovery."

Clay's belly tightened even more. "Only physical?"

"I believe you told me that she seemed confused about the time that had elapsed since her disappearance?"

"I thought she was lying," Clay muttered.

Willis shrugged. "Maybe. But there's also the possibility that she simply doesn't remember. The blow to her head was pretty severe. Add stress and mental trauma to that, and you could have yourself a case of selective amnesia."

Clay looked back down. "Will she get it back? Her memory, I mean."

"Probably, but when it comes to the mind, there's no guarantee."

"You mean I might never find out what happened to her?"

Dr. Willis tried to put encouragement in his voice, but he'd never been very good at hedging bets.

"There's every reason to believe that, with time, she'll make a full recovery. But until then, you'll have to be patient."

Clay sighed. It wasn't what he wanted to hear.

"Oh, I almost forgot," the doctor said. "There are a couple of detectives outside who want to talk to you."

Clay glanced at Frankie and then headed for the door.

Avery Dawson stood up as Clay stepped into the hall. Ramsey, his partner, was coming around the corner carrying a couple of cups of coffee.

"Dr. Willis said you wanted to see me?" Clay asked.

Dawson took the coffee Ramsey offered him, and led Clay to a quieter area.

"Thought you might like to know that there was a big midtown pile-up around two o'clock this afternoon. A Greyhound bus collided with a tractor-trailer rig and a couple of cars, one of which was a yellow cab."

Clay's jaw set. My God... Frankie's warning!

Dawson chose his words carefully. "We don't

know for sure if it was your wife, but when the cabdriver came to, he was missing his fare. He said she was a pretty young woman with dark, shoulder-length hair.''

Clay's eyes widened. "You think it was Francesca?''

Dawson shrugged. "Maybe. But if it *was* your wife, she was pretty damned lucky. Everyone else involved in the accident either went straight to the hospital or was taken to the morgue.''

"Jesus,'' Clay muttered. He dropped into a nearby chair and put his head in his hands.

And then something occurred to him. Something so obvious, he wondered if the detectives had already followed it up.

"Did anyone ask the cabdriver where he picked the woman up?''

Ramsey nodded. "At the bus station. Said he almost ran her over as she came running out of the terminal. Said when she got in, she was shaking, but he attributed it to the rain. Then, he said, she kept looking behind them, as if someone might be following.''

"What do we do now?'' Clay asked, standing again.

Dawson shrugged. "There's nothing to do. She was missing. Now she's back. Of course, if she volunteers any information, or begins to remember things, let us know. We'll check it out for you."

Clay stared. "Just like that?"

"Look, Mr. LeGrand, there's nothing else we can do for you. It's not a crime to run away from home."

"That's not exactly the way you looked at it two years ago," Clay snapped, and then turned and left them standing.

He stalked back to Frankie's room, so angry he couldn't think what to do next.

The doctor was gone. Except for the intermittent beeping of monitors, the room was silent. His gaze slid to Francesca's face. She hadn't moved since she'd been admitted. His belly knotted. What if she never woke up?

Clay dropped into a chair beside her bed and laid his hand over hers. At his touch, her fingers jerked spasmodically. He couldn't tell if she was resisting his touch or reaching for him. He sighed, his heart heavy as he let her go. At once her body stilled, and he stood up and strode to the window. Even unconscious, it seemed as if she didn't want him anymore.

"Clay?"

He spun. His mother was standing in the doorway.

"Mom, you didn't have to come back."

Betty LeGrand shrugged and held up a small overnight bag. "I thought you might need these."

He motioned for her to come in.

"How is she?" Betty asked.

"The same."

"Did I see her doctor in the hall?"

Clay nodded.

Betty set the bag down and took off her coat, draping it across a chair as she moved to the window where Clay was standing.

"So...are you going to volunteer what he said, or do I have to drag it out of you piece by piece?"

Clay sighed. "They said her memory loss is in keeping with the injury she suffered and that, hopefully, it will return in time. Also, she hadn't overdosed, and she's not suffering any sort of withdrawal. She has no illegal substances in her body. The only thing they found were slight traces of sedatives."

Betty pursed her lips, and turned toward the bed, gazing thoughtfully at Frankie.

"That doesn't surprise me," she said.

Guilt hit Clay hard. His voice deepened with bitterness. "Tell me something, Mom. I'm her husband. Why didn't I have as much faith in her as you did?"

Betty turned back to Clay. She hurt for her son, but she also hurt for Francesca.

"You know, my mother used to say that the deeper the love, the greater the hurt when things go wrong. You've been through hell, Clay. I would think it would be hard to be objective when you've been suspected of murder."

He moved to Francesca's bedside. "You know what's even worse?"

Betty followed, sliding her hand up the middle of her son's back, giving him a comforting pat.

"No, what?"

Clay swallowed several times before he could spit out the words. "I don't know how I feel about her anymore."

Betty closed her eyes briefly, struggling to find the right thing to say.

"That's understandable," she finally said. "But if the doctors are right, and her memory loss is for real, then think how Frankie will feel. In her mind, the last two years are nonexistent. Theoretically, she's still a newlywed. That means her heart is still yours, whether you want her or not."

Clay blanched. "I didn't mean I don't love her. I just don't know if I can trust her again."

Betty shrugged. "You won't know until you try."

Clay's shoulders slumped. "Okay, Mom. I get it."

Betty ached for her son. For the whole situation.

This was a nightmare, and what she had to tell him was probably going to add to the confusion. She bit her lip, judging Clay's mood against what she'd come to say.

"I went by your house before I came here," she said.

Clay thought nothing of it. His mother had been coming and going there for months now without his permission.

"And?" he asked.

"I thought Frankie might need a few things. I forgot that her clothes were all packed away. It took me a while to find them."

"Thanks," Clay said.

"You're welcome. But that's not what I came to tell you."

Something in his mother's voice wasn't right. He turned away from Frankie to stare his mother in the face.

"What aren't you saying?"

Betty put her hand in the pocket of her slacks and pulled out a wad of money.

"This was in the dryer, along with a pair of designer slacks and a blouse that were not meant to be tumble-dried. I'm afraid the clothes were ruined. However, except for a few wrinkles, I think these came through quite nicely."

Clay's mouth dropped, and when his mother put

the roll of bills in his hand, he felt like throwing up.

"My God," he muttered, fingering the hundred-dollar bills as if they were covered in filth. "How much is there?"

"One thousand, five hundred and fifty dollars."

He looked down in disbelief, his fingers curling spasmodically around the money.

"In the dryer?"

Betty nodded. "Two of the bills were still in the pocket of Frankie's slacks. They probably fell out of a pocket when the dryer began to tumble."

He dropped into a chair, still staring at the money. When he spoke, the sarcasm in his voice was impossible to miss.

"So. One of my nightmares about her was definitely false."

"What nightmare would that be, son?"

"The one about her being brutalized and starving to death."

"I'm sorry, Clay. I know this only adds to the confusion, but I think we shouldn't jump to any more conclusions. The best thing to do is just wait and see what Frankie has to say for herself when she wakes up."

Clay looked up. "It's not what she says that's the issue. It's if I decide to believe her."

Southern California

More than a day after the quake, the earth was still belching aftershocks, which hampered the efforts of the search and rescue teams. Going through the rubble of collapsed freeways and buildings was still the order of the day. Unfortunately, it was becoming easier to find the dead than the living. They were beginning to smell.

The more exclusive homes were often also the more isolated, and even though many reports had come in, searching them had taken a back seat to the mass devastation of the heavily populated areas. Rescue crews were relying on reports from police helicopters regarding areas to search. And when a helicopter pilot had seen half of a house in one of the canyons below, they'd radioed for help.

Pete Daley had been part of the San Francisco search and rescue team for more than ten years. He was an old hand at disasters and thought he'd seen everything, yet when the driver of their van took a sudden right into a heavily wooded area, he frowned.

"Are you sure this is the right road?" Pete asked.

His partner, Charlie Swan, shrugged. "No, but it's the only one here."

Pete rolled his eyes. "Then why are we—"

Charlie pointed through the windshield of the ambulance to the hovering chopper just visible in the distance.

"He isn't exactly leaving bread crumbs, but he's been circling for more than five minutes now. I figure he's over the spot."

Pete looked a little abashed and then sighed. "I haven't been paying attention, have I?" he asked.

"You do when it counts," Charlie said. "Now grab your gear. We're almost there."

A few minutes later they arrived at what was left of a great mansion, parking well out of the way of any walls that might still be prone to collapse. They grabbed their bags as the searchers began unloading their dogs. A few minutes later, some of the team entered the house, while the others made their way down the canyon to the wing of the house that had shattered below.

Almost immediately, one of the dogs began to whine, then it moved toward a huge pile of rubble at the foot of the stairs.

"We've got something," the handler yelled.

Searchers began clearing away debris and, moments later, uncovered a foot.

"Damn," Pete muttered, then knelt, expecting to touch cold, lifeless skin. Although he was wearing surgical gloves, when his fingers encircled the man's ankle, he felt warm, supple flesh.

"We got a live one!" he yelled. "Get this stuff off him fast."

Piece by piece, the debris was removed, each time the searchers making certain that something else didn't come crashing down upon him and finish the job.

"Look at that," Charlie said, pointing to the fallen beams and a piece of the wall that had formed a small alcove above the injured man. "That's what kept him alive."

Pete began taking vitals, while Charlie applied a neck brace and checked for broken bones. Everything about the victim was faint, even the intermittent whisper of breath slipping from between his bloody lips.

"See if that television chopper is still around. We've got a hot one, and he's not going to wait for Lifeflight!"

Within minutes, the injured man had been stabilized and strapped to a stretcher. A couple of workers began carrying him out to the lawn toward the waiting helicopter.

"I'll fly in with the news crew and be back as soon as possible," Pete said. "You go with the search dogs. There could be more survivors."

Charlie nodded and headed back to the mansion at a jog.

Pete shaded his eyes as he hurried beside the stretcher. Suddenly the man began to moan.

"You're okay, buddy," Pete told him. "We're going to take real good care of you."

"Woman...find my woman."

Pete frowned, then reached for his two-way. It crackled as he pressed the send button.

"Daley here," he said. "The victim is asking about a woman. Be on the lookout for another body nearby."

"Roger that," a voice said, and the connection was broken.

The man's eyelids fluttered, then he sighed and slipped into unconsciousness.

The *whap-whap* of the spinning helicopter blades soon made talking impossible, yet Pete felt obligated to give the man a last bit of hope.

"Hang on, buddy," Pete yelled as they began loading him inside. "As soon as we get you to a hospital, they'll fix you up real good."

Then he crawled in, directing the position of the stretcher inside the chopper, before settling down on the floor beside him.

"Take her up!" Pete yelled, and grabbed on to the back of a seat as the chopper suddenly rocked.

"Sorry," the pilot yelled. "Crosswinds."

Pete rolled his eyes and said a quick prayer. Moments later, they were airborne. Aside from a periodic check of the IV they'd started, there was little he could do except study the injured man's face.

He looked foreign, that much he could tell, but in L.A., that meant nothing. Black-winged eyebrows arched above deep-socketed eyes. The jut of his nose and the cut of his cheekbones bespoke what appeared to Pete to be a Middle Eastern heritage. Even though his skin was ashen and dust-covered, the even, toast-colored cast looked natural, rather than artificially tanned. Pete glanced back at the mansion, stunned by the sight of the devastation from the air, then shook his head in disbelief, amazed that the man was still alive.

"I'll bet you're one tough son of a bitch, aren't you, buddy?" But the man didn't answer.

A few minutes later, they began to descend. As they landed on the hospital roof, Pete made last-minute checks on the man's vitals, making sure the nurses would have all the information they would need. Moments later, a trauma team met them at the door. Pete jumped out, helping as they transferred the stretcher to a gurney.

Pete began relating vitals as they scooted the stretcher in place. As he stepped aside, one of the nurses got a clear view of his face.

"Oh my gosh! That's Pharaoh Carn!"

There was a moment of stunned silence as

everyone stared at their patient's face; then they began to run, pulling the stretcher as they went. Saving his life was uppermost in their minds. It didn't matter what he did for a living, but in L.A., Pharaoh Carn's ties to the mob were well-known.

Pete went as far as the door, then watched as the trauma team disappeared with the victim.

All the way back to the site of the search, he kept wondering about the woman Pharaoh Carn had lost. She must have been important to the man. He'd asked about her with his last conscious breaths. He wondered if they had found her. He wondered if she was dead.

Four

During the last day and a half, Clay had gone home only once, for a shower and a change of clothes. His parents had offered to take turns sitting with Frankie while he got some rest, but he'd refused. He was afraid. Afraid that if he left her, even for a minute, she would disappear again. So he slept in fits and snatches in a chair by her bed, and during the times that he was awake, he hadn't been able to take his eyes from her face.

She looked the same—and yet there were differences that ate at him. Her hair was shorter than it had been. He tried to picture her going about her life without him. Shopping for clothes and food. Getting haircuts and watching movies that made her cry. It seemed obscene that she had remained the same while he'd died inside.

But there were other differences besides the obvious. Her face was slimmer, her skin paler. There was a set to her mouth that hadn't been there before, as well as faint frown lines between her eyebrows. She had the look of a woman who had suffered.

And besides the mystery of the money, there was now the tattoo.

They hadn't found it until yesterday morning, when the nurses were changing the linens on Frankie's bed. As they'd rolled her onto her side to remove the dirty sheets, her hair had fallen forward around her face, revealing a small, gold-colored tattoo just below the hairline at the back of her neck.

"Well, now," one of the nurses said. "Would you look at that."

At their bidding, Clay had stepped forward, but when he saw the strange mark, his heart skipped a beat. He traced the shape with his fingers, trying to imagine her choosing to have this done, but the image wouldn't come. Frankie was deathly afraid of needles.

"It's sort of like a cross, but it's not," the nurse said. "I've seen them before but I forget what they're called."

"It's an ankh," Clay muttered. "An Egyptian symbol for eternity…I think."

The nurse gave him a curious glance but held her tongue. The whole floor was well aware of this couple's history. After all, this man's face had been on local television almost as often as the quarterback of the city's beloved football team, the Denver Broncos.

She smiled at Clay, then gave the sheets on Frankie's bed one last pat. "There you go. She's all fixed up. I'll be back later to change her IV."

Clay hated the pity he was getting almost as much as he'd resented the anonymous judgment of being a suspected murderer. He was glad when the nurses left. And while the discovery of the tattoo was strange, it offered no answers to the mystery of where she'd been. All he could do was wait for her to wake up. Hopefully, the rest could come later.

After thirty-three hours of steady rainfall, the Denver skies finally cleared. The streets glistened with a just-washed look as the last remnants of runoff flowed through the gutters. The early-morning air was sharp with the scents of autumn. Leaves had turned weeks ago, and the snowcaps on the Rockies were constant reminders of the coming winter.

She awoke to find Clay asleep in a chair beside her bed. She frowned, vaguely remembering a dream about palm trees that didn't make sense, then winced as the glare of new sun hit her eyes.

"Ooh," she moaned.

Within her next breath, Clay was awake.

"Francesca?"

She swallowed. Her tongue felt thick. "What happened?"

"You're in a hospital," he said. "Lie still. I'm going to get a nurse."

"Wait."

He was already gone. She sighed, then glanced around the room, trying to piece together the bits of her memory. It had been raining, and she'd been waiting for Clay to come home. She'd fallen asleep and...

At that point, everything stopped. She started over, replaying the memory a bit farther back.

She'd been out in the rain. But where, and why? She closed her eyes, willing her mind to go blank. Suddenly she saw herself running from a building. She could remember the water splashing up the backs of her legs and into her shoes. Remembered hailing a cab and feeling a sense of relief when she gave the cabby her address. But then her memory started to fuzz. She could remember them driving through traffic, but there was always traffic in Denver.

What next? She frowned. A bus? She flinched as it careened around a corner of her mind. Had there been an accident? Was that why she was here? She remembered hurting and then getting very wet. After that, the need to get home to Clay seemed to overwhelm anything else she might have remembered.

Someone began paging a doctor over the hospital intercom, interrupting her concentration. She tried to refocus, but all she could remember was taking the extra key from under the pot of dead geraniums on the front porch and going into the house.

She inhaled again, this time picturing the inside of her house. What had she done after she'd gone inside? Oh yes. The utility room. Her clothes were soaked, and she'd gone to the laundry and tossed them in the dryer. On the way through the kitchen, she'd taken a painkiller for the headache, then she'd filched one of Clay's T-shirts for a nightgown and crawled into bed.

Unconsciously, her fingers doubled into fists as she clutched at the sheets, trying to find her way through the maze of images flashing through her mind.

Suddenly something crashed in the hall outside her room. Before she could assimilate the noise, the door opened to her room. She gasped. A man stood silhouetted against the light. Even though her heart was telling her that the man had to be Clay, her mind was telling her different. The need to run overrode caution as she began kicking at her covers and yanking herself free from the machines they'd hooked up to her body.

Clay bolted, catching her just as she tried to crawl out of bed.

"Frankie, don't."

"Let me go!" she begged, and started to cry. "Please let me go. I don't want to die."

A shudder ripped through him. The wild, blank look on her face was terrifying—even more terrifying than the needle tracks had been. He didn't know this woman. When she drew back her hand and slapped at his face, he took the blow open-mouthed and staring. Before he could react, blood spurted everywhere as the needle from her IV went flying to the floor.

It was the color of red staining the pristine white of her sheets that broke his shock.

He grabbed her arms and started yelling for a nurse.

Her face was etched in fear as she kicked at both him and the covers over her legs. Moments later, the room was full of hospital staff and Clay was shuffled into the hall.

He dropped into a nearby chair and leaned forward, resting his elbows on his knees. His hands were shaking. His shirt was splattered with her blood. From where he was sitting, he could still hear her crying. A muscle jerked in the side of his jaw as he drew a deep, shuddering breath. The urge to cry along with her was strong. This was hell.

A short while later, her doctor emerged. Clay stood.

"Is she okay?"

The doctor nodded.

"What was that?" Clay asked.

"I'm not sure, but if I had to hazard a guess, I'd say she suffered some sort of traumatic flashback. We gave her something to calm her down. When she's better physically, you might consider some therapy."

A psychiatrist? Hell, what next? Clay exhaled slowly, then shoved a hand through his hair.

"Is she having a nervous breakdown?"

The doctor smiled. "No, Mr. LeGrand, nothing like that. As soon as she recovers, we'll see how much she remembers and then go from there."

Clay accepted the explanation, but there was something at the back of his mind that wouldn't let go. She'd been gone for two years. Her reappearance was as sudden and inexplicable as her disappearance had been. He hated to ask. It seemed like a betrayal of his feelings for Frankie. But for his own peace of mind, he had to know.

"Hey, Doc."

"Yes?"

"Could she be faking a loss of memory?"

The doctor paused, seriously considering the question, then shrugged. "She could be, but in my opinion, I doubt it."

Clay nodded. It wasn't exactly what he wanted to hear, but it helped alleviate some of his doubts.

"Mr. LeGrand, I know this is frustrating, but look at it from your wife's point of view, too. If there *was* something sinister about her disappearance two years ago, then she's the one who has the most to lose, right?"

The doctor patted Clay's arm and walked away.

Clay dropped into a nearby chair and leaned forward, staring at a spot on the floor. He felt as if he were going crazy. He didn't know who to trust or who to believe. He needed answers desperately, but until Frankie got well, that wasn't going to happen.

"Mr. LeGrand."

Clay looked up. It was one of the nurses.

"Yes?"

"Your wife is asking for you," she said.

Clay stood, but his hesitancy did not go unnoticed.

"It will be all right," the nurse said. "Head injuries are tricky, you know. I think she was just confused before. Don't take it personally. Oddly enough, she thought we were having an earthquake."

Earthquake? He vaguely remembered hearing about one somewhere on a news broadcast.

"She's been medicated, so she'll probably be groggy," the nurse added. "If you need us, just press the call button. Someone will be right there."

Clay moved across the hall toward Frankie's room as the nurse walked away.

Earthquake. He couldn't get the thought out of his mind. This was the third clue to add to the mystery of finding out where she'd been. First the money, then the tattoo, now this. He pushed the door open and walked inside. Her bloody gown and bedclothes had been replaced. The IV was back in her hand. Her eyes were closed, her face almost as pale as the sheets beneath her chin. Afraid to touch her for fear of setting off another panic attack, he stood, waiting for her permission to move.

Sensing his presence, Frankie opened her eyes. "Clay?"

He sighed, then started toward her, stopping near the foot of the bed. "Yes, it's me."

Her eyes filled with tears. "I'm so sorry. I don't know why I did that to you. I know this sounds stupid, but I thought it was an earthquake." She looked away. "I think I thought you were someone else."

His heart leaped. "Who, Frankie? Who did you think I was?"

A long moment passed as a frown creased her forehead. Finally, she shook her head and sighed. "I can't remember."

A chill ran up the back of Clay's spine. Could he believe her? He exhaled softly. What the hell could he do? Hold a grudge? What would that prove?

"It's okay," he said.

Frankie shook her head slowly. "No, it's not all right. None of this is all right." She held out her hand. "Come sit by me. I need to explain."

He pulled a chair up beside her bed. "I don't think you should be talking," he muttered.

"Sit by me...please," she begged.

He stood and scooted onto the edge of the bed.

Struggling with tears, Frankie bit her lower lip, using the pain to focus. His body language was obvious, and she didn't blame him for being defensive. But she had to make him understand. And then she sighed. Make him understand what? She was the one in the dark. How could she explain what was going through her mind when they were claiming she'd just lost the last two years of her life?

"Clay."

"What?"

"Have I really been gone all that time?"

His eyes narrowed angrily. "Oh yes."

Unaware that her chin was quivering, she bit her lip to keep from crying. She was scared. So scared. And Clay seemed so distant—even angry. Two years. *My God. Where would I go? And why don't I remember?*

She took a deep, shuddering breath. "Do you hate me?"

Clay's belly knotted. "No, Francesca, I don't hate you."

She glanced at his face. That dear, familiar face. Even though he was right beside her, the distance was obvious. Gripping the sheets with both fists, she stared at him until he looked away. As he did, tears filled her eyes.

Oh God. Please don't take him away from me.

Though she was almost afraid to ask, there was something she still had to know. She cleared her throat, trying to swallow her emotions, but it did little good.

"Clay?"

He looked up at her. "What?"

"Do you still love me?"

A shudder visibly shook him as he suddenly stood. "I have loved you since the day I saw you."

Her fingers clenched the sheets even tighter. "Why do I sense there's a 'but' in that answer?"

He hesitated briefly, but when he answered, his gaze never wavered.

"There's a difference between love and trust, Francesca. I still love you, but I guess I don't trust you anymore."

She bit her lip and then closed her eyes. This nightmare was too horrible to comprehend.

"I'm so sorry," she whispered, her voice thick with tears. "I don't know what to say to make this better."

"For starters, you could tell me where you've been...what you've been doing."

She shuddered. His voice was harsh. But there was an anger of her own that wouldn't let go. For some reason, she felt abandoned. This wasn't fair. She knew herself well enough to know that she would never have willingly walked out on Clay. And if someone had taken her away, even though she'd found a way to come back, it stood to reason that it might happen again.

"When I know, you'll know," she snapped, turning her face toward the wall.

Her anger startled him. And it was in that moment that the first inkling of trust began to renew itself. What if she was telling the truth? He needed to talk to the detectives to keep this out of the media.

After the quake: Day four

Even unconscious and barely alive, Pharaoh Carn still managed to make headlines. Of the seven bodies they'd pulled out of the rubble on his estate, he was the only one to survive. But the whys and how of it had yet to be told. Pharaoh was unconscious and unable to explain.

Duke Needham, Pharaoh's second in command, had been out of the country when the earthquake hit, and it had taken him a frantic day of plane hopping to get back to L.A., only to find the mansion in ruins and searchers still pulling bodies from the debris.

By the time he'd located the place where Pharaoh was hospitalized, he'd wasted another day. After finding his boss unconscious, he began searching for Pharaoh's woman. It wasn't common knowledge to anyone outside Pharaoh's compound that the woman even existed, but the ones who knew also knew that he had spent the better part of two years trying to win over a woman who seemed to hate the sight of his face.

After several days of diligent searching, all Duke knew was that Pharaoh's woman was not in a morgue. Whether she'd survived and been taken to another hospital had yet to be learned. It wasn't as if they could give out her name and see if she happened to turn up. It would have been like offering a reward to have stolen property returned to the thief. He never considered the fact that the woman could have escaped unharmed. Not after seeing the mansion.

So Duke waited, knowing that the next move had to come from Pharaoh, only Pharaoh was in no shape to tell anyone what to do. It was all he could do to draw his next breath.

There would be time enough later to retrieve that which had been lost.

Within hours of her awakening, Frankie's physical health took a remarkable turn for the better. By the next morning, she was allowed to sit up on the side of the bed, and by afternoon, with the aid of Clay's arm, she was walking up and down the hall. The mutinous thrust of her chin coincided nicely with the jumble of curls around her face. She looked like an unruly child, angry from an unjust punishment.

"I want out of here," she muttered. "I don't like being helpless."

Clay sighed. This wasn't the first time she'd said it, and from the look on her face, it wouldn't be the last. But if he was honest with himself, he would have to admit that he wasn't so sure he wanted the same thing. Here, she was under the watchful eyes of her doctor and the nurses, as well as himself. When they went home, he would be on his own again. Truth be told, he was scared. How could he face a normal day ever again, wondering when he left each morning if she would be home when he returned?

"Your doctor says you need to stay one more night. Just be patient, Frankie. You'll be home soon."

She headed toward a couple of chairs beneath a window overlooking the city, and sat down with a careful plop. She didn't know how to explain the urgency inside her, but it was there just the same.

From the moment she'd awakened in the hospital, she'd had an overwhelming urge to run. But why? And where? Clay was all that mattered to her. All that had ever mattered. And the little house they were renting from his folks was the first real home she could remember. She loved that house. She loved Clay. So why the panic?

"I know, but..."

She sighed, leaving her sentence undone, and looked down at her hands, frowning at the strange, dark red polish on her nails. The color was nothing she would ever have chosen. What else, she wondered, was different about her?

"Clay?"

"What?"

"Do I look different?"

"What do you mean?"

She frowned, blinking back angry tears. She hated this rootless feeling.

"I mean, physically. Am I fatter or thinner? Was my hair always this color? Do I have scars that didn't used to be there?"

Clay sat beside her and took her by the hand. She seemed so sincere. If only he dared believe.

"You're thinner, but not much. Your hair is shorter, but the color is the same."

She watched his lips moving as he spoke the words, and even though she heard him, her mind was remembering the way his mouth felt on her body. She stared at his fingers as they threaded through hers, and she shuddered. His hands. She'd always loved his hands. Strong and tan, they were callused from his work, yet with a few skillful strokes, could turn her bones into mush.

Suddenly she realized that he was no longer talking. She flushed, wondering how long he'd been silent. She looked up. His eyes were dark with secrets and pain. Pain that she'd put there. And there was anger, too. She flinched, then looked away.

Clay watched the expressions changing across her face and knew to the moment when her thoughts ran to love. He'd seen that look on her face too many times before not to recognize it now. It hit him, then, how drastically their expectations of life had changed. She thought of making love, while his thoughts ran toward fear and distrust. And then she turned away, once more revealing the tattoo to his gaze. He spoke before he thought.

"The tattoo...what does it mean?"

Frankie looked at Clay as if he'd gone mad. "What tattoo?"

He traced the shape of it with his finger. "The one here, at the back of your neck."

A shaft of panic dug deep in her belly as she pushed his hand away to feel her skin. Her skin became clammy, and her fingers started to shake. It was as if someone had just pointed out a spider crawling up her person.

"I can't feel anything," she muttered, and wondered why she wanted to cry.

He took her finger and placed it directly on the gold ankh.

"There."

Her eyes were dark and huge with shock. "What's it look like?"

Clay frowned. Fear wasn't the reaction he'd expected. Then he wondered exactly what he *had* expected.

"Like a cross with a loop on top. It's Egyptian, I think. It's called an ankh."

"This is my mark. In the eyes of the world, you will always be mine." The words echoed in her head.

Frankie closed her eyes. "Don't touch me," she whispered. "I'll never be yours."

She slumped forward, passing out in Clay's arms.

Five

The sun was weak but persistent as the nurse wheeled Frankie out of the hospital. When the cool air penetrated the thin sweater she was wearing, she shivered. It occurred to her then to wonder about her clothes. Had Clay given them away, believing her to be dead? Her lower lip trembled as she resisted the urge to cry. The familiarity of her world had been stripped away and she couldn't even remember being gone. My God, my God, how had this happened?

Sometimes she could feel something pushing at the edge of her consciousness, other times, her thoughts were a blur. She couldn't help but compare the emptiness she was feeling now to the emotions she'd suffered after her parents were killed. One day she'd had a mother and a father and a wonderful home. Within weeks, she had become a ward of the courts, living in an orphanage and crying in the dark for a mother who never came.

Now this.

The last thing she remembered was getting caught in the downpour and then coming home with a headache and crawling into bed. She'd woken up to a nightmare. Only this nightmare didn't fade, it was getting worse by the day. The emotional distance between her and Clay was as real as the air that she breathed, and it was scaring her to death. Clay was her rock. If he quit on her…

She shuddered. The consequences were impossible to consider.

"Cold, dear?" the nurse asked.

Frankie shrugged. It was easier to admit being chilled than to face how frightened she was.

"A little, I guess."

The nurse pulled the wheelchair back a bit into an alcove out of the wind.

"There comes your husband now," she said, pointing to a gray sedan.

Frankie didn't recognize the vehicle, but why should she? Her spirits plummeted even lower. In two years, a lot of things could change.

She watched as Clay parked and got out, her eyes narrowing as he came toward her. The first time she'd seen him, she'd been working in a restaurant. She'd looked up and caught him staring at her from across the room. Even then, she'd known they would be lovers. She sighed. Had she ever told him that?

Then she lifted her chin. The present was more than she could handle. There was no need dwelling on the past.

Silently, she continued to watch Clay's approach. He was so very much a man. Two years was a long time to be without a woman. Had he given up on her and found someone else? She moaned softly. The mere thought made her sick.

"Mrs. LeGrand, are you in pain?" the nurse asked quickly.

"I'm fine," Frankie mumbled, blinking back tears. She had to be. She had no other choice.

And then Clay was beside her. She met his gaze, trying to read his thoughts. His expression was bland, almost polite. She wanted to scream.

"Your wife is getting chilled," the nurse said, speaking to Clay as if Frankie was no longer present.

Clay's glance shifted to the stiff set of Frankie's shoulders.

"I'm sorry, honey, I didn't think," he said, and quickly shed his own jacket.

As Frankie stood up to walk to the car, Clay put it on her, working her arms into the overlong sleeves and overlapping its breadth around her waist.

Her tears came closer to the surface. He'd called her honey. Did that mean he was beginning to forgive, or was it just a word that he'd used out of habit?

"Drive safely," the nurse said as they bundled Frankie into the front seat of the car.

"Yes, ma'am," Clay said.

Moments later, they were pulling away from the hospital. Clay managed a smile and a pat on her leg before he lapsed into silence. Frankie couldn't bring herself to pretend that all was well between them anymore. She should have been elated to be going home, but all she could feel was an overwhelming sense of panic. And there was a certainty within her that wouldn't go away. She might not remember the last two years of her life, but she remembered her love for her man. She would not have left Clay of her own free will. Ever. And yet he believed that she had. That knowledge fed anger. The anger fed hurt.

As Clay stopped at a red light, another reality hit Frankie with a jolt. Accepting that her disappearance had not been of own accord, what reassurance did she have that it would not happen again? All she could think was, God, what a mess.

"Clay?"

He answered absently, his gaze focused on the red light as he waited for it to turn green.

"Hmm?"

"I don't have a job anymore, do I?"

Clay looked startled. "Why, no, honey." Then he added almost apologetically, "It's been two years."

She thought of the library, then looked away. "I loved working there." Her fingers curled into fists as the light turned and Clay accelerated through the intersection. "As soon as I'm better, I'll start looking for another job."

He frowned. The idea of Frankie being out of his sight was frightening. "There's no hurry," he said quickly.

"But we'll be needing the money. My salary always pays…I mean *paid,* the utilities. If I don't work, it'll put us in a bind."

Clay hesitated, choosing his words carefully so as not to insult her. "Not really—at least, not anymore. I bought Dad out a while back. The company is doing good. There's no rush."

She didn't know what to say. One of their dreams had already been realized and she'd had no part in its happening. Fear spiked. What else had he done in her absence? *Please God, just let him still love me.*

A few minutes passed, and the silence inside the car was growing more uncomfortable by the moment. Finally, for lack of anything else to say, Frankie said, "I was wondering about my clothes."

A muscle jerked in his jaw. "They're in the spare bedroom closet. Mom got them all out the other day and washed them."

"All of them?"

He nodded.

"I didn't take anything with me?"

He hesitated, then shook his head.

The tone of Frankie's voice shifted sarcastically. "And you didn't think that was strange?"

He inhaled sharply, angered by the accusation in her question. "Don't go there, Francesca. You don't know what the hell you're talking about. Two years ago this month, I came home, expecting to see my wife, and instead I found blood in the bathroom and a broken coffee cup and spilled coffee on the kitchen floor. Within an hour, I was the prime suspect in your murder, so don't give me 'strange.' Everything about it was strange."

In the middle of his answer, Frankie started to shake. She could still hear his voice, but the words were fading. Something flashed across her memory.

Hands upon her mouth.

A sharp prick in the flesh of her upper arm.

Someone whispering her name.

She gasped and put her hands to her head as if trying to hold on to the images, but they disappeared as quickly as they had come. She groaned.

"What?" Clay asked.

"I don't know. Something just…" She shook her head. "It's gone now. I don't know if it was a memory or my imagination."

Clay refused to be swayed by confusion and chose to ignore what she said.

"We're almost home," he said. "You'll feel better after you rest."

She flinched. His refusal to address her confusion was making her crazy.

"No, Clay, I won't," she snapped. "I won't feel better until I understand what's going on. I've lost two years of my life, and the way I feel, I'm losing my husband, as well. A good nap isn't going to cure a damn thing."

The color faded from his face. "You're not losing me," he muttered.

"Feels like it to me."

She looked at him for a long, silent moment—waiting for a more reassuring response, or, at the least, some sign of tenderness. It wasn't there. When he turned the corner and headed down their street, she looked away.

The tension between them lengthened. Moments later, he was parking in the driveway, and the business of getting her out of the car and into the house overtook the inquisition.

The house smelled damp, a holdover from the

recent rains. Clay helped Frankie inside, then stopped to turn up the central heat. As he did, she swayed. He reached to steady her, his hand brushing her breast, then lingering at the curve of her waist.

She watched his nostrils flare and then saw his mouth soften. She leaned forward, offering herself out of both love and desperation.

He didn't move.

She tensed, waiting for him to come closer, to take her in his arms and tell her how much she meant to him, how glad he was that she'd come home.

But the moment never came. She lifted her chin, her voice bitter with tears. "You know something, Clay? I never figured you for a quitter."

Then she took her bag from his hands and made her way down the hall without him. It was the longest twenty feet of her life.

Clay watched her go, wanting to go after her. But he kept remembering the years of believing she was dead—of being hounded mercilessly by the police and the press. A part of him was afraid to let go of the safety net he'd built around his heart.

"Coward," he muttered to himself, then stalked into the kitchen to make some coffee.

An envelope and a small pile of clothes were

lying on the kitchen table. He'd forgotten to put them away. He picked up the clothes, fingering the fabric and looking at the labels. He wasn't much of a judge of women's clothing, but it was obvious that these were not off any department-store rack. He dropped them on the table, reached for the envelope and looked inside, still incredulous that Frankie had been carrying this kind of money.

He turned toward the doorway. Frankie was coming down the hall. Suddenly he wanted to see her face when he showed her the money. If she had something to hide, he would know it.

She walked into the kitchen with an empty pill bottle in her hands. Her expression was closed, her body language posting an "off-limits" sign that any fool could have read.

"I have a headache. We're out of painkillers," she said.

He tossed the envelope on the counter and headed for the cabinet over the sink.

"Here you go," he said, shaking a couple out in her hands.

"Thank you."

Clay's conscience tugged. She looked so hurt, so confused.

"Francesca..."

"What?"

"Look, I'm sorry if I've hurt your feelings, but you have to understand my—"

"Why?"

He hesitated, frowning. "Why what?"

"Why do I have to understand your feelings? You don't seem inclined to understand mine."

He took a slow breath. He didn't want to fight, he just wanted answers.

"How can I understand anything, Francesca, when everything about you is still a big mystery?"

Tears surfaced again. "And no one regrets that more than I. But there's one thing I haven't forgotten."

His interest heightened. "What?"

"How much I love you."

He paled. The pain in her voice was palpable. "And I love you, too," he whispered, his voice shaking with emotion.

Her chin began to quiver. "Then why, Clay? Why are you keeping me at arm's length?"

His hands were shaking as tossed the envelope toward her. Money spilled from inside as it flew through the air.

"This was in the pocket of your slacks. Where did it come from?"

Frankie saw it fluttering to the floor, but her mind was already moving beyond the action to a scene from her past.

She rolled him over, shocked by the blood trickling from his lips. Then she gritted her teeth and thrust her hand in his pockets. She would need the money to help get away.

"Frankie?"

She looked up, her expression blank.

"I asked you a question."

"I'm sorry, what did you say?"

"I asked you where the money came from."

The answer came out of nowhere, surprising her more than it did Clay.

"I thought he was dead."

Clay jerked as if he'd been slapped, then grabbed her by the arm, forcing her to look up at him.

"What the hell did you say?"

She covered her face with her hands. "I don't know, I don't know," she mumbled.

But Clay couldn't let it go. "Who, Frankie? Who did you think was dead?"

Dark eyes—white teeth—smiling—always smiling.

Then the image disappeared, gone too quickly for her to see his face.

"I don't know," she moaned.

He cursed and turned away.

Suddenly it was all too much. Frankie sank to

the floor on her knees, desperate for Clay to believe. "For God's sake, give me a chance."

Clay turned, and in that moment, knew a terrible shame. "Ah, God, Francesca, don't do that."

He picked her up and carried her down the hall. Her quiet sobs tore at him as he laid her on the bed. When he turned her loose, she rolled away from him, curling herself in a ball as her shoulders shook from grief.

"Frankie, I—"

She put her hands over her ears.

Heartsick, he straightened, covered her with an afghan and started toward the door.

Suddenly she rolled over on her back, her tear-streaked eyes wide with fright. "Don't close the door!"

He paused and turned. The terror in her eyes and voice was impossible to miss.

"All right," he said.

"I don't like to be shut in," she muttered, then watched to make sure he did as she'd asked.

Clay's heart was hammering as he walked back to the kitchen. He paused in the doorway, remembering the fear in her voice as he knelt to pick up the money. A few moments later he stood, the wad of cash in his right hand. An echo of her cry sifted back through his mind.

I thought he was dead.

He looked down a the money he was holding and shuddered.

"Jesus," he muttered, and stuffed it back into the envelope, then dropped it in a nearby drawer. There would be time enough later to figure out what to do with it. For now, he just wanted it out of his sight.

Down the hall, Frankie lay on the bed, swallowing the last of her sobs and contemplating the emptiness of her homecoming. This was so wrong—so very, very wrong—and she didn't know how to make things right. Clay didn't believe her, and in spite of his assurances to the contrary, she didn't believe he loved her anymore. At least, not like he used to. She felt like she was coming undone. She rolled over on her side, pulling the afghan with her and closing her eyes.

Clay was in the kitchen now. The subdued banging of pans was not as subtle as it might have been. On any other occasion, it would have been comical, Clay trying to cook. Then she took a deep, shuddering breath. But he'd been doing just that for the better part of two years now, hadn't he? In fact, in his mind, he probably thought he'd been widowed.

A last angry tear slipped from under her eyelid and onto the pillow. But she wasn't dead. She was alive, and she was back, and he was going to have to learn how to live with the holes in her life until she found a way to fill them.

Las Vegas, Nevada

The sleek, private jet taxied to a stop a few yards shy of the white stretch limo waiting at the end of the runway. Moments later, the exit door opened. Duke Needham appeared at the top of the stairs, waved toward the waiting limousine, then disappeared back inside the plane. A short while later, the driver exited the limousine with a wheelchair in hand and hurried up the steps.

The scent of airplane fuel was faint upon the air, while overhead, a dull gray sky was dotted with gathering clouds, adding a bite to the wind. Minutes passed, and then Duke abruptly appeared in the doorway again, with the driver right behind him. Between them was Pharaoh Carn, wheelchair-bound, but bundled against the cold. They picked him up, chair and all, carrying him down the steps, setting him lightly upon the tarmac with hardly a bump.

Pharaoh was arriving without notice, intent on escaping to his Las Vegas home to recuperate. He had intentionally concealed his identity with a heavy coat and blankets. The dark sunglasses he wore effectively concealed his expression, but though his skin was a warm tan, it was obvious by the pallor beneath that he'd been ill.

Yet even in the wheelchair, his presence demanded attention. The tilt of his head, a wave of his hand, a sharp tone to his voice, and both men jumped to do his bidding.

Duke leaned forward instantly, his behavior concerned and submissive. Words were traded. Minutes later, the limousine was gone, and there was nothing to mark their passing but a bit of paper that had blown out of the plane.

Moonlight reflected on the rain-washed steps, while inside Pharaoh's Las Vegas home, he slept. But his rest was constantly disturbed by strange dreams. Twice he woke abruptly, believing that the floors were shaking. Each time he closed his eyes, he could still feel Francesca's hands against his chest, fighting him, pushing him. And he could feel himself falling, rolling head over heels down the stairs. He groaned. Betrayal was the sharpest pain of all.

At the sound, a woman's voice was at his ear, her hand soft upon his brow.

"Mr. Carn, are you in pain?"

He flinched. That damned nurse. If he was well enough to be released from the hospital, he was well enough to sleep on his own. Never in his life had he shared a room with a woman, not even Francesca, and he wasn't about to start now.

"Of course I'm in pain."

"Just a moment, sir. I'll get your medicine."

"I don't want medicine. I want some peace and quiet. Just get out. If I need any pills, I can get them myself."

"But, sir, Mr. Needham said—"

Pharaoh rolled over, and even in a prone position, his demeanor demanded compliance.

"I gave you an order," he said softly. "Get out of my room—and do it now."

The nurse scurried. It was the best way to describe the hasty panic with which she left.

The moment he heard the door closing behind her, he began to relax. The air in the room seemed lighter, the walls less confining. Gingerly, he turned onto his side, wincing slightly as he accidentally put too much pressure on healing ribs.

"Damn, damn, damn," he moaned as a muscle suddenly went into spasm. But the nurse was gone, and there was no one here to help rub it out. He gritted his teeth, forcing his injured body to relax until the pain began to lessen. Finally he took a slow, deep breath, exhaling softly. The worst was over.

Then he amended that thought. The worst *wasn't* over. It was just beginning. He couldn't rest until he knew what had happened to Francesca. The thought made him crazy. It wasn't fair. She belonged to him. He'd known it almost from the first day he'd seen her.

He shifted restlessly, trying to find a more comfortable spot on the mattress.

His eyes closed, and finally he dreamed...of the beginning, when Francesca Romano had entered his life.

By the age of thirteen, Pharaoh Carn had accepted the fact that people didn't like him. In fact, he'd capitalized on it by terrorizing the other orphans of Kitteridge House. He was the undisputed ruler of his domain, in the classroom as well as at the home. But it wasn't just his looks that set him apart. In New Mexico, where the Native American face was a familiar fixture, his dark skin and black hair were nothing remarkable. It was his hate that made him different. His hate was a rage. His rage was a power. He was vicious and cruel and took pride in the fact that everyone—including the teachers—was afraid of him. At least they had been—until her.

He'd been sitting in the director's office, awaiting his latest punishment, when a social worker had arrived with the little girl in tow. The first thing he'd noticed about the child was her hair. It was almost as dark as his. And her eyes—brown and rounded in fear—shimmered with unshed tears. She was clutching a small teddy bear in one hand and a shred of an old blanket in the other. Her shoes were scuffed, and the ribbon someone had tied in her hair earlier had slipped from its bow and was hanging down the back of her head.

She looked at him and then poked her thumb in her mouth.

He glared at her.

Only this time the glare didn't work. He watched as her gaze scanned his face, picking apart his features with undisguised interest.

He glared harder. Stupid kid. He'd been stared at all his life. Just because she was little, that didn't mean he was going to take any crap from her, either.

But his angry expression seemed to have no impact on her. In fact, when the social worker sat down, the little girl took her thumb from her mouth and moved toward him, dragging her blanket behind her. To his discomfort, she walked all the way across the room, stopping only inches from where he sat. Her wide-eyed stare discomfited him, and for the first time in his life, Pharaoh Carn didn't know quite how to react.

"Get lost, kid."

She barely blinked.

He had no way of knowing that her father's hair had been black like his, and that her mother's skin had been as smooth and brown as his own. All he saw was a little kid who should have been afraid, but wasn't.

"Francesca, come here, please," the social worker said, but the little girl didn't move.

Pharaoh saw the woman stand, and he could tell by the set of her mouth that the kid was going to catch hell. In that moment, something gave way inside him that he hadn't known was there.

"It's all right," he mumbled. "She ain't botherin' me."

The woman hesitated, then shrugged and sat back down, keeping a close eye on the pair, nonetheless.

"So, how old are you, kid?"

The little girl held up four fingers.

He nodded, then leaned back, thinking to himself that, for a kid, she was pretty cute. And her eyes—they cut right through his armor to the boy beneath.

They stared at one another. Finally Pharaoh tried another approach, searching for something else that might elicit a verbal response.

"So, your name is Francesca, is it?"

Clutching the teddy bear a little tighter, she considered the question and then nodded.

"My daddy calls me Frankie," she finally said. And then her lips trembled, and the tears that had been threatening suddenly spilled. "My mommy and daddy went away. They went to heaven without me."

Pharaoh flushed. Damn, this was too intense. What was he supposed to do now? He looked up, certain that someone was going to blame him for her tears, but no one seemed to be paying them any attention. To his dismay, the flow increased. He leaned forward, his elbows on his knees, as he lowered his voice.

"Look, kid, don't cry, okay? I ain't got no daddy either. That's why I'm here. That's why we're all here."

She absorbed his words. "Are you sad, too?" she finally asked.

Pharaoh straightened abruptly. "Hell no," he muttered, then flushed again as he realized he shouldn't have cursed in front of the kid. "But that's because I'm grown-up. When you grow up, you won't cry, either."

Then, because he didn't want someone to accuse him of making her cry, he took the end of her blanket and gave it a swipe across her cheeks.

"Here," he said, pinching the end of her nose with a piece of the blanket. "Blow."

* * *

Pharaoh woke with a start, then glanced toward the clock. It was just after four in the morning, and he needed to pee. He considered ringing for the nurse, but shoved the thought aside. He was home. Surely he could manage that much on his own.

With a groan, he sat up, gingerly inching his way to the side of the bed. Everything about him hurt, but the deepest pain of all was in his heart. There was an emptiness inside him that time couldn't heal. Francesca was missing. They hadn't found her body in the rubble of his home, so he wouldn't let himself think that she'd died. But the hospitals were full of people who'd been injured, some still unidentified.

Gritting his teeth against the bone-jarring pain, he stood, slowly making his way into the bathroom. A few minutes later, he came out, glanced at the bed and the jumble of sheets, and walked to the window instead.

The security lights were bright against the darkness. In the circle of illumination, he could see movement beneath the shrubs. Probably an armadillo. He made a mental note to mention it to the gardener tomorrow. Then he amended the thought. It was already tomorrow.

He laid the flat of his hand against the cold windowpane.

"Be alive, Francesca...and be ready, because I'm coming for you."

Six

It was just after two in the morning when Clay suddenly awoke. The house was dark, the bedroom silent, but his instincts told him something was wrong.

Frankie!

He bolted from bed, pulling on his jeans as he ran across the hall. The door to her room was open, her bed empty. Panic hit his heart first as he relived every horror from two years ago. He pivoted sharply, then started up the hall toward the front of the house. Almost immediately he saw flickering lights on the living-room wall and frowned. Had he left the television on?

Then he saw her on the sofa, wrapped in her favorite blanket and crying quietly in the dark. The remote hung loosely from her fingers as she sat, mesmerized by the images on the screen.

He took a deep breath, willing his panic to subside. All he could think was, thank God, thank God. Silently, he moved toward her, stopping behind where she sat, then leaning down to press his cheek against the back of her hair.

"Francesca, what are you doing awake?"

She jumped and looked up, relaxing only after she saw it was Clay.

"You startled me," she said, and then added, "I couldn't sleep."

He cupped her cheek, wiping away tears with the ball of his thumb, then kissed the side of her face.

"Are you all right?"

For days, he'd been so cold—so distant. His unexpected sympathy was her undoing. Her words were a jumble of tears and disjointed sentences as she nodded, then pointed the remote at the screen.

"Movie...so sad...loves her so much."

Clay glanced at the empty video box on the table, then hid a smile. It was one of his mother's movies, and, as he remembered, pretty damned sad at that.

"But it ends good," he offered.

Slightly mollified by his remark, she sniffed. "It does?"

He looked down at those dark, tear-stained eyes and wanted to kiss her. As much as he wanted to give in to the urge, he stood fast. He'd been behaving like a fool ever since she'd come home. She would probably slap him.

"Yes, it does."

She sniffled, then wiped her face with the end of her blanket.

"Promise?"

"I promise," he said softly; then he eyed the empty end of the sofa she was sitting on. "Want some company?"

Frankie's heart stopped. Could this be an offering of peace? "Yes, please."

He circled the sofa, but instead of settling beside her, he scooped her up, blanket and all, and sat her in his lap.

Frankie held her breath, waiting to see what came next.

"Comfortable?" he asked softly, settling her firmly into the crook of his arm and rewrapping the blanket across her legs.

Frankie's heart was pounding. "Yes," she whispered.

"Warm enough?"

Words left her. She nodded.

"Where's the remote?"

She handed it to him, watching as his thumb centered on the volume and upped it a notch.

"Can you hear that okay?" he asked.

Over the thunder of my heart? "It's fine."

"Okay, then."

Once again she managed to became lost in the

heroine's confusion. It wasn't until the last scene was playing that she let out a sigh of relief. She looked up at Clay, her eyes bright, her heart lighter.

"I love happy-ever-after endings, don't you?"

He smiled and nodded, but his belly was in a knot. After everything he'd put her through, she was still the gentle, forgiving woman that he'd fallen in love with and married. Why hadn't he seen that before? Why, when she'd virtually returned from the dead, had he seen nothing but negatives? He should have been down on his knees thanking God, not looking for lies.

"Frankie, I am so sorry."

She stilled. The moment she'd been praying for was finally here, and she was afraid to move for fear she would wake up and find herself dreaming. She bit her lip, then tentatively reached for him, cupping the side of his face. His eyes closed as he turned toward her touch, then he kissed the palm of her hand.

"I don't do drugs," she said, her voice shaking.

He leaned forward until their foreheads were touching. "I know, baby, I know."

"I don't know how the needle marks got on my arms, but I didn't—"

"Hush," Clay begged, and pulled her into an embrace.

Frankie shuddered. Of all the emotions she was feeling right now, the most overpowering was that of being safe.

"I'm not lying to you. I want to remember."

"I know," Clay said. "And you will...when it's time."

She sighed. "I don't know where I was, but I came back to you, didn't I?"

Clay's conscience pricked. Why hadn't that been enough?

"Yes, Francesca, and I will be forever grateful that you did."

A long silence ensued before Frankie spoke again. This time, it was for him that she worried.

"It was terrible for you, wasn't it?"

His arms tightened around her as he remembered the endless days and nights of torture, imagining her in every terrible situation—at times believing her dead. He nodded.

"I'm sorry this happened to us." She sighed, her voice full of regret. "We were so happy."

Clay looked up. "And we will be again. It just takes time to get past the shock." He tried to smile. "Sometime after the first year had passed, I guess I gave up hope. In my heart, I believed you were dead. It was the only reason I could think of for why you would stay away."

Frankie wanted to cry all over again, only this

time for her and Clay, not for the movie. "I can understand that, but I obviously didn't give up on myself or on us. I came back to you, Clay. All I ask is that you bear with me a while. Help me find out what happened—and make sure it never happens again."

Clay's smile disappeared. "Was that a warning, or were you being prophetic?"

"Neither," she said shortly. "Just facing a fact. I know I would never willingly leave you...so in my mind, there's only one other reason for it happening."

"What?"

"Somebody took me." She shuddered. "What frightens me is that if it happened once, it could happen again."

Given everything they knew so far, she could be right. Danger could be anywhere, but they wouldn't know what to look out for until she could remember where she'd been.

"Come to bed," he said. "There's time enough to worry about all this later."

Frankie hesitated, almost afraid to ask as Clay helped her up from the sofa. "With you?"

Clay tunneled his fingers through her hair and drew her close to his chest. "Yes, baby, with me— if you're willing to sleep with a reformed jerk."

She wrapped her arms around his waist. For the

first time since she'd regained consciousness in the hospital, she was beginning to believe everything would be all right.

"I suppose I could set aside my prejudices for the night," she said.

He grinned. "Come on. It's late, and you need to rest. Just because you're out of the hospital, that doesn't mean you can run roughshod over doctor's orders."

"I was sitting down," she protested as he led her into their room.

"And now you're going to lie down," he said, straightening the covers as she crawled into bed.

Moments later, he was lying beside her. An uneasy silence ensued.

The sound of her breathing tugged at his heart. He hadn't known how precious that small sound was until he'd lost it. Even though the bed was king-size, the surface seemed to have shrunk. For some reason, he felt hesitant to trespass into her space without her consent. It took a while for him to realize that the time she'd been lost had been longer than the time they'd been married. It seemed foolish, but he almost felt as if he was sleeping with a stranger.

And then her voice broke the silence, and the moment he heard it, everything fell into place.

"Clay?"

"What, honey?"

"Will you hold me?" she asked.

Once again, he was struck with remorse that his own wife felt obligated to ask for what should have been an understood right.

"It would be my pleasure," he said softly, and opened his arms.

Moments later, Frankie's head was pillowed on his shoulder and one arm was across his chest. Soon the even rise and fall of her breathing told him that she'd fallen asleep. But sleep wouldn't come for Clay. He kept thinking of what she'd said about being afraid it would happen again. What if she was right? What if she was in danger? Here they were, going about their lives as if nothing had happened. What was it the detective had said about the woman the cabby had picked up at the bus station? Oh yes, she'd come running out of the terminal as if she was being chased. His heart skipped a beat.

At the time, the scenario had seemed so far-fetched that he'd been inclined to ignore it. But what other explanation could there be? Her disappearance had been baffling. Her return was just the same. The fact that she'd been injured before she'd had time to explain could be nothing more than an unfortunate stroke of fate.

With a reluctant sigh, he reached down and

pulled the covers up over her shoulders, then closed his eyes and tightened his hold. Outside, the air was cold, the wind sharp. A new day was about to dawn.

Pharaoh Carn sat before the window overlooking the back of his estate, sipping a cup of coffee and contemplating the dawning day. A rabbit's-foot key ring dangled from the ends of his fingers as he gazed across the grounds.

His night had been restless, his sleep disturbed more than once. Every time he closed his eyes, his mind went into replay mode. The rolling floor—the fear on Francesca's face—falling backward down the stairs.

After that, his memory faded. The rest was just bits and pieces: a man's face leaning over him; being loaded onto a helicopter; and then his days in the hospital. The endless hours of strangers' faces, and the poking and prodding and pain, all in the name of medicine. And in the background of it all, the knowledge that for the second time in his life, he'd lost his luck.

He palmed the rabbit's foot, knowing that this would not be enough mojo to offset the loss of Francesca, but at the moment, it was all he had. He put down his cup and then stood, before slowly making his way toward the fireplace and the brown leather sofa nearby. With a groan, he sank into its depths, stretching out on the four-cushion length and closing his eyes.

He needed to rest. He couldn't seem to concentrate for more than minutes at a time. The organization he had created demanded an authority figure in constant attendance. His weakness was dangerous. In his world, only the strong survived, and money and power were the ultimate goals. Strength equaled power. Power equaled control. And to continue to reign over the world he had created, he had to stay in control. But the silence of the room was seductive. Before he knew it, he had fallen asleep, once again slipping into the past through his dreams.

Albuquerque, New Mexico

Ten-year-old Frankie Romano giggled at the boy outside the schoolroom window. For the past six years, Pharaoh Carn had been the single most important person in her life. For a child stunned by the tragedy of her parents' deaths and starved for the affection she'd been used to, his attention had been her salvation.

Although he no longer resided at the home, Pharaoh Carn was now an employee there. A year ago, the courts had declared him an adult, and he'd moved out and into an apartment nearby.

On the surface, he appeared no different than any other teenager of his era. But looks were deceiving. Pharaoh had a taste for luxuries, but without the education or patience it took to acquire them, he had turned to a life of crime. It was easy, it was fast and it presented a challenge that he couldn't resist. He wanted everything—and he wanted it now.

By the age of sixteen, Pharaoh had involved himself with a local gang. It hadn't been easy. His time was restricted more than the normal teenager's, but he quickly learned how to bypass the system in which he was caught.

The past three years with the gang had been his only on-the-job training. Heisting cars had become a cinch, and he'd long since graduated from breaking and entering to armed robberies. Although he had yet to kill, he'd used a gun more than once in the act. Now that he was on his own, he drove a nice car, bought fancy clothes and sported a two-carat diamond stud in one ear. His good looks, dark eyes and thick, curly hair were a draw for the young women. He took from them what he wanted and tossed them aside like empty beer cans when he was through.

But with Pharaoh's exit from the orphanage had

come a hitch in his plans for the future. He was young and strong and greedy. He wanted it all, and he wanted it now. But the flaw was having to leave Francesca behind.

Superstitious to a fault, he firmly believed that Francesca Romano was his luck—that, with her, would come his full power. But she was only ten. It would be years before she could join him. Yet when that day came, Pharaoh firmly believed that, with her at his side, he would come into his own.

So he had taken a job as a groundskeeper at Kitteridge House. If he couldn't take her with him, the least he could do was protect his future.

Over the years, he'd become her confidant, her protector and, at times, a substitute father figure. The little girl had brought out the only good there would ever be in Pharaoh Carn. From the day of her arrival, the people at the home had begun looking at him in a different light. It was as if they were seeing him anew through Francesca's eyes. Everyone knew that children couldn't be fooled, and it was obvious that Frankie Romano saw something in him that the others did not. Her dependence upon him and the adoration she gave him elevated him to something important—even something special. With her in his life, he could do no wrong. So when he saw her in the classroom with her chin in her hands, gazing longingly out the window toward the playground swings, he couldn't help but make himself known.

He watched her focus shift as he walked into her line of vision. When her expression changed and she began to smile, he felt lighter than air.

The teacher tapped her pencil on the edge of the desk and then pointed straight at Francesca.

"Frankie, pay attention!"

Frankie jerked at her teacher's angry tone and looked up, embarrassed at being caught daydreaming.

"Yes, ma'am," she said softly.

When the teacher's attention returned to the blackboard, Frankie dared a last look, but Pharaoh had wisely moved away. It didn't matter, though. He would see her again. He was never far.

After sleeping the rest of the night in Clay's arms, Frankie woke up alone in their bed. Her heart ached as she rolled, laying her hand on his pillow and feeling the lingering warmth. He hadn't been gone long.

She fisted the pillowslip in her fingers and closed her eyes, remembering that they used to wake up making love. But she wasn't going to feel sorry for herself. Not today.

Last night had been a revelation. Who could have known when she'd gone to bed so miserable and unable to sleep that the morning would bring her such joy? Sighing softly, she got out of bed.

She dressed quickly, pulling on a pair of Clay's sweats and a long-sleeved T-shirt, then headed for the bathroom to brush her teeth and hair. Her scalp was still tender, and she winced as the brush bristles scraped the point of injury. She paused for a moment, staring at herself in the mirror. On the surface, she looked the same. But there were too many variables in what she couldn't remember to fool herself into believing in appearances. Nothing would ever be the same again. Not between herself and Clay, no matter how much forgiveness was passed from one to the other. And certainly not for her. Someone had stolen two years of her life.

Suddenly she heard footsteps coming down the hall, and her heart jerked, but in fear rather than anticipation. Somewhere inside, her subconscious was warning her to run.

"Frankie?"

At the sound of Clay's voice, she went weak with relief and exhaled softly. "In here."

He pushed the door aside, then grinned wryly when he saw what she was wearing.

"Remind me to move your clothes back into our closet," he said as he set down the tray of coffee he'd been carrying.

She dropped the hairbrush back in the drawer

and threw her arms around his neck. Her grip was fierce as she hugged him.

"What's this all about?" Clay asked. "Not that I'm complaining, mind you."

"Nothing," she muttered. "I'm just glad it's you."

He frowned. "Who else would it be?"

Uncomfortable with the thought, she buried her face against his chest. "I don't know. Sometimes, as I'm turning around, I almost expect to see someone else's face."

Clay tried not to let his voice mirror his concern. "But that sounds like a good sign. Maybe you're beginning to remember."

She sighed. "I hope so. I feel like there's a hole in my mind, and every so often a little bit of my past leaks out. I keep trying to focus on the images, but the harder I try, the more vague they become."

"Just remember, you're not there alone," he said, then gave her a long, silent look.

"What?" Frankie asked.

"Where do we go from here?"

Her heart skipped a beat, and her voice faded. "You mean us?"

Instantly, he touched her face. "No, baby, no, not us."

"Then if not us, what did you mean?" she asked.

"You should know that until you remember something, the police can't go any further with your case. The way they look at it, you left me and now you're back. Unless you can give them a reason, they don't see a crime, only a wife who walked out on a marriage."

Frankie paled. "I didn't do—"

"I know that," Clay said. "But legally, that's the way it stands."

Her shoulders slumped. "So what are you saying?"

He watched her mood shifting from joy to despair and hated to be the one to bring it all up. But after what she'd said last night about fearing it could happen again, he wasn't going to sit around and wait to see if she was right.

"When you disappeared before and the police began trying to make a case against me, I hired a private investigator to try and find you on my own."

Her face crumpled. "Oh, Clay. I didn't know."

He shrugged. "There's a lot you don't know," he said. "That's okay. What I'm asking you is, what do you think about hiring him again?"

She looked up, startled by the request. But the longer she thought, the more intrigued she became.

"Do you think we could afford to?"

He frowned. "Francesca, that's not the point. The better question is, can we afford not to?"

She sighed, wrapped her arms around herself and turned away. Clay was right behind her. He pulled her back against his chest and cradled her where they stood.

"Talk to me, Frankie. Tell me what you're thinking."

Before she could speak, the phone rang. Clay crawled across the mattress to the other side of the bed to answer.

"Hello?"

"Clay, it's me, how's Frankie?"

"Oh, hi, Mom. She's good," he said quietly, watching the way Frankie's body moved beneath his clothes as she took a pair of socks from a lower drawer. He grinned. Those were his socks, too.

"Are you going to work today?" Betty asked.

He thought of the job in progress and knew he should, but it was Frankie's first day home, and he wasn't about to leave her alone.

"No, not today. Dad's already there, isn't he?"

"Yes, he left around seven."

"Good," Clay said. "I'll give him a call later, but I thought I'd spend the day here with Frankie. I'm not comfortable leaving her alone just yet."

"And that's part of why I called. I'm offering

my services as nurse, or baby-sitter, or mother-in-law, or whatever is needed,'' she said.

Frankie moved to the bureau and got a band to tie back her hair. Clay kept thinking of the mornings after she'd disappeared, when he'd stood in this very room, wondering how he was going to find the guts to keep living without her. And now she was back. He shuddered with a sudden longing to be with his wife in the most intimate way.

''Clay, you didn't answer me,'' Betty said.

He blinked. ''Sorry,'' he muttered. ''I guess I'll pass today, but we'll take you up on the offer another time. Maybe tomorrow, okay?''

''Sure, honey. Just give me a call. I can be there in fifteen minutes.''

''Will do.''

''Bye. Give my love to Frankie.''

''Yeah, I'll do that,'' he said, and hung up the phone.

Frankie turned, the hairbrush in one hand, the band in the other.

''Who was that?''

''Mom. She was offering to hang out with you for a while until you felt stronger.''

Frankie frowned. ''I love your mother, and I would love for her to visit, but I don't need a keeper.''

''That's debatable.''

Before Frankie could argue, he took the hairbrush out of her hands and set it back on the bureau.

"Come here," he said softly as he pulled her close. "I have something to give you."

Frankie smiled hesitantly. "And that would be?"

"Mom said to give you her love. This is the best that I can do." His mouth skirted the edges of her lips, then centered.

Frankie swallowed a groan and wrapped her arms around his neck.

When he came up for air, Frankie sighed. "Is that the best *you* can do?" she whispered.

Clay's eyes glittered darkly. "Hardly, but it's all you're going to get until I think you can handle it."

Frankie almost blushed. "*Handle* it? Might we be just the least little bit overconfident?"

Clay moved away from her. "I don't think so," he drawled. "*We* have been celibate for a hell of a long time."

She tightened her hold around his neck. "Then don't you think it's about time we corrected that problem?"

Seven

Clay's heart skipped a beat. Over the past months, he'd imagined this moment in the nights when he'd been unable to sleep and had come to accept that memories would be all he had left of his wife. But no more. The reality of her return was now. There were no doctors hovering or police in the next room. Only him—and her—and the love that once bound them. Would she forgive him? Could he trust her? He sighed. Finally, none of it mattered.

He cupped her face with his hands, concerned for her injuries, that this would be too soon.

"Are you sure?"

Her chin quivered. "Sure that I love you? That I want to make love to you? Oh, Clay, what do you think?"

He exhaled slowly, then lowered his head. Finally there was nothing to be heard but the shifting of one body to another as she lifted her lips for his kiss. Within seconds, their joining went from sweet to insanity.

She moaned, yielding to his onslaught as he backed her against the wall. One hungry kiss led to another, then another, until they were both shaking and gasping for air. He tunneled his fingers through her hair. When she winced, too late he remembered her injury and drew back in remorse.

"Sorry, so sorry," he muttered, and started to move away when she caught him, pulling him back, then yielding to the instinctive thrust of his hips.

"Careful, Francesca."

"I don't want to be careful. I want to be loved," she begged.

He groaned beneath his breath. Refusing her—or himself—was impossible. He took her in his arms again, gently kissing her face, her eyelids, then finally her lips. They were warm and soft and yielded to his demands all too easily. But he wanted more—so much more.

Frankie's head was swimming. His passion engulfed her. Shaking, she broke free from his kiss to look up at his face.

"Clay..."

His voice was just above a whisper. "What, baby?"

"Take me to bed."

A muscle jerked at the side of his jaw as he picked her up and carried her across the room.

When he laid her on the sheets, she pulled him down with her. They rolled, tangling themselves in the covers of the unmade bed.

Immediately, Clay began to pull at her clothes. His message was urgent and impossible to misunderstand. He wanted her naked, and he wanted her now.

Frankie gladly obliged, tugging at his shirt and jeans as well, until the only thing between them was passion.

Clay raised himself onto one elbow, pausing momentarily to look down at his wife. His smile was brittle, his breathing short and shattered. Two years of celibacy had all but destroyed his control.

"Francesca...sweetheart...I don't know if I can—"

Frankie put her fingers against his mouth. "This is for you."

His groan ripped the quiet of the room as her body made way for him to come in. He began to move almost instantly, thrusting deep inside her. Thoughts came and went, passing through his mind like near-spent bullets, and tearing through the loneliness that had been his sole companion.

Been so long...feels so good.

She wrapped her legs around his waist, pulling him deeper. He groaned again. It was going to be over too fast.

Suddenly the blood was hammering against his eardrums and his body was on a plane all its own, moving without thought, chasing a feeling that kept trying to catch hold.

And then it was upon him—pushing, pushing, driving him harder, deeper. He heard a soft cry, then a deep, aching groan. It was himself that he heard—and he was coming undone.

It was five minutes after three in the afternoon when the doorbell rang. Clay exited the kitchen on the run, anxious that it not wake Frankie, who was taking a nap. Their morning had been exhausting for her, but so healing for them both. Making love to her today had been like making love to her again for the very first time.

When he saw his dad's car through the window, he frowned, hoping that something hadn't happened on the work site. Hastily, he combed his hair with his fingers, then opened the door. The wind was sharp, the air brisk.

"Hey, Dad, come in out of the cold," he said quickly, and shut the door behind them as Winston LeGrand slipped inside.

"Damned miserable today," Winston muttered, shrugging out of his overcoat.

Clay eyed his father's mood as he hung the coat

on their hall tree. As always, it was impossible to read his emotions.

"How about a hot cup of coffee?" Clay asked. "I just made a fresh pot."

"Don't mind if I do," Winston said, rubbing his hands together as he followed his son into the kitchen.

Curious, he looked around as Clay got down a cup. "Where's Frankie?"

"Taking a nap."

Winston nodded, taking the hot cup of coffee and cradling it between his cold palms like a hand warmer.

"She all right?" he asked.

Clay leaned against the counter. "She's getting there," he said quietly.

"Remembering anything?" Winston asked.

"Not enough to help—yet."

Winston nodded and took a slow sip of coffee.

"Everything okay on the site?" Clay asked.

"Yeah, sure."

"I appreciate you stepping in to help me like this," Clay said.

Winston nodded again and took another sip of coffee.

Several long, uneasy moments passed between the men, with Winston busying himself cooling his coffee and Clay watching him blow into the cup.

"So, what do you think?" Winston finally asked.

Clay sighed. He knew what his father was getting at. He'd been so angry and distrustful before, it only stood to reason that his parents would be curious about his state of mind.

"I think I acted like a jackass," Clay muttered. "Thankfully, Francesca seems to have a penchant for men with long ears and a tail."

Winston managed a grin. "It was a rough call," he said.

Clay nodded. "Maybe so, but the least I could have done was listen to her side first."

"Well, you have to admit that the needle marks were incriminating as hell. Add to that the fact that she was oblivious to the two passing years, and you have a woman with a lot of explaining to do."

"I guess," Clay said. "But it doesn't make me feel any better to know that the whole time I was grilling her about where she'd been, she was suffering from a serious concussion." He shuddered. "It's a damn wonder I didn't let her lie there and die."

"But you didn't, and that's that," Winston said. "By the way, your mother told me to tell you that she'll be here around eight tomorrow morning."

Clay looked startled. The thought of walking out the door and leaving Frankie behind made him ill.

"I don't know... I was thinking that maybe I'd spend another—"

Winston took his son by the arm. "Clay."

"What?"

"It's not your fault."

"What's not my fault?" Clay asked.

"Frankie's disappearance. And just because she's back, that doesn't mean you have to stay here with her for the rest of your lives. If your marriage is going to have a chance of surviving this, you both have to get back to a normal way of life as soon as possible."

Logically, Clay knew his father was right, but emotionally, he didn't think he was ready.

"I'll think about it," he muttered.

Winston set his coffee cup down on the counter and looked at his watch.

"Well, think hard, then, because you only have seventeen hours before your mother shows up. After that, you're out the door."

Clay sighed. He knew his father was right. When Betty LeGrand got a notion in her head, there was no stopping her.

"I'll talk to Frankie about it when she wakes up."

"Talk to me about what?" Frankie said.

At the sound of her voice, both men turned. Clay

frowned. She looked as if a good wind would blow her away.

"We didn't mean to wake you," he said.

"You didn't," Frankie countered, and smiled hesitantly at her father-in-law. He was so like Clay, not only in looks, but personality, as well. She wondered if he had judged her as harshly.

"Well?" Winston drawled. "Aren't I going to get a hello kiss?"

A wide smile broke the somberness of her face as she walked into his arms. Winston's shirt smelled of cigars and diesel and the cold, but the bear hug he gave her more than made up for it all.

"I wasn't sure you wanted one," she said softly.

Winston cocked an eyebrow at his son, then looked back at her. His eyes were twinkling. "And why wouldn't I want a kiss from my only daughter?"

Frankie wanted to cry. It was rare praise from a closemouthed man, and for that, she cherished it all the more.

"For that, you may have two," she said, and kissed him on either cheek.

Winston blushed, but his smile never faded. "Well, now. I delivered my message, and the tip was probably more than I deserved, but I'll take it with pleasure."

Clay chuckled. It did him good to see his father a little distracted.

"Okay, you two," Frankie said. "I'll take the affection, but I still want an answer. I'm here. What are you going to talk to me about?"

Before Clay could answer, Winston blurted out his message again. "Betty said she'd be over tomorrow to spend the day with you, so that Clay could go back to work."

Frankie looked puzzled. "Of course I'd love to spend the day with her, but I don't need a babysitter, you know."

Clay tensed. How does a man tell his wife he's afraid to leave her alone for fear she'll disappear?

"Look, you guys, except for a headache now and then, I'm fine. The doctor said so." She looked at Clay, frowning. "If you needed to be at work, you should have said something sooner. I would have been fine on my own."

Winston frowned. "Didn't mean to start such a fuss," he said shortly. "I delivered your mother's message. It's up to you two to let her know if you change the plans. I'm going home now. Call if you need me."

"Yeah, okay, Dad," Clay said. "And thanks for helping out."

"No problem," Winston said.

Moments later, they heard the front door slam and then the sound of a car driving away.

Frankie was still waiting for Clay to answer, but he seemed overly concerned with washing the coffee cup his father had used. Finally her patience ran out. "Clay, don't ignore me."

He turned. His expression was blank, his posture stiff and unyielding.

Frankie sighed. "What's this all about?"

Water dripped from his hands as he stared at her from across the room. Long moments passed as Clay struggled with an answer. Finally, it was the truth that came out.

"I'm afraid to leave you alone."

Her face paled and she jerked as if she'd been slapped. "Why?"

He swallowed, hating the fear in his voice. "What if it happens again? And before you get mad, you have to be honest. You've already voiced the same fear."

She kept staring at him. Although her accusation was silent, his belly knotted, all the same. He knew what was coming, but so help him God, he didn't know how to stop her from asking.

Finally she shuddered and then blinked. A single tear slid down her cheek.

"You weren't talking about kidnappers, Clay.

You were talking about me...walking out on you again.''

"I wasn't... I mean, I don't think you..."

She covered her face with her hands, but before he could get to her, she looked up, and the fire in her eyes stopped him cold.

"I won't say it again," she said quietly. "There's no need to defend myself to a man who doesn't trust me. So call your mother. Call the neighbors. For the love of God, Clay, call the police for all I care. I don't know what more I can say."

Then she walked away, and Clay knew, as sure as he knew his own name, that it was going to take more than making love to make this go away.

Steam rose from the heat of the water as the shower jets pelted on top of Frankie's head. Twice she worked her shampoo into a lather and then rinsed, each time taking care not to rub too hard on the sore spot. Finally, with her hair squeaky-clean and her body tingling from her bath, she turned off the water and stepped out of the tub. Without thought, she wrapped her wet hair turban-style, and began to dry off with another towel.

The mirror was foggy, the room warm and filled with mist, and yet she felt chilled. Without Clay, she felt weightless and empty. Yes, he was still in the house, but not in her heart. They'd made love, but they had yet to make up. He might love her, but he didn't trust her. That was a fact she had to accept. A part of her almost understood—but there was another part of her that knew if the situation had been reversed, she would have been down on her knees thanking God for his return.

Quickly she toweled herself off and reached for her robe. The thick, pink terry cloth swaddled her body as she tied the belt in a knot. Then she turned to the mirror and gave it a swipe with the hand towel so she could see to comb out her hair.

As she did, something scratched against the back of her neck. She felt inside the collar of the robe, trying to find the source of irritation, but nothing seemed evident. Then she turned sideways and looked in the mirror, pulling at her collar and still trying to see what was poking her skin.

Suddenly her gaze shifted from the robe to her neck. There, just below her hairline, was a fleck of something gold. Frowning, she rubbed at the place, wondering if she'd missed some shampoo, but nothing came away on her hands. She looked again. Whatever it was, was still there. She could just see the bit of color.

Curious, she got a hand mirror from the drawer and turned her back to the mirror. Her gaze focused, then her heart skipped a beat.

My God! It was the tattoo. Although she remembered Clay mentioning it before, she'd completely forgotten about it.

Suddenly her vision blurred, and in her mind she saw the same golden image on a man's bare chest. Fear hit with a gut-wrenching gasp. The mirror fell from her fingers and onto the floor. As it shattered, she screamed.

Clay was in the living room when he heard her scream. He bolted from the chair and dashed down the hall into their room, hitting the bathroom door with the flat of his hand, ready to fight. But the only thing that escaped as he entered was the steam from her shower. He saw her first, then the broken glass, then yanked her off her feet before she could move. He carried her into the bedroom, then sat down on the mattress with her in his lap, his hands shaking as he checked her for cuts. There were none.

"Sweetheart, what happened?"

She looked up, her expression blank. "Clay?"

His heart skipped a beat. Oh God. Where had she gone?

Then her focus shifted, and he saw recognition returning. Her chin quivered as she reached toward the back of her neck and began digging at the surface of her skin as if something foul was stuck there.

"That thing on my neck. Get it off. Get it off."

Startled by her panic, he grabbed her hand before she could do herself harm.

"Easy, baby," he said gently. "It's just a tattoo."

She shuddered, then moaned. "Who did this to me?"

Her fear shamed him. He wrapped his arms around her, holding her close.

"I don't know, Francesca. I wish to God I did, but I don't."

She began to sob. Clay pulled her closer, rocking her where they sat.

"It will be all right," he said gently. "One of these days we'll have the answers, but until then, we have each other, okay?"

"I don't have you," she kept sobbing. "Not anymore. Not anymore. He ruined it all."

Clay froze. Did she realize what she'd just said? He took a slow breath, anxious not to upset her further. But he couldn't let the remark go unchallenged.

"Who, baby?" he asked softly. "Who ruined it all?"

Suddenly quiet, she caught her breath on a sob.

Slowly she sat up, staring at him. "The man," she muttered.

"What man?" Clay countered.

She closed her eyes, trying to look at his face, but as hard as she tried, her inward eye could not move past the tattoo on his chest.

"Frankie?"

She shook her head as she opened her eyes. "I can't see his face."

"How did you know it was a man?" Clay asked.

"Because I saw his bare chest." Then she shuddered. "There was a tattoo, just like the one on my neck." She moaned. "I don't want it there. Get it off."

Clay gritted his teeth. He would like nothing better, but short of laser surgery, which he didn't think she was up to yet, he didn't know of a way.

"We will, baby, when you're stronger, okay?"

She kept shuddering, her voice shaking with every breath. "Promise?"

He hugged her close. "Promise."

Finally she began to relax. Minutes later, her eyes closed, and Clay knew she was drifting off to sleep. He removed the wet towel from her hair and then laid her down and covered her up.

For a moment he worried about the damp tangles on her pillow, then shrugged off the idea of drying her hair and hung the wet towel on a hook. She needed to sleep. Besides, he was afraid that his wife had endured far worse things than going to bed with wet hair.

It was almost morning when the dream began, but time had no meaning for Frankie. There was nothing but a numbing fear and the knowledge that she was going to die...

The floor beneath her feet began to roll. Outside the window, trees were dipping and swaying, while others tumbled to the ground. As she watched, the ground beneath the window split, like cracks in hot chocolate cake. The earth was coming undone. She clutched at the bars on the windows, screaming for help, but there was no one to see. No one to care. Everyone here worked for him.

Behind her, an onyx statue suddenly toppled from its pedestal onto the floor, shattering with a sound like a gunshot into thousands of pieces. She spun at the sound, staring at the falcon's head that had separated from the form of a human body. She shuddered. Horus, the ancient Egyptian god of light and heaven, was in pieces on the floor.

Another rumble of earth against earth sent her scrambling for the door. This place had been her prison, but it wouldn't be her tomb.

Frantically, she began to hammer her fists against the surface, screaming aloud over and over.

"Help! Somebody help me! Let me out! Let me out!"

Suddenly the door opened. Just for a moment she thought it was Horus himself, right down to the hawklike eyes. And then Pharaoh grabbed her wrist, yanking her from her gilded cage into the magnificence crumbling down around them.

"Run, Francesca!" he shouted. "Run for your life!" he cried, and pulled her after him.

She ran, but not with him. In her mind, she was running to Clay.

Frankie sat up abruptly, Clay's unspoken name on her lips. Sweat was pouring down her face, and her heart was hammering as if she'd been running. He was asleep beside her, his arm stretched out toward the place where she lay. Still shaken by the dream, she pushed the hair from her face and crawled out of bed. Almost instantly, Clay sensed her exit.

"Frankie?"

"I'm just going to the bathroom," she said quietly, and tiptoed into the other room.

Once inside, she closed the door and turned on the lights, staring at herself in the mirror over the sink. The woman looking back was a stranger. She didn't know how, and she didn't know why, but she knew now that for the last two years she'd been living with someone else. Not willfully, but she'd been living with him just the same.

"How could you do that?" she whispered to herself.

As soon as she gave life to the question, the answer was already in her mind. She'd hadn't been living, she'd been enduring. And she'd done it for Clay. For the chance that somehow—some way—she would find a way to get back to him.

Well, she'd done it. She was home where she belonged. But the question remained, was she safe? Or were her fears going to prove her right? Would that hawk-man come after her again? The urge to run away was strong. They could move. They could hide. They could...

She stopped, disgusted with herself for letting panic take control. That wasn't the way she intended to live her life. Until Clay, her whole life had been uncertainty. She wanted her world back the way it had been before she'd disappeared. She refused to live life on the run.

As she stared, struggling with the turmoil in her mind, an idea began to emerge. If the man came again, she would not be the victim. The hunter would become the hunted, and she would be waiting.

* * *

Betty LeGrand smiled at her daughter-in-law over her Caesar salad. They were having lunch at one of Betty's favorite downtown restaurants.

"Is your chicken good?" she asked, pointing her fork at Frankie's grilled chicken and pasta salad.

"Mmm," Frankie said, smiling and nodding around the bite in her mouth.

Betty forked another bite of salad, chewing thoughtfully as she watched Frankie's face. The girl was thinner, but that was to be expected. Betty prayed for the day when Frankie's memory would come back. It was the devils you didn't know that plagued you the most.

Frankie chewed thoughtfully as she reminisced over the past morning. True to her word, Betty had been at their house by eight o'clock. Clay had been out the door about thirty minutes afterward, and, except for trips to the bathroom, Frankie had yet to be alone. But after last night's revelation, she no longer cared. She had bigger fish to fry than fussing over being smothered in love.

"Betty, I want to thank you for showing me the clippings."

Betty laid down her fork. "I wondered about bringing them, and then I put myself in your place and knew that if it was me, I'd want to know."

Frankie nodded. "You were right. Reading the reports of my disappearance and the hell that Clay went through afterward has put an entirely different spin on understanding his behavior now."

Betty's gaze was solemn. "I wasn't trying to take Clay's side in all of this. I just wanted you to know what we all went through."

Frankie sighed. "If only I knew what *I'd* gone through, as well, we'd all be a lot better off."

Before Betty could respond, the cell phone in her purse began to ring. She rolled her eyes. "That's either Winston or Clay."

Frankie's eyes suddenly sparkled. "A hot-fudge sundae says that it's Clay."

Betty grinned, well aware that she was probably going to lose the bet, but it didn't matter. Lunch was on her anyway.

"You're on," she said, and answered the phone. "Hello. Oh, hi, hang on a minute, will you?" Then she waved at a passing waiter. "Two hot-fudge sundaes, please, and put them on my ticket."

"Yes, ma'am," the waiter said, and slipped through the crowded tables to place the order.

Betty winked at Frankie and then returned to her call. "Sorry, son, I was just making good on a bet. Now, what was it you were saying? Yes, she's fine. Here, you ask her. I'm going to the ladies' room."

Betty handed Frankie the phone and winked as she left the table.

"Clay?"

He sighed. Just hearing her voice took the angst out of his gut. "Hi, baby. Having a good time?"

"Oh sure," she said. "We've done lunch, and we're going to do a little more shopping before we head home."

"Just don't overdo, okay?"

"I won't."

There was a moment of silence, then she heard him sigh again. "I love you, Francesca."

Her heart tugged. "I love you, too," she said softly.

"I'll see you this evening."

Her heart hurt for the doubt she heard in his voice, only this time she knew it wasn't her he didn't trust. It was fate.

"I'll be waiting."

She disconnected, then laid down the phone. There were tears in her eyes when she looked up, but she quickly blinked them away. This wasn't a time for self-pity.

Moments later, Betty returned. No sooner had she sat down than the waiter appeared with their desserts.

"Dig in," Frankie said. "When we're through, there's someplace I need you to take me."

"Sure thing," Betty said, taking her first bite. "Mmm, good."

"It sure is," Frankie said. "Thanks."

Betty dug her spoon into the chocolate-covered mound. "My pleasure, believe me."

Frankie giggled.

"By the way, where do you want to go?" Betty asked.

Frankie shrugged. "Wherever they sell guns."

Betty paused, staring at Frankie as ice cream dripped from her spoon onto the table.

"Excuse me? I misunderstood you. I thought you said guns."

Frankie's expression hardened. "You heard me right. I'm going to buy one, then learn how to shoot."

Betty shuddered. This was so unlike the tender-hearted girl her son had married. "But, Francesca...a gun?"

Frankie's gaze never wavered. "I was a victim once. It won't happen again."

"Are you going to tell Clay?" Betty asked.

"What do you think?" Frankie asked.

Betty sighed. "I think not."

Frankie tensed. "Are you going to tell him?"

Betty hesitated, then, against her better judgment, took another bite of her sundae. When she looked up, Frankie was still staring at her from across the table.

"What?" she asked around a mouthful of ice cream.

"Well, are you going to tell him?" Frankie asked.

Betty never blinked. "Tell him what?"

Frankie sighed, unaware how tense she'd been until Betty had spoken. "Thank you," she said quietly.

Betty's lips firmed. "Just don't make me sorry."

"Hey, Dawson."

Detective Avery Dawson looked up. His partner was waving at him from across the room.

"Long distance for you on three," Paul said.

Dawson picked up the phone. "Denver Police Department, Dawson here."

"Detective Dawson, I'm Captain Paul Fornier, L.A.P.D."

Dawson sat up from his slump. "Captain, how can I help you?"

There was a slight pause. Dawson could hear papers shuffling.

"Hello? You still there?" Dawson asked.

Fornier cleared his throat. "Sorry," he said shortly. "I was trying to find my notes. Yes, here they are. As you know, things have been in a hell of a mess out here, what with the earthquake and all.''

''Yes, we've been keeping up through the national news,'' Dawson said. ''Were you hit bad?''

''The department didn't suffer as much damage as my home, but we're all still standing,'' Fornier said. ''However, that's not why I called. A flyer for a missing person came across my desk yesterday that matches the description of a Jane Doe we have in the morgue.''

Dawson frowned. ''And how does that pertain to us?''

''Your name and department were listed as the point of contact. I'm calling to check on the status of the case as part of a process of elimination.''

''Oh, right,'' Dawson said, and reached for a pen and a clean piece of paper. ''What's the name?''

''Francesca LeGrand.''

Dawson tossed down the pen and kicked back in his chair.

''Well, I can answer your question on that one real quick. Throw the flyer away. Francesca LeGrand is no longer missing.''

''Oh? What happened, did her body turn up?'' Fornier asked.

''Nope. Like the proverbial prodigal son, she came back on her own.''

"Alive?"

"And breathing," Dawson added.

"Well, now, in our business, that doesn't happen every day, does it?" Fornier said. "Okay, then, that's one down for me and only a couple hundred more to go."

"Yes, sir, I know what you mean," Dawson said. "Anything else I can do for you?"

"No. No. I think that just about covers it," Fornier said.

"All right, then," Dawson said. "Good luck to you all."

Fornier chuckled in the phone. "We're going to need it."

Dawson started to hang up when he realized Fornier was still talking.

"I'm sorry," Dawson said. "What did you say?"

"Out of curiosity, when did Mrs. LeGrand show up?"

"Just a few days ago," Dawson said.

"All right, and thanks again," Fornier said.

Dawson disconnected, then sat, staring at the files strewn on his desk. The conversation wasn't any different than others he'd had before, and yet there was something about it that bothered him. He went back over the words in his mind, volleying Fornier's questions with his answers. It wasn't until he got to the last part that it hit him. Why did it matter to Fornier when Francesca LeGrand was taken off the missing list? If she was here, she could not be there, certainly not in a morgue.

His gut clenched as he reached for the phone.

"Operator, I need the number for the Los Angeles Police Department. Yes, the main number will be fine."

A few moments later, he was counting the rings.

"Los Angeles Police Department, how may I direct your call?"

"I'd like to speak with a Captain Fornier, please," Dawson said.

"I'm sorry, sir, but there's no officer by that name in this department."

Dawson suddenly felt light-headed, as if he'd stood too abruptly.

"Are you sure?" he asked.

"Yes, sir," the receptionist said. "I'm looking at the directory as we speak, and there's no one here by that name."

Dawson was shaking as hung up the phone. Even though the LeGrand case was technically active, he and Ramsey had come to a private conclusion that Francesca's story about being taken from her home by force was all a lot of bull, especially since she'd returned under her own steam. But this phone call put another spin on the story. If she'd been telling the truth, he'd just given some very important information to a man who'd lied about his identity. The thought made him nervous. He got up from his desk and headed across the room to his captain's office. If things were about to go sour, he didn't want to be the only one in the know.

Eight

"How about that one?" Frankie asked.

The clerk at the gun shop arched an eyebrow. The woman might not know anything about guns, as she claimed, but she had a good eye. He lifted the small handgun from the case and laid it on the counter in front of her.

"Good choice," he said. "Like the others I showed you, this is also a 9 mm Glock. It's a G26 model, which is small and lightweight, making it easy to carry, and it fits nicely in your hand. And it fires eleven rounds, which is more than sufficient for normal protection. Here, hold it," he urged. "See how it feels."

Frankie picked it up, palming the grip and sliding her finger against the trigger.

"This one has the same features as the other Glocks you showed me, right?"

"What do mean?" the clerk asked.

"I mean about accidental firings, say, if it was dropped."

"Oh, yes, of course," the clerk said. "In fact, that's the beauty of a Glock. It employs three internal safety mechanisms, all based on the trigger, remember? Simply put, it won't fire if you don't pull the trigger."

Frankie nodded, looked down the barrel and took aim at a paper target on the opposite wall.

"Have you ever fired a gun before?" he asked

"No."

"I highly recommend some lessons." Then he smiled to soften what could be construed as criticism.

"I'm going to sign up at the Foothills Shooting Center in Lakewood. Do you know of it?"

"A good establishment. I'm sure you'll get all the instruction you need there."

Frankie nodded again. There was little more to be said, and truth be told, she was still a bit uncomfortable with the fact that she was seriously considering the purchase of a gun.

She looked at it then—at the way her fingers curled around the grip, the way it warmed from the heat of her body. The longer she held it, the more it began to feel like an extension of herself. It should have felt strange, even uncomfortable, but it didn't. Instead, it balanced out her fears, making her feel as if she was on even ground with her faceless captors.

Then she shuddered. Even arming herself was no guarantee that she would be safe. There were too many unanswered questions. She couldn't afford complacency until she had answers for her missing years. Simply owning a gun would not save her from future danger, but it did give her an emotional edge she badly needed.

She felt the clerk's gaze, and for some reason was reluctant to face him. She hadn't expected it, but there was a feeling of guilt associated with the purchase of a weapon. It was as if she was admitting to the world that her life was in disarray, and that she was willing to resort to violence to fix it.

Added to that, this was a big step she hadn't discussed with Clay. Then she reminded herself that Clay wasn't the one in imminent danger. She glanced out the window toward the car where Betty was patiently waiting, then took a deep breath.

"How much?" she asked.

"It's six hundred and twenty-seven dollars, plus tax." Then he added, "There'll be a three-day waiting period before you can pick it up."

She nodded. "I'll be back."

"That's fine, then," the clerk said. "I'll need you to fill out some papers."

She proceeded to do as he asked, and a short while later exited the gun shop. She gave her mother-in-law a nervous smile as she slid into the passenger seat.

"Did you do it?" Betty asked.

"Yes."

"I hope you know what you're doing."

Frankie's smile faded. "What I do know is that I'm never going to be a victim again."

Betty's eyes darkened with sympathy as she reached for Frankie's hand and gave it a squeeze.

"I'm so sorry this has happened to you," she said softly. "But I want you to be careful. People die daily from accidental gunshot wounds."

Frankie's lips thinned into a hard, angry line. "If I ever pull the trigger of a gun, it won't be an accident."

Betty paled. This was a side of Francesca she'd never seen.

"Could you? Kill someone, I mean."

"If I felt my life or Clay's was threatened, yes."

"You're that sure?"

"I'm that sure," Frankie said, and then looked away.

They headed home in silence. Only when Betty was turning down the drive did Frankie speak again.

"Clay is already home," Frankie said, then remembered to add, "Thank you for lunch and for chauffeuring me around."

Betty parked, and gave Frankie a hug. "Oh, honey, it was my pleasure. When you disappeared, I grieved as if I'd lost my own child. Being with you like this is something I thought I'd never get to do again. All you have to do is ask."

"I will, and soon," Frankie promised. She exited the car on the run.

The wind was sharp. It felt like snow. She reached the door, her fingers shaking from the cold as she fumbled with the knob, but before she could turn it, Clay was standing in the doorway.

He smiled a welcome and pulled her into the warmth of the house, shutting the door behind her. "Come here to me," he growled and opened his arms.

Frankie sank against him, snuggling her face against his red sweatshirt and savoring the strength of his embrace.

Clay rubbed his chin against the crown of her hair, loving the way she felt in his arms and thanking God that he was able to hold her once more.

"You and Mom had a pretty long day. Are you tired?"

She sighed. "Sort of, but it was good to be with her. I love her a lot, you know."

He smiled. "Yeah, I know. She thinks you're okay, too."

He pulled back enough that he could look at her face. "How about a hot bath before dinner?"

She nodded and then frowned as she remembered. "Oh, Clay, I didn't even think of dinner or shopping for groceries. Do we have anything to cook?"

"It's already done, so don't worry," he said.

Her shoulders slumped. "I'm not paying much attention to my side of the deal, am I?"

He frowned. "What deal?"

"You know, the one where you work and I take care of the house."

"Even if it was only part-time, you were working, too," he muttered. "Besides, who ever said anything about a deal, Francesca? What happens to you, happens to me, and vice versa. As far as I'm concerned, you should still be in bed, and you're damn sure not going to start keeping house until you're stronger."

She managed a smile. "Okay."

"Now, how about that bath?" Clay asked.

"You talked me into it," she said. "I won't be long."

"Take your time, honey. The baked potatoes are still in the oven, anyway."

She hurried away, ridden with guilt that Clay was doing all these wonderful things for her while she was going behind his back, keeping secrets.

But she reminded herself that she wasn't just doing it for herself, she was doing this for the both of them.

Sweat beaded across Pharaoh's upper lip as he rolled over in bed. He reached for the rabbit's foot, rubbing it between his fingers as he tried to block out the pain. Frustrated with his slow recovery from his injuries and the drowsiness the pain medication was causing, he had quit taking it a couple of days earlier. Now, while his mind was clear again, his body was objecting. He gritted his teeth and made himself focus on the small pair of Egyptian statues sitting side by side in an alcove in the wall opposite his bed.

Isis, in ancient Egypt, wife to Osiris and revered as mother of all things, lady of the elements, the beginning of time.

Osiris, resting right beside her, was, to the same ancient Egyptians, the ruler of the underworld, the prince of the dead.

Pharaoh clenched his teeth as another spasm of pain gripped his body. He closed his eyes, willing his mind to ignore the pain and to remember the world from whence he'd come. The rich, indolent world of ancient kings—the blast of desert sands and never-ending heat, the cool waters of the Nile and the shade of date palms. It was a lot easier to assimilate than facing the fact that he'd been abandoned at birth with no earthly idea of his lineage and raised in a New Mexico orphanage.

Within the madness of Pharaoh Carn's mind, he'd settled the mystery of his birth by reincarnating himself from a world he'd never seen. And it had been his name, Pharaoh, that had given him the key to unlocking what he believed was his past.

Pharaoh touched the ankh tattoo in the middle of his chest as he stared intently at the statues, searching for himself in the features of their cold marble faces.

His mind jumped from his past to the present as Francesca's image shifted through his mind. A muscle jerked at the side of his jaw as he tried not to picture her lifeless body lying nameless in some California morgue. And while his heart told him she was still alive, logic said otherwise. If she'd lived through the earthquake, they should have found her by now. And he'd sent Stykowski to Denver days ago and had yet to hear from the man. He gritted his teeth in frustration. The least the son of a bitch could do was call.

A knock sounded softly on the door.

"Come in."

Duke Needham opened the door, but stopped in the doorway.

"Boss, I'm sorry to disturb you, but we've got trouble on the docks in Houston."

Pharaoh's mind quickly shifted from the personal to the business side of his life.

"What?" he snapped.

"It's the DEA. They just confiscated the *Little Egypt* and everything on her."

Pharaoh's face flushed angrily. His personal yacht had always been off-limits. Someone in the DEA wasn't earning the money Pharaoh was paying him.

"Help me up," he muttered. "I've got some phone calls to make."

Duke hurried to the bed and pulled his boss upright. "What do you need?" he asked once Pharaoh was on his feet.

"To get to my office," he snapped. "Find that damned nurse and see what she did with the wheelchair."

"Yes, sir," Duke said, and left on the run.

A few minutes later, after ordering the permanent removal of one Dabney Carruthers from the face of the earth, Pharaoh hung up the phone.

"The little bastard," he muttered. "I'll teach him to fuck with me. I liked that yacht."

Clay woke abruptly from a dreamless sleep, then rolled over in bed, casting a sleepy eye at the clock. 5:45 a.m. He hit the button on the alarm before it could go off and wake Frankie, then rolled back, snuggling beneath the covers for a few more minutes.

Frankie faced him as she slept, and he could just see the outline of her features, that delicate face with the china doll features framed by a thick tangle of black hair. He reached for her, wanting nothing more than the tenuous connection of skin against skin. But when he touched her, she moved toward him, snuggling her cheek against his chest and burying her nose beneath the covers.

His heart lurched. For a man as big and self-sufficient as he was, it was frightening to be this in love—to know that someone this small held such power over his life and happiness.

He wrapped his arms around her, loving the feel of her body next to his, knowing that this woman—this beautiful, fragile woman—was his wife. But his greatest fear came not in facing his weaknesses, but in knowing he had not protected her. He'd promised to honor her and keep her all the days of their lives, and he'd barely lasted twelve short months. That didn't say much for his ability to keep promises.

He watched as Frankie shifted within his embrace, feeling her heartbeat and the softness of her breath against his skin. Inside his belly, an angry fire began to burn. He *would* honor his vows. He *would* take care of his own.

Frankie stood at the window, waving goodbye as Clay backed out of the driveway. Winston and Betty LeGrand's second car was now parked on the street in front of their house, and there was a new cell phone on the hall table by the front door. Frankie let the curtain fall shut and turned away, absorbing the quiet. It was the first time she'd been alone since her return, and she didn't know whether to be elated or afraid. In the back of her mind, the constant threat of the unknown continued to loom. However, Clay had done all he could to make sure she never felt stranded again. And while the car had given Frankie a sense of freedom, the phone was insurance for Clay. Now he could contact her anytime, anywhere, and assure himself she was safe.

Frankie stared at the living room in silence, debating with herself about going through with her plan. The gun she'd ordered was ready to be picked up. But was she ready to take this step? Not only was she lying to Clay, she was lying to herself. Yes, she wanted protection, but there was also a part of her that wanted revenge. Someone had stolen two years of her life. My God, why couldn't she remember?

With a sigh, she headed for the kitchen, telling herself that she would do the dishes and start some laundry. There was still time to think about the gun. She could always change her mind.

She loaded the dishwasher, then wiped off the table and countertops. As she hung up the dishcloth to dry, her gaze fell on the small corner drawer where Clay had stashed the money they'd found in her clothes. In spite of last-minute nerves, she opened the drawer and took out the bills, staring at them as if at any moment they were going to explain their presence.

But nothing happened.

No flash of memory.

No revelation.

Frowning, she thrust the money back in the drawer. There was laundry that needed to be done. That was what she should be concentrating on, not complicating their lives even more by deceit.

As she separated the clothes, her gaze fell on Clay's Harley-Davidson T-shirt. It was old and faded and all but in rags, and it was her favorite nightshirt. She smiled and lifted it to her chest, hugging it to her and thinking of the man who was her husband.

When she'd worked at the library, she'd almost been jealous of the way her co-workers had acted when he would come to pick her up. Usually wearing clothes he'd worn on the job, the soft, faded denims and blue chambray shirts had molded themselves to his tall, muscled body like the fig leaf on Adam—covering what mattered, but leaving little to the imagination. His nose had been broken once in high school and had a slight bump on the bridge. His eyebrows were thick and dark and had a tendency to arc when he was intrigued. His chin was strong, with a stubborn thrust, and his eyes were a dark, brooding blue. But his bad-boy looks were deceiving. He was sexy as hell, but as faithful and honest as they came.

She sighed, then dropped the shirt into a pile with dark clothing and finished her task. A few minutes later, the washing machine was churning and the dishwasher was beginning the rinse cycle. She stood in the middle of the kitchen floor, looking for another task. Again her gaze fell on the kitchen drawer. She bit her lip and turned away.

"Focus," she muttered, and moved into the living room and switched on the TV.

A talk show and seven commercial breaks later, she was no more settled than she'd been when she sat down. She glanced at the clock on the wall over the mantel. It was almost ten. Two hours before lunch. At least six hours before Clay would be home for dinner.

As the program ended, a brief news update came

on the air, mentioning the possibility of snow before morning and then segueing into a report about the continuing cleanup of the devastating earthquake in southern California.

As the newscaster began to speak and the pictures flashed onto the screen, the skin on her body began to crawl. Blood drained from her face as she stared at the broken buildings and the devastation on the people's faces.

"Run, Francesca, run!"

She jerked and turned, certain that someone was behind her, but there was no one there. She bolted from the sofa and ran to the door, making certain that it was securely locked, then went all through the house, repeating the procedure on all the other doors and windows until she was positive she was still alone.

As she stood in the hallway, listening to the quiet and waiting to see if the voice would reappear, something in her memory began to resurface.

She was running—running. There was a long flight of stairs. Windows shattered like gunshots. She frowned, trying to see beyond the door standing ajar. There was green, lots of green. And many, many trees. And they were falling. Everything was falling. She shuddered and closed her eyes as the image solidified in her mind.

Then someone grabbed her. Pain shot up the

back of her neck as she was slammed against a nearby wall.

She heard herself scream, "I want to go home!"

She could see his dark eyes, blazing with anger as he held her fast.

"But you *are* home, Francesca. You belong to me now."

She could feel herself fighting, struggling without success against the hold he had on her throat. She was choking. She couldn't breathe.

"Let me go," she had begged. "I don't want to die."

And then she pushed and he fell. Down the rocking staircase, head over heels, landing facedown on the floor in the foyer. Blood seeped from beneath his head, spilling onto the dark-veined marble and mixing with the falling plaster and broken glass.

The floor rocked. She pitched forward, skinning her knees and hands as she slid down the top three steps before she could stop. Dust was thick in the air now. Something exploded beyond the walls of the house, and as it did, all the lights went out. Ignoring the pain, she bolted down the stairs just seconds before they came undone, only to trip and fall over the man's prone body. When she looked up, she was nose to nose with the unconscious man.

And then everything began to fade.

"No," Frankie muttered, trying desperately to get back the memory she'd been in. She closed her eyes, trying to make herself concentrate on his features. She needed an identity before she could she go to the police. But the image wouldn't come. All she could see was the cut of his lapel as she rolled him over on his back and took the wallet from his body.

Then she gasped and opened her eyes. The money! That was how she'd gotten the money!

She headed toward the kitchen on the run, telling herself if she could touch it, maybe the answers would come. But when she took the bills out of the drawer, all she got was a sick feeling in the pit of her stomach. Maybe she didn't need the gun now. In her vision, the man had looked dead. But something kept pushing at her, refusing to give her ease. At that last moment at the top of the stairs, had he tried to kill her or save her?

She closed her eyes. "Please, God, help me remember," she whispered, but nothing more came.

Clutching the money with both hands, she held the bills against her stomach as if they were some sort of shield. Her thoughts kept jumping from one scenario to another, but what she kept thinking was little more than supposition. All she remembered was just enough to keep her scared. But as she stood, her fear began to morph into a cold, angry purpose. She headed for her bedroom to change.

A short while later, she exited the house, giving the neighborhood a cursory glance as she headed for the car at the curb.

Mrs. Rafferty from across the street waved at her as she retrieved her morning paper. Frankie waved back and smiled. So one thing hadn't changed. Mrs. Rafferty still liked to sleep late. She was obviously just starting her day.

As she opened the car door to get in, Mr. Davidson, who lived one block over, came by with his dog. He didn't wave. But it wasn't because he was unfriendly. The white cane that he carried before him said it all. He was blind.

Frankie slid behind the steering wheel, and it was only after they had passed that she realized the guide dog he was using was not the same one he'd had before. She watched in the rearview mirror as Mr. Davidson and the dog turned the corner. It was one more sign of how life had gone on without her.

Just before starting the car, she rechecked the address of the gun shop. It occurred to her as she drove away that part of her memory might be gone, but the part of her that mattered most—her will to survive—was strong. Wherever she'd been, she'd still found her way back to Clay.

* * *

"Here you go, Mrs. LeGrand. Sign here, and we'll have you ready to go."

Frankie signed the receipt, carefully counting out seven one-hundred-dollar bills as the clerk put her gun in its case and slipped it into a sack.

"How much extra ammo are you going to want?" he asked.

Frankie looked up. "I don't know. Enough to learn how to shoot, I guess."

He reached for a handful of boxes and dropped them into the sack with the gun. "This will get you started," he said. "But it's going to add to your cost."

She took another bill from the envelope and laid it with the others. The money meant nothing to her. Wherever it had come from, she was going to put it to good use.

"If you plan on carrying this, you'll have to apply for a permit," the clerk said.

She looked startled. Another hitch in her plans. This was getting complicated.

"How do I do that?" she asked.

"You apply through the chief of police."

"Where do I get the form?"

He took her money from the counter. "I might have one," he said. "Let me get your change, then I'll look."

He disappeared into his office, leaving Frankie alone out front. The bell jingled over the door. She spun, suspiciously eyeing the man dressed in camouflage clothing who'd just entered. He paid her no mind, but went straight to a shelf and began going through some magazines there.

She turned, looking nervously toward the place where the clerk had gone. Suddenly she wanted nothing more than to be free of this place and everything it represented.

Then she looked down at her package, and her shoulders slumped. By taking the responsibility of her own freedom and safety onto her shoulders, she would never feel free again. She glanced up as the clerk reentered. It still wasn't too late.

"Here you go," the clerk said, handing Frankie her change. "And here's the form you need. Fill it out, send it to that address. After that, it's up to them. Okay?"

Her hands were shaking as she stuffed the change in her purse. By the time she got to the car, she felt nauseated. She opened the door, slid behind the steering wheel and closed the door. The solid thump and the ensuing silence were deafening.

The air felt close as she glanced down at the package on the seat beside her. All she could think was, what had she done?

Suddenly the need to hear Clay's voice was overwhelming. She took her cell phone from her purse and dialed.

"LeGrand Construction, this is Joe."

"Joe, this is Francesca, Clay's wife. If he isn't too busy, may I speak with him?"

"Sure thing, Mrs. LeGrand. Hang on a minute. I'll get him for you."

Frankie closed her eyes, concentrating on the background noises she could hear through the receiver. The rapid fire of nail guns was loud and steady. The roar and grind of heavy machinery in constant motion, as well as the boisterous banter of men at work, reminded her that this was Clay's world. Once it had been so familiar to her. Now she felt like an outsider. But before she could dwell on the fact, Clay's voice was on the phone. She went limp with relief.

"Frankie...baby...is something wrong?"

His sympathy was her undoing. She bit her lip as tears slid out from beneath her lids. "No, nothing's wrong."

"Joe said you sounded upset."

She glanced at the package again. The urge to tell him was strong—so strong—but he'd borne the burden of her disappearance for too long as it was. She couldn't burden him with the depth of her fears. So instead of telling him the truth, she lied.

"I'm not upset. I just wanted to hear your voice, that's all."

"You sure you're okay? You sound like you're crying."

She choked on a sob, hoping it would pass as a laugh.

"You're a worrywart," she said. "Are you going to be late coming home?"

"I don't think so," he said.

"Good, that will give me time to make something special for dinner."

"Don't overdo," he warned. "Anything will be fine." Then he lowered his voice. "The only thing I'm really hungry for is you."

This time Frankie managed a real laugh. "Like I said, I'll make something special." Then she added, before he could hang up, "I love you."

"I love you, too, Francesca—more than you will ever know. See you later, baby."

"Yes, see you later," she echoed, but the line was already dead in her ear.

She tossed the phone aside and looked at the parcel again, only this time the glitter in her eyes wasn't tears. She started the car and pulled out of the parking lot. Within minutes, she was on her way to Lakewood to the Foothills Shooting Center. Maybe she was wrong in not telling Clay, but she'd set this in motion. The least she could do was follow through.

If she'd looked back just then, she might have seen the customer from the gun shop come running out of the store. But she was too focused on the traffic in front of her to worry about what might be coming behind.

Nine

At the tap on her shoulder, Frankie lowered her gun and turned, lifting the headpiece from her ears to hear her instructor's remarks.

"You're still jerking the trigger, Mrs. LeGrand. Just relax and squeeze it, remember?"

She nodded, then readjusted the headpiece as she turned to face the target once more. Mentally reviewing the set of instructions she'd been given, she gripped the gun with both hands and took aim.

Focus.

Inhale.

Exhale.

Squeeze.

The scent of gunpowder was strong in her nose as the handgun bucked in her hand, but this time something within her felt different. When her instructor mouthed "good job" and gave her a thumbs-up, she knew that she'd hit the target.

Smiling with satisfaction, she took aim again and repeated the steps.

Again and again and again.

* * *

"Hey, Dawson, the chief wants to see you."

Glad for a reason to abandon the endless paperwork, Avery Dawson tossed his pen aside and got out of his chair. Even if the reprieve was only momentary, it was welcome. A couple of minutes later, he walked into his superior's office.

"You wanted to see me, sir?"

The chief handed him a piece of paper.

"This just came across my desk. I want you to check it out."

Dawson frowned as he glanced at it.

"A request for a carry permit?"

"Not just *any* gun permit. Look at the name."

Dawson's mouth dropped. "Son of a—! Francesca LeGrand?"

"My sentiments exactly," the chief said. "I want you to find out what's going on in her head. I'm disinclined to sign something like this for a woman with her history."

"But what do you want me to do? There's no law against her owning a gun, or, for that matter, applying for a permit to carry."

"Aren't you the investigating officer on her disappearance?"

Dawson nodded. "Yeah, although that's pretty much hit a dead end since she's back."

"Still, there are her claims of being taken against her will," the chief reminded him.

"I know, sir, but short of some new leads, we're right where we've been for the past two years—with nothing to go on."

"What about the phone call you got the other day about the identification of a Jane Doe?"

Dawson's conscience pricked. "I told the captain, but so far, we've been unable to turn up any answers."

"What does your gut tell you?" the chief asked.

Dawson hesitated, then said what he thought. "That it was more than a coincidence."

"Have you contacted the LeGrands about the call?"

"No, sir. Captain said there was no need to worry them unless we had something solid."

The chief frowned. "A phone call is solid. They have a right to know. Tell them."

"Yes, sir," Dawson said.

The chief stood, then walked to the window, looking out into the streets and the dusting of snow that was falling.

"She still has nothing to say about her disappearance?" he asked.

"No, sir."

The chief pointed toward the permit. "Something tells me she's keeping secrets. And I don't like secrets on my watch. She obviously feels threatened or she wouldn't be arming herself. I don't like vigilantes, Dawson. Check it out. I don't want someone turning up dead because she went paranoid. Do you get my drift?''

"Yes, sir.''

Then the chief added, ''Let me know what she says.''

"Yes, sir. I'll get on it first thing tomorrow.''

Marvin Stykowski stepped off the sidewalk and slipped behind a tree as Francesca LeGrand came out of the shooting center. He'd been tailing her for a day now and knew it was past time to check in with his boss.

It had taken him the better part of two days to locate the house, then another half day to see if she was there. He was pushing his luck in not calling Pharaoh, but there were things that he'd had to attend to before he'd been able to begin the search—like finding a supplier and getting a stash. After he started the stakeout, he wouldn't have time to run and make buys. And going cold turkey on the job wasn't a smart way to fly.

No one in Pharaoh's organization knew Marvin was an addict, and it would have gotten him in very deep shit had the fact ever become known. To Stykowski, Pharaoh's rule of no dope was a joke. They bought and sold the stuff. The fact that he was one of his boss's best customers should have been a plus for him, not a thing to hide.

He watched as Frankie drove away before he headed back to his own car. There was no need to hurry. He knew where she was going. All he had to do was find a phone and call home.

And it would have happened, if he hadn't run a red light. The cop on the corner nailed him before he'd gotten halfway down the street. When he heard the short burst of a siren and saw the red lights, his heart took a nosedive. Frantic that the blow in his glove box not be detected, he did a stupid thing. He hit the accelerator instead of the brake.

Twenty blocks and five minutes later, he was facedown on the ground, with handcuffs being snapped on his wrists.

"Hey, man, that's too tight!" he shrieked.

"Then lie still, sir," the policeman said.

Marvin groaned. Pharaoh was going to kill him.

Frankie was taking the roast from the oven when she heard Clay's truck pulling into the drive. Hastily, she set the roast aside, and checked the stove, making sure that all the burners were off. With only moments to spare, she dashed down the hall, disappearing into their bedroom just as Clay came in the front door.

"Hey, baby, I'm home."

"In here," Frankie yelled, tossing the last of her clothes on the bed and heading for the shower.

Hot water came quickly, sending a billow of steam into the air. She stepped inside, moving under the water jetting from the showerhead. Quickly she grabbed the shower gel from the shelf, squirted it all over her body and rubbed it into a lather. Minuscule bubbles now covered her skin, lingering on the edge of her chin, on her breasts and on the tips of her fingers.

"Something sure smells good," Clay said as he walked into the room and began unsnapping his work shirt. He was cold and tired and glad to be home.

"Hey, Frankie, are you almost through in there?" he yelled.

She stepped to the back of the shower and quietly undid the latch on the door.

"What did you say?"

Clay set his work boots near the closet as he headed for the bathroom.

"I said, are you almost through in there?"

She stifled another giggle. "I'm sorry, I can't hear you."

He was reaching for the shower door when it

suddenly came open. Frankie's hand came out, and she grabbed him by the shirt. Before he knew it, he was standing beneath the spray, his clothes plastering themselves to his body.

Frankie laughed and pushed his shirt farther open, running her fingers across his bare belly. He groaned. One hunger was forgotten as another took its place.

"You're gonna be sorry," he warned, grabbing at her arms, but she was soap-slick and slipped out of his grasp.

She laughed and pulled at his shirt, trying to get it off his shoulders as he took her in his arms.

"You little witch."

"You have on too many clothes," she taunted, and slid her arms around his waist.

When her breasts flattened against his chest, he lowered his head with a groan.

"My God, Francesca, you take my breath away."

"Take mine, too," she begged, lifting her face for a kiss.

Their lips met, his hard and demanding, hers soft and yielding. Play moved to need, and they both began tearing at his clothes, pulling off the sodden shirt and tugging at the jeans clinging to his legs.

Erect and aching, Clay reached for the water,

turning it off and leaving them isolated in the steam-filled enclosure.

Droplets clung to her skin like miniature jewels. Clay's eyes glittered hungrily as he began to cup her breasts. Before Frankie knew it was coming, his hand was between her legs and her knees were threatening to buckle. Her head lolled back against the wall as she grabbed for him to keep from falling.

Within seconds, she was on her back in the bottom of the tub and Clay was driving himself into her. A snap from his shirt was rubbing against her shoulder, and his jeans were wadded up near her feet, but she didn't feel them. All her senses were focused on the precision-like motion of their water-slick bodies.

Time ceased. There was nothing that mattered but the pounding of flesh to flesh and the end that was drawing near. Tighter and tighter he wound her, pushing past boundaries to a point of detonation.

And then it came, hitting her with the power of a fist to the gut and shattering every inhibition she'd ever had. She wrapped her legs around his waist and let go with a cry that echoed eerily within the small stall. Moments later, she felt him shudder, then heard him groan. Two final thrusts and Clay collapsed on top of her, trembling in every muscle and struggling to catch his breath.

"Sweet mercy," he mumbled, and tried to get up, but Frankie pulled him back down.

"Wait," she said softly. "Don't leave me yet."

He slid his arms around her body, and rolled until he was on the bottom and she was reclining with her back against his chest, her head beneath his chin. He shuddered, then took a deep breath, trying to steady his racing heart.

"My God, Francesca..."

She lifted his hand to her lips and pressed her lips against the palm. "I know," she whispered. "I know."

A minute passed, and then another. The air began to chill as the steam dispelled. When Frankie shivered, Clay wrapped his arms closer around her.

"I'm sorry, baby, are you getting cold?"

"A little."

He frowned, loath to turn her loose, but aware that the last thing she needed was to get sick.

"Here," he said gently, starting to help her up. "I'm going to take a quick shower before dinner, and you need to get into some clothes before you catch cold."

Frankie turned in his arms and leaned forward, brushing her lips against one side of his mouth and then the other. Then she pulled his shirt and jeans from the bottom of the tub. After wringing them out as best she could, she tossed them on the floor and reached for the faucet.

"What are you doing?" Clay asked.

"Running your bath," she said quietly. "And then I might be persuaded to scrub your back, too."

He grinned. "Why all the special treatment?"

Her smile was taunting as she stood, well aware that she was enticing him all over again. She reached on the shelf above for a clean washcloth and grabbed the shower gel on her way back down. She knelt before him, pouring a dollop of the soap in her hand, then reaching for his belly.

"Don't you think you deserve it?"

When her fingers encircled his manhood, he closed his eyes and groaned.

"I don't know if I deserve this or not," he whispered. "But I'll wring your sweet neck if you stop."

It was already morning, and Clay was reluctant to get up. He eyed the clock, willing the alarm not to ring. But the closer the hand moved toward six, the more he had to face the inevitable.

He turned off the alarm and then slipped out of bed, taking his clothes with him to the living room to dress so he wouldn't wake Frankie. As he reached the doorway, he looked back. She had always slept with the abandon of a child, one arm outflung, sometimes a foot hanging off the bed. It was something he had teased her about. But ever since her return, she slept in one place with the covers wrapped around her like a shell. He frowned. If only she could remember what had happened. She wasn't just his wife. She was his life—his reason for living. And she was asleep in his bed. Just as he'd left her before.

Something in him recoiled; then he shrugged off the fear, angry with himself for the thought. It had been almost a week since he'd felt this much panic. It was probably because of last night. Making love to Frankie was wonderful, but it also underlined what a number her disappearance had done to his own sense of self.

Disgusted with himself for such negative thinking, he headed for the living room to dress. A short while later, he was in the kitchen, pouring water into the coffeemaker and planning his day. When he reached for the coffee filters, there were none. Never one to let details get in his way, he wrote them down on the grocery list, then reached for a paper towel. It wouldn't be the first time he'd substituted like this. He poked it down in the well, and reached into the kitchen drawer to his right, where a pair of scissors was kept. With a couple of deft snips, the excess paper was removed.

Humming to himself, he spooned the coffee into the filter, shoved the well back in place and turned on the pot. Absently, he tossed the scissors back in the drawer and had started toward the refrigerator when the skin suddenly crawled on the back of his neck. He turned, his heart pounding as he retraced his steps and opened the drawer.

The envelope.

It wasn't there.

His heart tightened, then skipped a quick beat.

He opened the next drawer, then the next, and the next, until every drawer was pulled out. The blood slid from his face, and for a moment he felt sick. He didn't like what he was thinking, but there was an indisputable fact that couldn't be ignored. Fifteen hundred dollars was missing, and he wondered how long it had been gone.

"Clay, what on earth are you doing?"

He turned, staring at the laughter on Frankie's face and thinking to himself how much she had changed. There had been a time when she couldn't have kept such a secret—when he would have known by the look on her face that she'd been telling a lie. But now? He shuddered.

"Where is it?" he asked.

"Where's what?" she asked.

"The money."

Instantly, her expression closed. His heart sank. It was instinct that made him look at her arms, where the needle tracks had been. When he did, Frankie caught the look and exploded.

"Damn you, Clay, I thought we'd come further than this."

His eyes turned cold; his voice deepened with disappointment and anger.

"Yes, Francesca, so the hell did I."

An angry flush spread across her cheeks. "I didn't sniff it up my nose or shoot it in my arms, if that's what you're thinking."

He crossed the room and grabbed her by the shoulders, all but shaking her.

"I don't know what the hell to think," he muttered. "The woman I married didn't keep secrets and lie."

She flinched. The pain from his accusation was as great as if he'd just struck her. She lifted her chin, her eyes glittering with unshed tears.

"That's just it, Clay LeGrand. I'm not the same woman you married. My naiveté is gone—forever. Something happened to me that I don't understand. But whatever it was, I know one thing for certain. I will never be the same."

Then she grabbed Clay by the arm and began dragging him down the hall.

"What are you doing?" Clay asked.

"You wanted the money."

His heart stopped. Oh God. What if she'd just moved it? And, like an ass, he'd jumped to every conclusion but a logical one.

"Look, Frankie, I'm sorry if—"

She spun, her eyes brimming. "Shut up, Clay. Just shut up."

Heartsick, he paused at the doorway to their bedroom. When she walked into the closet, he followed, completely unprepared for what she slapped in his hand.

"Here," she said. "This is what I bought, and this is what's left of the money."

Repelled by the feel of the gun in his hand, he stared at it, then at her, as if he'd never seen her before.

"Why?"

Her chin quivered, and she started to shake.

"Because I'm afraid, Clay. I'm afraid every waking minute and even when I sleep. Just when I think everything is going to be okay, bits and pieces of faces and places slide through my mind like small, ugly ghosts. When they do, I feel as if I'm going to choke."

Clay's hands were shaking as he laid down the gun and the money. He cupped her face, his words colored with regret.

"Why didn't you tell me you were beginning to remember?"

Her expression crumpled. "Because I don't know what it is that I see. Sometimes it's only a picture on a wall, or the view from a window. Sometimes I wake up imagining that the floor is rolling beneath my feet. I jump at sounds, and sometimes even an odor can undo me." Finally her tears spilled over. "Most times I just think I'm going crazy."

He took her in his arms, pulling her close and rocking her where she stood.

"You're not crazy," he muttered. "And I promise that I will never doubt you again. Just trust me enough to tell me what's going on. You don't have to face this alone. Somehow, we'll find out what happened."

"But how?"

Clay's expression hardened. "The private investigator. I should have called him sooner. His number is at the office. I'll call him as soon as I get to work, and I'll call Detective Dawson, as well. Maybe he'll have something new to tell us."

Frankie nodded, but when Clay started to pull away, she clung to him, loath to let him go.

"Come here," he said softly. "Let's get you into something warmer, then you can keep me company over a bowl of cereal."

"I feel like such a baby," she muttered as he dug out a pair of sweats and tossed her one of his shirts.

Clay glanced at the gun. "You aren't acting like one," he said. "Can you shoot that thing?"

Her jaw set. "I'm learning."

"You're kidding."

"No. I've been taking lessons at the Foothills Shooting Center in Lakewood."

He looked at her with renewed respect. "You're serious about this, aren't you?"

"Dead serious," she said, and then pulled the sweatshirt over her head.

It was almost noon when the doorbell rang. Frankie laid down her paring knife, rinsed the tomato juice from her fingers and grabbed a towel on the way to the door. Through the window, she could see a dark blue sedan parked at the curb. She pulled back the curtain, recognizing the detective assigned to her case. Her heart skipped a beat. Clay had promised to call him. This quick response gave her hope that there would be news. She opened the door.

"Detective Dawson, this is a surprise," she said. "Come in."

Avery Dawson stepped inside, closing the door behind him. This woman looked nothing like the woman he'd interviewed in the hospital. Her skin was glowing, and there was a smile on her face. Her clothes were casual, and there was a scent of home cooking in the air. She didn't look like a woman about to go over the edge, but the fact still remained that she had bought a gun, and that his chief wanted some answers before the permit was signed.

"Thank you, Mrs. LeGrand. I apologize for any inconvenience, but I was wondering if I could ask you a few questions."

"Sure," Frankie said. "May I take your coat?"

Dawson shook his head. "No, I won't be long, I promise."

"At least come into the living room. It's chilly here in the hall."

Dawson followed her, taking a seat on the sofa opposite her chair.

"When Clay told me this morning that he was going to call you, I never expected this quick a response. Do you have any news?"

Dawson frowned. "I haven't spoken with your husband, Mrs. LeGrand."

Her smile slipped. "Oh?"

"No, ma'am. Actually, I'm here at the request of my chief. You applied for a carry permit?"

She frowned. "Yes, I did."

"Which I take to mean you recently purchased a gun?"

There was something in the tone of his voice that offended her. All of a sudden she felt as if she was being interrogated, when she was the one who'd been victimized. She leaned forward, draping the towel she carried across her lap and resting her elbows on her knees.

"Yes, I recently purchased a gun. I wasn't aware that such purchases were routinely investigated like this."

Dawson resisted the urge to fidget. "Normally, they're not," he said.

"I see," Frankie said. "Please continue."

Dawson was at a loss for words. Suddenly he felt awkward, and he didn't like the feeling. He was used to being the one in control.

"Look, Mrs. LeGrand, I'm just following orders."

She remained silent, although her eyes were accusing.

Dawson searched for a question that might make some sense.

"What were you thinking...you know...your state of mind...when you decided to buy a gun?"

Frankie shook her head in disbelief. It was all she could do not to scream.

The tone of her voice rose an octave. "Tell me

something. Is this the kind of detecting you normally do? Because if it is, then no wonder no one could find me.''

Dawson flushed. ''Look, Mrs. LeGrand, I—''

Frankie stood abruptly. ''No, you look, Detective. Someone stole two years of my life from me. I don't know where the hell I've been, or how I got home, therefore I have no way of recognizing danger should it return. Yes, I bought a gun because I don't feel safe. And after this conversation, my confidence in the Denver Police Department is nil. I am taking lessons from an instructor at Foothills Shooting Center. I am not crazy. I am afraid.''

''Yes, ma'am, I can understand that. But surely you can see the chief's position. In the wrong hands, guns can do great harm.''

She smiled sarcastically. ''Well, sir, that's a great public-announcement slogan, but it's certainly not news. Why don't we just be honest with each other? You people have convinced yourselves that I'm some sort of a nut who abandoned her husband, then, for reasons of her own, pulled a con to come back. Is that about right?''

Dawson flushed again. It was close enough to his original opinion that he had trouble looking her in the eyes.

''No, ma'am, that's not what I said.''

''Oh, no, I heard what you *said*,'' Frankie said.

"It was the *way* you said it to which I take offense. I did nothing wrong, Detective Dawson, and yet I'm the one under scrutiny. Do you know how that makes me feel?"

It was all he could do to meet her gaze. "Like I said before, I'm just following orders."

"Fair enough," Frankie said. "And since you're here, you won't mind if I ask you some questions?"

He stood, suddenly uncomfortable with her cold, angry stare. "Ask away," he said.

"Do you have any new leads on my case?"

He thought of the phone call, then the gun, and shook his head. "No, ma'am. Not since the cabdriver who picked you up at the airport."

She nodded. "Then get out your notebook. For the past few days, I've been remembering things. Nothing that makes any sense, but still things, just the same."

Dawson scrambled for his pen as Frankie began to pace.

"Wherever I was, there was an earthquake. I don't know for sure, but I think it was the reason I got away. And everything was green. Lots of grass and trees—even palms, like California," she added.

Dawson's heart skipped a beat as he remembered the phone call from L.A.

Then she stilled, and the animation on her face all but died.

"Sometimes I can almost see his face." Then she sighed, her shoulders slumping as she gave Dawson a quick glance. "But I can't. However, I did see a tattoo on his chest."

Dawson looked startled. "What kind of tattoo?"

She lifted her hair and turned. "Like this one," she said. "Only it was in the center of his chest."

Dawson leaned forward, staring intently at the small ankh tattoo.

"How long have you had that?" Dawson asked.

Frankie turned. "I couldn't tell you. All I know is that it wasn't on me when I disappeared."

Dawson was making furious notes.

"And once I had the impression that there were bars on the windows in my room. Do you think I could have been in jail?"

"Not with the scenery you've described. Besides that, if you'd been in jail and escaped, your description and picture would have gone out on the wire."

She relaxed slightly. "Good. I couldn't imagine why I would be there, but it makes me feel better to hear you say that."

"Is there anything else? Anything at all? Even the most inconsequential thing could be a key to something important."

A frown creased her forehead as she thought. Finally, she shrugged.

"Not that I can remember."

He put his notebook in his pocket, and at that moment he made the decision not to tell her about the phone call from L.A. He wanted to talk to Clay instead. "I'll be going now. If there's anything else—anything at all—don't hesitate to give me a call."

She nodded and led him toward the door. She started to open it when he stopped her.

"Mrs. LeGrand, there's something I want to say."

She waited.

"Off the record," he added.

She nodded.

"For what it's worth, I believe you."

She almost smiled. "For what it's worth, I thank you."

Moments later, he was gone, leaving Frankie with the impression that her world was more complicated than ever. It occurred to her that she hadn't ask him about the carry permit. She shrugged. It didn't matter to her whether it was signed or not. She had the gun. She knew how to use it.

GET *THE BEST* FREE...
2 FREE
BOOKS!

MIRA BOOKS, the brightest star in women's fiction presents...

The Best of the Best™

Superb collector's editions of the very best fiction novels by the world's best-known authors!

To get your 2 free books, affix this peel-off sticker to the reply card and mail it today!

2 FREE BOOKS!

Plus, receive a FREE BONUS GIFT!

2 FREE BOOKS!

HURRY! Return this card promptly to get **2 FREE Books** and a **FREE Bonus Gift!**

The Best of the Best ™

YES! Please send me 2 free books from "The Best of the Best" collection as explained on the back. I understand that I am under no obligation to purchase anything further as explained on the back and on the opposite page. ***Also send my free bonus gift!***

Affix peel-off **2 FREE BOOKS** sticker here.

Name: _____
(PLEASE PRINT)

Address: _____ Apt.#: _____

City: _____

State/Prov.: _____ Postal Zip/Code: _____

383 MDL CPQE

183 MDL CPQF
BB2-99

® Offer limited to one per household and not valid to current Best of the Best subscribers. All orders subject to approval. Books received may vary. ® and TM are trademarks of Harlequin Enterprises Limited.

PRINTED IN U.S.A.

◄ DETACH AND MAIL CARD TODAY! ▼

The Best of the Best™— Here's How it Works:

Accepting your 2 free books and gift places you under no obligation to buy anything. You may keep the books and gift and return the shipping statement marked "cancel." If you do not cancel, about a month later we will send you 3 additional novels and bill you just $4.24 each in the U.S., or $4.74 each in Canada, plus 25¢ delivery per book and applicable sales tax, if any.* That's the complete price, and — compared to cover prices of $5.50 each in the U.S. and $6.50 each in Canada — it's quite a bargain! You may cancel at any time, but if you choose to continue, every month we'll send you 3 more books, which you may either purchase at the discount price…or return to us and cancel your subscription.

*Terms and prices subject to change without notice. Sales tax applicable in N.Y. Canadian residents will be charged applicable provincial taxes and GST.

If offer card is missing write to: The Best of the Best, 3010 Walden Ave., P.O. Box 1867, Buffalo, NY 14240-186

BUSINESS REPLY MAIL
FIRST-CLASS MAIL   PERMIT NO. 717   BUFFALO, NY

POSTAGE WILL BE PAID BY ADDRESSEE

THE BEST OF THE BEST
3010 WALDEN AVE
PO BOX 1867
BUFFALO NY 14240-9952

NO POSTAGE
NECESSARY
IF MAILED
IN THE
UNITED STATES

Ten

Clay flipped through the Rolodex on his desk, searching for the name and number of the private investigator he'd hired once before. A couple of minutes later, he was on the phone to Harold Borden, P.I. It rang once, then twice, then a half-dozen times. He kept waiting for Borden or the answering machine to pick up, but nothing happened.

It had been more than a year since he'd talked to the man, and there was always the possibility that he was no longer in business, although the idea was vaguely surprising. Harold Borden had struck Clay as the kind of man who would die of old age on the job, not puttering in his garage or out on the golf course killing time between meals.

Just when he was about to hang up, the call was finally answered. Clay could hear the short, gasping breaths of someone who'd been running.

"Borden Investigations."

"This is Clay LeGrand. I'd like to speak to Mr. Borden, please."

Borden put down his coffee and sack of doughnuts and sat with a thump.

"You're talking to him. And hello to you, too, Clay LeGrand. It's been a while, boy. How the hell are you doing?"

Clay's footsteps sounded hollow on the floor of his portable office as he strode to the window overlooking the construction site.

"Good…and not so good."

Borden reached for an applesauce doughnut, took a bite, then talked as he chewed. "Give me the good news first."

"Francesca came back."

Borden almost choked. "The hell you say!" He took a quick swig of coffee, then leaned forward in disbelief. "How? When? And, more important, where has she been?"

Clay sighed. "That's the bad news."

"I take it this call isn't social," Borden said.

"No."

"Wait," Borden muttered. "I can't find a pen… Oh, here's one. Okay. Shoot." Then he went back to his doughnut as Clay started to talk.

"I came home from work and found her asleep in our bed. All I can tell you for sure is that she was in an automobile accident within an hour of her arrival in Denver. Not only does she not remember where she's been, she has no memory of ever being gone."

"And your problem is…?"

Clay took a deep breath. "Frankie believes she's in danger. She claims there's no way she would have left willingly. And we both know there's no such thing as some crazy just letting someone go—especially after two years."

"Yeah, right," Borden said. Then he added, "Don't take this wrong, but what do you think?"

"I believe her."

"Okay. So what do you want from me?"

Clay combed his fingers through his hair. "This is where it gets tough. I know what I want, but I don't have much info to give you."

Borden turned to a fresh page in his notebook. Ever since he'd quit the case, he'd been bugged by the knowledge that he'd somehow let this man down. Now was his opportunity to rectify the situation.

"What *do* you know?" Borden asked.

"The police talked to a cabdriver who picked up a woman at the bus terminal who fit Francesca's description. The cabby claimed the woman acted strange—almost afraid. But other than a few errant memories that don't make much sense and a gold ankh tattoo on the back of her neck, Frankie knows nothing."

"What the hell is an ankh?" Borden asked.

"Picture a cross, except that the top is a loop rather than a straight line."

"Oh, yeah. One of those Egyptian-looking things."

"Yes, that's it."

"Anything else?" Borden asked.

"Well, Frankie says that the man who was holding her captive had a matching tattoo on his chest. She also thinks that wherever she was, there was an earthquake. And, as you know, California recently had a big one."

Borden's interest piqued. "It's a place to start."

"Yeah, that's what I think," Clay said.

Borden leaned back in his chair, mentally reviewing the file he'd collected on Francesca.

"You know, I mentioned this to you before, but we never went anywhere with it. What do you think about delving into her past while we're at it?"

Clay frowned. "I still don't think Francesca has a secret past."

"No, you misunderstand me," Borden said. "I don't mean that kind of past. I'm talking about her childhood."

"She grew up in an orphanage," Clay reminded him.

"I know, and I know it's a long shot, but maybe there's something there that could help us."

Clay sighed. "Right now, I'm willing to try anything."

Borden made a few more notes. "The children's home was in Albuquerque, right?"

"Yes."

Borden fiddled with the pen, tapping it lightly on the top of the desk as his mind jumped from one scenario to another.

"You know, Clay, any branch of child welfare is usually pretty closemouthed about releasing information to outsiders. I can check out some things with no problem, but in my opinion, your best bet is to take Francesca and go back for a visit. Talk to the people who work there. Ask about her friends. Her habits. Why wasn't she adopted? Stuff like that. The worst that could happen is that you just take a trip to Albuquerque. The best is that she might remember something that will help."

Clay's mind was turning as he glanced at the calendar on the wall. If his dad would step in and help out again, he might just make it.

"That's a good idea," he said. "I'll talk to Frankie about it tonight."

"Good," Borden said. "In the meantime, I'll go at it from my end. Together, we might come up with some answers we can use."

"Thanks, Harold. I appreciate you getting on this so quickly."

Borden frowned. "I owe you one, boy. Remember, I worked for a year looking for that girl. It's just good to know she's back, however it happened. Say, are all your numbers still the same?"

Clay gave him their cell-phone number to add to the file.

"Okay, that should be it," Borden said. "Keep in touch, and I'll do the same."

Clay hung up, feeling better about the situation than he had since the day Frankie had come home. He was on his way out the door when the phone rang. He answered absently, his mind still focused on his conversation with Borden. But when he heard Avery Dawson's voice, his interest changed.

"Detective, I was going to call you today."

"So your wife said," Dawson answered.

Clay frowned. "You talked to Frankie?"

"Yes. Just a little follow-up stuff for the chief before he signed her permit."

Clay frowned. "Permit? What permit?"

Dawson hesitated. It hadn't occurred to him that Frankie would have kept it a secret, but it was too late to back out now.

"The carry permit," he said.

"Oh, that," Clay said. "For a minute I forgot. So is everything all right?"

"Yeah, I guess. I think the chief will probably okay it."

"Is that why you called me?"

Dawson frowned. "No. Something happened at work the other day that I thought you should know. Someone called, identifying himself as an officer with the Los Angeles Police Department. Said he was following up on some runaway posters in trying to identify a Jane Doe."

Clay's gut clenched as he thought of all the trips he'd made to morgues across the country, looking for Frankie. At least that was something he wouldn't have to do again.

"So what does that have to do with my wife?" he asked.

Dawson took a deep breath. "Here's where it gets weird. He asked about a missing-person poster on Francesca LeGrand. Said the Jane Doe fit her description. I told him it couldn't be her, and to throw away the flyer, because the woman was no longer missing. I told him we got lucky, that she was alive and had come back on her own."

Clay was listening but had yet to make a connection that made sense.

"So," Dawson continued, "we traded a few pleasantries, and I'd started to hang up when the guy had one more question. He wanted to know when she'd come back, so I told him. It wasn't until I hung up that I began to wonder why it would matter to the guy when she came back. If she was here, she couldn't be the woman in the morgue.''

"Right," Clay said. "So what's the problem?"

He heard Dawson take a deep breath, and when he did, Clay's gut began to tighten. It was almost as if he knew what the man was going to say before he said it.

"I don't know," Dawson said. "Chalk it up to my suspicious nature, but I called right back to the L.A.P.D., asking to speak to this officer. The receptionist told me that no one by that name worked there."

Clay's legs went weak. "So what are you saying?"

"That someone wanted to know about Francesca LeGrand and lied about the reason why. Considering the situation as we know it, I find that extremely bothersome."

"Sweet mercy," Clay muttered. "She was right. She's still in danger."

Dawson frowned. "I don't know about that," he said. "But I felt obligated to tell you about the call. Take whatever precautions you feel necessary. We're investigating on our end, but truthfully, there's precious little to investigate. We checked phone records. All we know is that the call came from a pay phone in Las Vegas.''

''Did you tell Francesca about this?'' Clay asked.

''No, considering what she's been through, I thought it best to tell you. You tell her what you see fit.''

The urge to take Frankie and run was strong, but Clay knew it would not solve the problem.

''Look, Detective, I'm taking Frankie back to Albuquerque to the orphanage where she grew up, just on the off chance that something there might be the key to what happened to her.''

Dawson made a quick note. ''Not a bad idea,'' he said. ''Especially considering the lack of evidence otherwise. When are you leaving?''

''As soon as possible,'' Clay said. ''If I learn anything interesting, I'll be sure to pass it on.''

''Keep in touch,'' Dawson said.

''Count on it,'' Clay said. ''And thanks for letting me know.''

A few moments later, Clay was on the phone again, but this time to his dad. Within the hour, Winston LeGrand was on the site and Clay was on his way home.

Pharaoh Carn was restless, and it wasn't the forced inactivity from his healing wounds that made him so. His body ached, but it was getting better. Each day his staying power increased. Today he'd been at his desk for almost four hours. Only days earlier he'd all but collapsed after two, but there were some positives to offset his frustration. His empire was spinning smoothly once more.

Ever since his return to Las Vegas, the phone had been ringing nonstop with calls from his business associates. He should have been pleased, but there was no way he could rejoice in his own survival when the woman who belonged at his side was gone. He wouldn't hazard a guess as to how long he could hold it all together. And no matter how hard he tried, and how much money he spent making it happen, his ride at the top wouldn't last—not without Francesca.

Before her return to his life, he'd been doing okay, but he'd been on the outskirts of the big time, one of the hundreds of middlemen for the Allejandro cartel.

The day he found her, he'd been on his way back to L.A. from Seattle, after cleaning up a small internal problem. The fact that Pepe Allejandro was now minus one brother-in-law was immaterial to the fact that Allejandro's missing millions were still intact.

Rolling the rabbit's foot between his fingers, he leaned back and closed his eyes, remembering that day on the plane. It had been so many years since he'd seen her, yet he would have known her face anywhere.

Until he'd picked up the paper, the flight had been monotonous. And when he'd first seen the picture, he almost passed it by. It was of little importance—something a Denver photographer had taken of a young woman laughing in the rain. But it had been picked up by the Associated Press and run in papers across the country. When recognition dawned, his center of gravity had literally shifted.

It was Francesca. *His* Francesca.

He felt light-headed, then weighted down by the distance of miles between them. His first urge was to move, and then he remembered where he was. Frustration set heavily on his shoulders as he faced the fact that, until they landed, he could do nothing.

He thought about her during the rest of the flight, remembering her childhood years at Kitteridge House and how she had dogged his footsteps. Remembering that he'd been there for her when her parents had not, remembering that as she'd grown, his feelings for her had changed from those of a boy for a child to how a man loved his woman.

When she had not returned those feelings as he'd expected, he'd chalked it up to her youth.

When she grew up, things would be different, and until then, he would bide his time.

And then he'd screwed up. He called it his five years' worth of stupid. By the time he'd gotten out of prison, Francesca had turned eighteen and left the orphanage for parts unknown. He still remembered the panic of knowing that, like everyone else, she had disappeared from his life.

By the time the plane landed in L.A., Pharaoh's mind was set on going after her. But first things first. Pepe Allejandro would be waiting to know the outcome of the trip. It wouldn't do to keep him waiting.

Four hours later, Pharaoh was on his way home, still trying to digest his windfall. Pepe had been extremely pleased with Pharaoh's performance— so pleased that he'd just promoted him to a district all his own. That it was in a seedy section of L.A. rife with gang wars didn't bother Pharaoh a damn. This was his chance to prove himself, and he wasn't going to blow it.

And there was another fact that he couldn't ignore. All of this had happened after he'd found Francesca again. He started to grin. It was just like before. The teachers at the home had viewed him as nothing but a troublemaker doomed to failure— and then she'd come along. After that, it had been harder for them to judge him as bad when that sweet-faced baby had given him her devotion. That was when he'd known she was more than his friend. She was his luck.

He rubbed the palms of his hands on the fabric of his slacks, smiling with inward glee as he looked down at the newspaper again. If Francesca thought getting rained on was fun, she would be delirious when she saw his face. And he *would* find her. In his mind, success depended on it...

But that had been then, and this was now, and Pharaoh was philosophical enough to know that the things worth having never came easy. His body protested as he shifted in his chair. He didn't want to think of his disappointment again, but finding her hadn't been all he'd imagined it would be. He hadn't expected such violent objections from her. He hadn't planned on keeping her under lock and key, but one day had turned into another and then another, and before he knew it, she'd been with him for months. The months had turned into years, and she still turned her face from him—pleading to be let free, begging to go back to her husband. Ironically, it was nature, rather than man, that finally thwarted him. He hadn't counted on an earthquake rocking his carefully laid plans.

He turned toward the window, staring out at the gray, cloudless sky. Something was wrong, he knew it. Stykowski was way overdue to check in, which made him nervous. But then, he reminded himself, since the earthquake, everything was still a mess. Two of Allejandro's best men had been killed in a car on a crumbling piece of freeway, several had been injured and one was still missing. The infrastructure of the entire organization was in disarray. The men Pharaoh often counted on were being used in other capacities, and he had been forced to use second-rate men like Marvin Stykowski for his personal business.

Pharaoh tossed the rabbit's foot onto the desk and cursed. His mistake had been not in keeping Francesca locked up, but in letting her husband live. And yet, as often as he thought about letting her go, his greed would not permit it. With her, the wealth he had amassed was staggering. His power within the cartel was only less than that of Allejandro himself.

But he was tired. Tired of thinking. Tired of waiting for his carefully orchestrated world to start coming undone. He needed Francesca. And he needed to rest. He glanced toward the bookcases against the east wall. He would rest, but later. There was something more important he needed to do.

With a halting step, he moved toward the books, running his fingers along the shelves, counting down the titles until he reached the eleventh one from the end. He pulled, and as he did, the wall opened soundlessly. He stepped inside the passageway as the door slid shut behind him.

The passageway was narrow and winding, with false turns and dead-end halls, meant to confuse an intruder. But Pharaoh knew where he was going, and the closer he got, the more rapid his steps became. He likened the feeling within these walls to being inside a womb. The massive cinder blocks were reminiscent of the great blocks of stone from which the pyramids had been made, and the narrow hallway down which he was walking was not unlike the passageways inside the tombs of ancient Egyptian kings. The closer he came to the light, the more rapid his heartbeat became.

A faint odor of incense greeted him as he reached the entryway. Instinctively, his gaze moved toward the pair of dark marble statues against the wall. Their majestic features were etched in stone, capturing the godlike quality that had marked them throughout the centuries. He inhaled deeply, drawing strength from their images. His legs were shaking from exertion, and his rest was well past due, but the discomfort was unimportant compared to what he derived from being here.

He moved, stopping only inches from the statues. Deep within the bowels of this house, the sllence was almost deafening. The sound of his heartbeat, the exhalation of each breath, each served as a reminder that he alone was still among the living. His gaze moved across the first statue, separating the high, noble forehead from the large, sightless eyes, measuring the cut of her cheekbones against his own—envisioning the touch of her lips upon his brow.

Isis.

If he'd had a mother, she would have been like this—noble and magnificent.

He exhaled slowly. The sound was like a wail within the small, cloistered walls. There, in the shadows, he waited for a sign. Somewhere within him, time ceased. Unaware of the cold, hard marble on which he stood or the weakness within his bones, he listened with his heart, knowing that an answer would come.

And when the image of Francesca's beautiful face suddenly flashed before his eyes, he shuddered. The need to hear her voice, to feel the texture of her skin, was a visceral ache. But he had his answer. He knew, as certainly as he knew his own name, that Francesca LeGrand would be with him again.

Only after the plane lifted off from the Denver airport did Clay breathe a slow sigh of relief. Detective Dawson's phone call had put a rush on his plans like nothing else could have. He glanced at Frankie, who was sitting in the aisle seat beside him. Her knuckles were white, her jaw tensed. He slipped his hand over hers and leaned sideways, whispering in her ear.

"It's okay, we're off the ground," he said softly.

Her eyes were wide and filled with fear as she met his gaze. "I've done this before," she muttered.

He frowned. "I thought this was your first—"

Suddenly he understood. She was remembering.

"Tell me," he urged.

"I feel sick," she whispered.

He glanced up. The Fasten Seat Belt sign was still on, and the plane was still climbing. Getting her to a bathroom wasn't going to be easy.

"Hang on, Frankie, I'll ring for an attendant."

"No," she muttered, grabbing at his hand before he could follow through. "Not sick like that."

His frown deepened as he cupped her face, tilting her chin until she was forced to meet his gaze.

"Sick how, baby?"

She shuddered again. "With fear. I feel sick with fear. When we left Denver, we left in a plane." Then she closed her eyes. "The ground was so far below. There were clouds...we were flying through clouds. The engine sounded different—smaller, I think. I could see the man's hands on the controls—the instrument panel was all lit up in front of us."

"Can you tell where you are?" Clay asked. "What do you see below? Is it green? Is it—"

"Mountains! I see mountains—and there's a huge city below."

He patted her hand. "This is good, Frankie, real good. This means that more of your memory is coming back."

Her joy began to fade. "But it doesn't tell us a damn thing about where we landed."

"All in good time," he promised. "All in good time. Right now, let's just concentrate on going back to Kitteridge House. You're bound to have left some friends behind."

"Yes, of course you're right," she said.

He grinned. "Always."

She snorted softly beneath her breath and then gave him a wry grin. "You are such a man."

He leaned even closer, whispering softly against her ear, "And don't you forget it."

She arched an eyebrow and smiled. "As if you would ever let me."

His grin widened. "Hey, I'm only doing what I can to justify my existence."

She laughed, and the sound warmed his heart. A few moments later, the tension had passed. Even after Frankie had drifted off to sleep, Clay kept a close, anxious watch. He couldn't quit thinking that the more she remembered, the more desperate their situation would become.

It was sunny in Albuquerque when they landed, but there was a chill in the air. Frankie pulled her jacket a bit closer around her and hastily took her seat on the passenger side of their rental car, while Clay loaded their bags in the trunk. A security guard nodded at her as he passed. She smiled back. Nothing out of the ordinary there. If only her life was as uncomplicated as that.

Clay slammed the trunk shut, then, moments later, slid behind the wheel, giving her a quick wink as he put the key in the ignition.

"Okay, baby, we're loaded. I think we should get a motel first. We'll call Kitteridge House from our room, make an appointment to see the administrator and then find a good restaurant. How does that sound?"

"Like a plan," Frankie said. "I'm starved."

A short while later, Clay carried their bags into their room while Frankie searched the phone book for the number to the orphanage. Her heart skipped a beat as she found it.

"Clay?"

He paused at the door to the bathroom and looked back. "What, honey?"

"This feels weird."

He frowned. "How so?"

"I don't know. It's almost as if I'm coming back home under false pretenses. How much am I going to tell the administrator about what happened to me? Whatever I tell, it's bound to sound crazy."

"No, I don't agree," Clay said, and sat down on the bed beside her. "Look at it this way. They've been in the business of helping children for years, right?"

She nodded.

"Well, just because you've grown up, that doesn't mean they won't help you again. They fed you and clothed you, and, I would suppose, there were some there who even loved you."

A boy's laugh suddenly echoed inside her mind. She shuddered.

Clay saw the shadow cross her face. When she shivered, he took her in his arms. "What is it, baby?"

She wiped a shaky hand across her face. "I don't know. I had a flash of something, but it's gone." She sighed. "Just another teaser, I suppose."

"Want me to make the call?" Clay asked.

Frankie hesitated, then straightened. "No, I'll do it. Just don't go far, okay?"

"I'm with you, Francesca—all the way."

Eleven

Frankie leaned back in the seat, bracing herself for the flood of memories as Clay drove onto the grounds of Kitteridge House. The first time she'd come through these gates, she hadn't been tall enough to see out of the car window. She could remember the bare branches of the trees, angling toward heaven with skeleton-like arms—and being afraid. Everything that had confirmed her identity was gone: her parents, her home—even her own toys. All she'd been allowed to bring were her clothes, a small teddy bear and her blankie.

She sighed. As she remembered, even the blankie hadn't lasted long. One day it went to the laundry and never came back. As she'd grown older, she'd often wondered if that had been their way of weaning her from her past, or if it had truly been lost, as they'd claimed.

"Are you okay?" Clay asked.

Frankie nodded. The concern on his face was touching.

"I'm fine," she said quietly. "Just a lot to absorb."

He nodded, remembering himself at the age of four and trying to put himself in her place. He couldn't imagine the devastation of losing his mom and dad, and he felt like crying for the little girl that she'd been.

The driveway began to circle, and he slowed to take the turn. It hit him then that Frankie was coming back to Kitteridge in somewhat the same manner she'd arrived. Then she'd lost her parents, now she'd lost the past two years of her life. But the trauma was still the same.

"It's really big," Clay said, seeing it through the eyes of a contractor.

"And old," Frankie added.

The carefully kept grounds were somewhat Southwestern in style, although large shade trees with ornamental benches beneath were interspersed about the grounds. Along with some decorative borders, the occasional cactus garden could also be seen. Clay knew that whatever grew green in Albuquerque came from irrigation and vast sprinkler systems.

The buildings, while large, were lacking in ornamental design. A two-story edifice, without benefit of awnings or porches, served as the hub, with other wings angling out from the main entrance like spokes in a wheel.

Kitteridge House had been founded by Gladys Eugenia Kitteridge in 1922, for the safety and preservation of motherless children. Over the years, the guidelines had changed some, allowing in children who had been abandoned, as well. Although they weren't all orphans, which meant they were not all adoptable, they had one thing in common: they had nowhere to go except here.

As they passed a groundskeeper, Frankie turned to stare. She didn't recognize him, but it stood to reason. It had been eight years since she'd been here. A lot of things would have changed.

"It seems smaller than I remember."

Clay smiled. "No, baby. Your world just got larger, that's all."

She laid her hand on his thigh, taking comfort from his strength. "*You* are my world."

An ache hit his gut. *Please, God, let me keep her in mine.* He parked in front of the main entrance, then killed the engine. Francesca was waiting for him to make the next move. He gave her a wink.

"I love you, too," he said softly. "And just for the record, we'll continue this discussion later— back at the motel."

"Sounds marvelous. Now, let's get this over with."

"Are you still scared?"

She looked out the windshield. There was a small group of children walking from one building to another. She glanced at her watch and knew where they were going. Since this was Saturday, chances were they were going to the gym.

"No, I'm not scared—at least, not of this place or these people. It's what I don't know about myself that's making me crazy."

Clay opened the door and then grabbed her by the hand. "Come on, baby. We'll slay the dragon together."

As they exited the car, a gust of wind hit, running chill, breezy fingers down the back of her neck. She shuddered.

"Cold?" Clay asked.

"A little."

"Then let's run," he said, taking her by the hand.

By the time they reached the entrance, they were laughing and her dismal mood was over. Clay opened the door, the smile still on his face, and almost bumped into a tall, gray-haired woman who was standing in the doorway.

"Oops, sorry," he said quickly.

She smiled politely, but her smile widened as her attention focused on Frankie.

"Francesca Romano, I knew it would be you."

"Miss Bell!" Frankie cried, and gave the tall woman an impulsive hug.

Clay began to relax. If this was any indication, at least the visit would not be traumatic.

Addie Bell looked over Frankie's shoulder. "This would be your husband, I presume?"

Frankie smiled. "Yes, ma'am. Clay, Miss Bell is the administrator of Kitteridge House. Miss Bell, this is my husband, Clay LeGrand."

Addie extended her hand, taking note of his firm handshake and the straightforward look in his eyes. He just might do, she thought.

"My name is Adeline," she said shortly. "But you may call me Addie." Then she looked back at Frankie. "When the secretary told me that a Francesca LeGrand had called for an appointment, something told me it would be you. Where do you live now?"

"Denver," Frankie said.

Addie nodded. "I hear it's a lovely city, although I've never been there myself. So, what brings you to Albuquerque, dear? Business or pleasure?"

The knowledge that Addie Bell had never let her down made Frankie feel safe. Suddenly the embarrassment she'd been feeling was gone. All she wanted to do was get her story told and let someone else share the burden. She bit her lip, but it was not enough to stop a sudden sparkle of tears in her eyes.

"I don't know how to categorize what's happened to me, but we're in trouble," she said.

Addie's smile slipped.

"Let's go to my office, where we can be comfortable. I'm sure we can straighten everything out. But first, I want to hear everything, from the moment you walked out of our doors until this very minute." Then she glanced at Clay and almost winked. "Well, maybe not everything, but you know what I mean."

With one backward glance at Clay, Frankie let Miss Bell take her by the hand and lead her down the hall, just as she'd done so many times before. He followed behind, watching the way the tall, elderly woman leaned down, so as not to miss a word of what Frankie was saying. For a moment he couldn't put his finger on what he was thinking. And then it hit him.

Trust.

Frankie trusted this woman in a way she trusted few others. At that point, the last of his reservations about bringing her here disappeared.

* * *

To say Addie Bell was stunned by their story would have been putting it mildly. Yet Francesca was here, and if Addie was any judge of character, as afraid as a woman could be.

"Good Lord! Are you serious?" Addie asked.

Frankie felt weak with relief. "Yes, ma'am."

"Two years—and you have no idea where you were taken?"

Frankie's shoulders slumped. At that point, Clay felt obligated to join the conversation.

"No, she doesn't. Except she thinks there was an earthquake right about the time that she got away."

Addie gasped. "There was one in southern California only a short time ago."

"We know," Clay said.

Addie leaned forward, staring intently into Frankie's face.

"Francesca, you truly believe that you were held all that time against your will?"

Frankie glanced at Clay, taking comfort in the way her heart always settled when she looked at his face, then turned back to Addie.

"Oh yes, ma'am. There is no way on God's earth that I would have willingly left Clay. He's my life." She sighed. "So you see how lost we are. Besides the police, who I have learned spent most of that time trying to prove Clay had murdered me, there was a private investigator Clay hired trying to find me, as well. In fact he's in California now, following up on the little I remember."

"And he found nothing?"

Frankie shook her head. "Not yet. Whoever took me didn't do it for money. There was never a ransom note."

She hesitated, knowing what she said next would hurt Clay, but she was sure it wasn't something he hadn't already considered.

"When I first came back, everyone thought I'd been doing drugs. There were a lot of needle marks on my arms. But it turned out that the only drugs in my system were sedatives."

She took a deep breath, wishing there was another way to say the ugly truth, but there wasn't. "I don't think I was physically abused. Except for the injuries I'd suffered in the wreck, I was physically sound. But I can't say the same about sexual abuse, because, God help me, I can't remember."

Addie looked horrified. "And yet you came back."

Frankie shook her head. "Yes, but I don't think I was turned loose. I think I escaped. And because of that, I have no way of knowing if I'm still in danger."

At this point, Addie Bell circled her desk and

took Frankie in her arms. "My dear! My dear! I don't know what to say." She glanced at Clay. "It must have been difficult for you, as well."

Clay shrugged. "I have her back. Nothing else matters."

Addie nodded approvingly and gave Frankie a quick pat on the cheek as she turned back to business.

"Obviously you didn't come here just to tell me this. How can I help? What do you want to know?"

Frankie looked to Clay for help.

Clay stood, and then began to pace.

"When I hired the P.I. the first time, we were looking for clues in Frankie's current life that might give us some answers. You know, like people she'd come in contact with at work—people who might hold a grudge against me. Even the random nut who just crossed her path—things like that. But the fact that she'd been taken from home led us to believe the random aspect of her disappearance was less likely. Someone had to have known our habits—to know that I left for work early each morning and didn't come home until dark. To know that I wouldn't panic if I called home during the day and got no answer."

"And the investigator found nothing?"

"Absolutely nothing," Clay said, then put his

arm around Frankie's shoulders as she slid beneath his embrace. He gave her a quick hug before he continued.

"This time, when I contacted the P.I., he suggested we start from the beginning, which means as far back as Frankie can remember. That's why we're here. Is there anything—any instance, any person—you can think of who would have instigated something this bizarre?"

"Oh my, no," Addie muttered. "Nothing untoward ever happened here at Kitteridge House. Unlike some of the other children, Francesca didn't have any family left. And she was so small when she came to us, I doubt she has many memories of her life before."

Frankie sighed. "It's true. I vaguely remember what my parents looked like, but I'm not even sure where we were living when they were killed."

"Why wasn't Frankie adopted?" Clay asked.

Addie shrugged. "Who knows? Several times we thought it would happen, but each time we would get close, the people decided on a baby instead."

"I remember one couple who had another daughter," Frankie said. "That little girl didn't like me at all. I remember they brought me back."

"And we were happy to get you," Addie said. "Francesca was such a sweet child. Everyone loved her.'' Addie's mouth suddenly twisted in a disapproving slant. ''Even that strange boy. Hmm...at the moment, I forget his name. Anyway, before Francesca's arrival, he was intolerable. Such a troubled, angry young man. But they formed a bond, you know. It was quite a sight. She was just four. He was almost in his teens. Francesca's affection changed him somewhat, even if he didn't have the epiphany we all hoped for.''

Something stirred in the back of Frankie's mind. Almost a memory, but not quite. She waited, focusing on the feeling and hoping that more would come.

Clay saw her grow quiet. Almost too quiet. He leaned over and touched her shoulder.

''Honey, are you okay?''

She jumped. ''Sorry, what did you say?''

He frowned. ''Miss Bell was talking about your friends. Is there something specific you remember?''

''No. Oddly enough, I don't remember any boy like that.''

Addie Bell stared at Frankie as if she'd suddenly grown warts.

''You aren't serious?''

Frankie shrugged. ''I don't remember being special friends with any boy.''

Addie's frown deepened. ''This doesn't make

sense. In fact, as you grew older, we all began to worry about the relationship. He became so persistent, almost obsessive. I used to fear for your safety.''

Frankie stiffened. ''You mean he would have hurt me?''

''Not in the way you're thinking,'' Addie said. She suddenly paled. ''Oh my,'' she muttered, and sat down with a thump.

''What's wrong?'' Clay asked.

''I just remembered something.''

''What?'' Frankie cried.

Addie's hands were shaking as she adjusted the collar of her blouse. ''It couldn't be anything,'' she said. ''I'm sure I'm making too much out of something so inconsequential. Besides, it was all so long ago.''

''Please, Miss Bell, let us be the judge of that.''

Addie's lips tightened into a hard, grim knot.

''You were such a pretty little thing, but when you began to mature, your beauty was quite remarkable, as it is now.''

Frankie blushed.

Addie continued. ''This boy…oh, why can't I remember his name? Anyway, this boy had become a man.'' She glanced at Clay. ''All of our children leave us when they turn eighteen, you know, and he'd been out on his own for some time, yet he kept making excuses for coming back, even getting himself hired as a groundskeeper for a short period of time. It took us a while to figure it out, but he'd come back to be near Francesca.''

The skin on the back of Clay's neck began to crawl. Obsession like that was unnatural, especially a man's for a child.

''How did I react?'' Frankie asked.

''Oh, at first you thought nothing of it. After all, he was such a familiar part of your childhood, '' Addie said. ''But as time passed, I think you became uncomfortable. In fact, I think you were beginning to fear him. And then one day he didn't show up for work. We learned a few days later that he'd been arrested, and later he was sent to prison.''

Frankie leaned forward in her seat. ''You mean, I never saw him again?''

Addie shrugged. ''Oh, I have no way of knowing that, my dear, but when he was released from prison, he did come back here looking for you.''

She shifted nervously.

Clay knew there was more.

''What happened?'' he asked.

''He flew into a rage when he learned you were gone. Broke things in my office, called us all kinds of names. Kept screaming something about Francesca belonging to him.''

Frankie shuddered. Again, something fluttered through her mind. Something dark. Something ugly.

By now Clay was making notes. He wanted to remember all the details to give to Harold Borden.

"His name, Miss Bell. If you could just remember his name," Clay urged.

Addie nodded. "Of course. Let me get my files. It was a strange name, I remember that." She opened a drawer in the file cabinet behind her. "Let's see. I believe the year he turned eighteen was the year we had the fire in the gym. We thought he'd set it, you know."

Frankie's eyes widened. "You mean he was really bad, even then?"

"Oh my, yes, I'm afraid so, my dear."

"Then why did I like him?" Frankie muttered.

Addie shrugged as she continued to dig through her files.

"He wasn't unkind to you. In fact, quite the opposite. Besides, who knows what goes on in the mind of a child? You'd just lost your parents and had come to a place that was strange and frightening. For some reason, he filled a need in your life."

Frankie leaned closer to Clay.

Minutes passed as Addie Bell continued to

search. Finally she stepped back from the cabinets with a file in her hand.

"Aha!" she cried. "I have it."

"His name...what was his name?" Clay asked.

She looked up. "Such a strange name for such a strange child. Here's his picture. Dark skin, black, curly hair. We weren't sure about his ethnicity, but we suspected at least one of his parents was from the Middle East. And the name Pharaoh—so Egyptian, but who knows?"

When Frankie saw the picture, panic shafted through her so quickly that it took her breath away. She meant to inhale and heard herself moaning instead. The room began to spin. She reached for Clay and felt nothing but air.

In the distance, she could hear Clay shouting her name, but she was too far away to answer. She slid out of the chair and onto the floor without making a sound.

Frankie sat on the motel bed, wrapped in her robe and staring at the seascape on the opposite wall. Steam from the adjoining bathroom spilled into the room like a faint blanket of fog, all but obscuring the seagull shower curtain and the lighthouse bedspread.

Clay was still in the shower. He'd spoken earlier

with Borden, and now they were waiting for Detective Dawson to return their call.

The absurdity of the room's decorations was lost upon Frankie. She was too upset to notice that the motel decor would have been better suited to an oceanside city rather one built on a desert. Every so often her heart fluttered and then skipped a beat. And while she knew the arrhythmia was due to stress, there was no way of alleviating the worry. Not when every day brought a new set of problems.

She lay back on the bed and closed her eyes, picturing the face from Addie Bell's file. He would be older now. But there would be no way of disguising his skin or that thick, curly hair. And his eyes. She shuddered. The lack of expression had been frightening.

She rolled over on her side and tucked her hands beneath her chin, replaying the events of the day. She'd fainted. There was no getting around the fact. And while she knew there was a part of her that remembered the boy, she had no way of knowing if she also remembered the man. Even more, what was it about him that had been so awful that the mere sight of his face would make her react as she had? According to Miss Bell, she had not returned Pharaoh Carn's affections.

Even if she bought into the theory that her abductor was this person from her past, then how, after all these years, had he found her? The authorities at Kitteridge House had not known her whereabouts. They couldn't have told. All in all, her life had been very low-key until her disappearance. It wasn't as if she and Clay were the kind of people who regularly made the society pages. Frankie had never even had a parking ticket, so it couldn't have been through the courts.

And then suddenly she sat up.

"Clay!"

The water was still running.

She rolled out of bed and bolted into the bathroom.

"Clay!"

Startled by the sound of her voice, he yanked back the shower curtain. Soap ran from his hair and onto his neck, while the washcloth dripped on the floor.

"What's wrong?" he asked.

"My picture."

"What picture, baby?"

"You're getting water on the floor," she said, yanking the shower curtain back in place. "You rinse. I'll talk louder."

"What picture?" he echoed, and then stepped beneath the showerhead to rinse out the shampoo.

"The one of me in the rain that ran in the papers. Remember?"

The soap was gone, and so was Clay's patience. He turned off the water and stepped out of the tub, wrapping a towel around his waist as he did. Her agitation was obvious, but he was still in the dark.

"Yes, I remember. But I don't know what you're getting at."

"Suppose," she said, beginning to pace, "just suppose that this Pharaoh person who was obsessed with me as a child is the one who abducted me."

Clay sat down on the closed lid of the commode.

"I'm listening," he said.

"All afternoon I've been trying to make sense of it all. If he cared so much about me, wouldn't you wonder why he waited so long to come get me?"

"Yeah, maybe," Clay muttered. "But remember, Miss Bell said that he did come looking for you, but you'd already graduated and left Kitteridge."

"Right. But didn't she also say that he pitched a big fit because no one knew where I was?"

He nodded.

"Then consider this. If one day he happened to find me, how do you think he would react?"

Clay stiffened. "How are you suggesting he *happened* to find you?"

"I know it's a long shot, but in an odd sort of way, it almost makes sense. Remember the picture the Denver paper ran of me in the rain? The one that was picked up by the Associated Press?"

"Yes...so?

"It was only a couple of weeks before the day I disappeared."

Clay's expression stilled. "Son of a—"

"It's just a theory," she cautioned.

Clay stood. "But it's a damned good one, Francesca."

She smiled. It felt good to be doing something positive toward solving the mystery of her past.

"So what do you think?"

"I think I'm calling Borden back, and when Dawson calls, I'm going to add this to the list of things he needs to know." Then he added, "You realize we could be making a mountain out of a molehill. Pharaoh Carn could be happily married and living an ordinary life in some suburb."

"Not according to Miss Bell," Frankie reminded him. "Boys who set fires and run with criminals rarely wind up in the suburbs."

"Be careful, goddammit," Pharaoh groaned, glaring at the physical therapist who was putting him through his workout.

"I'm sorry, Mr. Carn, but you won't regain full strength unless you use these muscles."

He cursed beneath his breath, which didn't seem to faze the therapist.

"Now, Mr. Carn, I need you to roll over on your stomach for me."

Pharaoh rolled, enduring the therapeutic massage because he had to. The man's long fingers dug deep into unused muscles, causing Pharaoh to wince once again. He raised himself up to argue, but before he could speak, Duke hurried into the room with a phone in his hand.

"Boss, it's for you."

"I'm busy," Pharaoh said.

"I think you might want to take it. It's long-distance from Denver."

"It's about time," Pharaoh muttered as he reached for the phone.

"Hello?"

"Boss, it's me."

Pharaoh frowned. Finally Stykowski was checking in.

"Where the hell have you been?" he growled. "And why haven't you called?"

"Hurry up, Stykowski," the guard said. "You don't have all day."

Marvin Stykowski glanced over his shoulder at the jailer, then nodded.

"Who's that?" Pharaoh asked. "Who are you with? I told you to keep this low-key."

"Uh...I ran into a little bit of trouble," he said.

Pharaoh stiffened, then gave Duke a look that prompted him to remove the therapist from the room.

"What kind of trouble?" Pharaoh asked.

"I got picked up, boss. I'm in jail."

Ignoring the pain of movement, Pharaoh rolled until he was sitting on the side of the massage table. Not by the tone of his voice, or the choice of his words, could anyone have told he was seething.

But when Duke came back in the room, he knew. The expression in Pharaoh's eyes had gone flat. He tensed, wondering what Stykowski had done wrong.

"Picked up for what?" Pharaoh asked. "And where are you now?"

This was the admission Marvin hated to share. "For possession, boss. I ran a red light, and they found it in my car. I'm in jail, trying to make bail."

Blood thundered through Pharaoh's ears, and it was all he could do to concentrate.

"When is your arraignment?" he asked.

"In a couple of hours."

"There will be a lawyer at your arraignment,

You will make bail, and then you will get your ass back to Las Vegas before midnight, do you understand me?''

"Yes, Boss," Marvin said.

"Don't screw up again," Pharaoh warned. "I don't like mistakes."

Marvin paled. It was only now that he could hear the true anger in Pharaoh Carn's voice.

"I'll be there, boss. You can count on me."

"We'll see," Pharaoh said.

"Uh, boss, about the other…?"

Pharaoh frowned. "Save it," he snapped. "You've got company, remember?"

Marvin glanced at the guard. "Yeah, right. I'll fill you in when I get there."

As soon as the line went dead in Pharaoh's ear, he flung the phone across the room, shattering it against the wall.

"Do you want the therapist back?" Duke asked.

Pharaoh nodded. "Hell, yes, let's get this over with. It's getting so I can't depend on anyone but myself. I've got to get well."

Pharaoh had been at the library window for hours—sometimes sitting, sometimes standing—contemplating the city, the lights, and now watching the headlights of a car as it came up the winding road to his estate. Fury sat in his belly like a rock, seething, rolling, with nowhere to go.

Finally the car pulled up to the main gates. Beneath the security lights, the driver's red, curly hair and goatee were a giveaway to his identity. Stykowski.

Pharaoh reached for the intercom. "Let him in," he snapped.

The gates opened inward, making way for the car to come through. Pharaoh watched Stykowski park. He saw the bravado in his walk. Only after the man had been given entrance to the house did Pharaoh turn his back on the window.

He rolled his rabbit's foot back and forth between his fingers like worry beads as he strode to his desk. They would be here soon. Duke had his orders. The minute Stykowski arrived, he was to bring him in here.

Pharaoh tossed the rabbit's foot onto his desk and then opened a drawer just as the knock sounded on his door.

"Enter!"

Marvin Stykowski sauntered inside.

Pharaoh stepped back from the desk and fired without aim. Luckily for Duke, who was only a few feet away, he was a good shot. The bullet ripped through Marvin Stykowski's brain before he could register fear. Blood spattered across Duke's face, like blowing rain against a window.

Duke gasped and then froze—afraid to move, afraid to breathe. The look on Pharaoh's face was terrifying. Never, in all the years that he'd worked for this man, had he seen him in such a rage. Duke took out a handkerchief and began wiping his face.

"Get rid of that puke," Pharaoh muttered, then tossed his gun back in the drawer and pushed it shut.

Duke stuffed his handkerchief in the pocket of his suit and went for the phone.

Within minutes, the body was gone.

Pharaoh was standing at the window with his hands behind his back, again contemplating the Las Vegas skyline as if he'd never seen it before.

"This is a powerful city," he mused.

"Yes, sir, that it is," Duke muttered.

"I should have waited to ask him what he'd learned in Denver," Pharaoh said.

"If you say so, boss."

Pharaoh turned, then frowned, as if looking at Duke for the first time.

"Your clothes are ruined. Tomorrow, go downtown to my tailor and get yourself a new suit. I like my men well dressed."

Personally, Duke was just happy to still be

breathing, but he would certainly do as the man said.

"Yes, sir. I will. Will there be anything else tonight?"

Pharaoh frowned. "I need someone I can trust to go to Denver. Who do you suggest?"

Duke shrugged. "I don't know, Mr. Carn. Everything has been so messed up since the quake, I don't know who's where, or if they're even alive."

Pharaoh sighed. "And therein lies the problem, right, Duke? It's the fault of that damned quake. Oh well, I suppose we'll have to make do. See if Simon Law is available. He's done work for me before."

"Yes, sir. I'll get on it right away."

Pharaoh waved his hand and gave Duke a benevolent smile.

"It can wait until morning. Get yourself a good night's sleep. God knows we can all use one."

"Yes, sir. I will, sir," Duke said. And even though he knew the gun was still in the desk drawer, the flesh tightened in the middle of his back. Later, as he took off his bloodstained clothes and stepped beneath the shower, he wondered which would be worse—knowing you were going to die, or getting it in the back, completely unaware.

Twelve

The motel television was playing softly in the background. Frankie was smiling at the cheese string hanging from Clay's second helping of delivery pizza when the telephone rang. She jumped, watching anxiously as Clay dropped the slice back in the box and reached for the phone. Frankie hit the mute on the remote as Clay started to speak.

"This is LeGrand."

Avery Dawson shifted the receiver to his other ear.

"Got your message," he said. "What's up?"

It's Dawson, Clay mouthed to Frankie, then reached for his notepad. He didn't want to forget anything.

"Plenty," Clay said.

"Where are you?" Dawson asked.

"Still in Albuquerque. We found out some stuff you might find interesting."

"I'm listening," Dawson said.

"We spoke to Adeline Bell, the administrator at

Kitteridge House, which is the orphanage where Frankie grew up. It seems that there was a young man who was obsessed with Frankie, from the time of her arrival at the age of four up to the time he got sent to prison.''

"Obsessed, huh?''

Clay frowned. ''That wasn't my word, it's the term Adeline Bell used. I'll give you her number. Talk to her yourself. She didn't paint a very healthy picture of their friendship, if you know what I mean.''

"Okay, I'm still listening. So he went to prison. What for?''

"I don't know for sure,'' Clay said. ''But Miss Bell said by the time he got out, Frankie had turned eighteen and was already gone. She said he raised holy hell when he found out he'd lost touch with her.''

"And that was how long ago?'' Dawson asked.

"Frankie's been out of Kitteridge for a little over eight years. I'm not sure about when he got out of prison. All we know is he came back looking for her.''

"Yes, but...''

"There's more,'' Clay said. ''Frankie claimed she didn't remember any such person, which seemed to surprise Miss Bell. Yet when Frankie saw a picture of the young man, she fainted.''

Now Dawson was paying attention. "Damn. Did she identify him as the man who abducted her?"

Clay hesitated. "No, she hasn't remembered anything that detailed. All she's been able to say about her abductor is that he has a tattoo on his chest, remember?"

"Yeah, that Egyptian thing." Then Dawson sighed. "Look, Clay, I know this sounds promising, and I will certainly check it out. But you do know that we can't make a case like this without some actual physical evidence."

Clay wouldn't look at Frankie. He knew that she would be able to tell that Dawson wasn't all that fired up about what he'd just said, and after the way her day had gone, he hated to disappoint her again.

"Yes, we're aware of that," he said shortly. "However, we would appreciate it if you would check the man out. He has a record. It shouldn't be all that difficult to locate him."

"Sure, what's his name?" Dawson asked.

"Pharaoh. Pharoah Carn."

Avery Dawson rocked back in his chair.

"Not *the* Pharaoh Carn."

Clay frowned. "You know him?"

Frankie gasped, then leaned forward, her own pizza quickly forgotten. "What?" she whispered.

Clay pulled her forward, then held the receiver

so that they could both hear what Dawson was saying.

"No, I can't say that I know him personally," Dawson said. "But I certainly know *of* him. However, it remains to be seen if the Carn you're talking about is the same one I'm thinking of."

"What's so special about your Pharaoh Carn?" Clay asked.

Dawson snorted beneath his breath. "I wouldn't call him special. More like notorious."

Frankie's fingers curled as her pulse reacted. She glanced at Clay, her eyes wide with shock.

"What has he done?" Clay asked.

"Nothing the law could prove," Dawson said. "But in certain circles it's a well-known fact that he's Pepe Allejandro's number-one man."

Clay's gut tightened. "Allejandro...as in the California crime family?"

"One and the same," Dawson said. Then he added, "Jesus Christ, LeGrand. If we're dealing with these people, neither one of you will be safe."

"There's something else," Clay said. "A couple of weeks before Frankie disappeared, the AP ran a picture of her. It didn't amount to anything except a pretty girl laughing in the rain, but it ran in papers all over the United States. She thinks that might be how he found her."

"Well now, why didn't this ever come up before?" Dawson asked.

"It wasn't me who thought of the connection, it was Frankie," Clay said. "So how soon can you find something out?"

Suddenly, Frankie bolted out of bed and headed for the bathroom. Clay was torn between following her and needing to finish this conversation.

"I'll do some checking," Dawson said. "We need to know where this Pharaoh Carn grew up. And where he's been for the past two years, and, even more to the point, where the hell he is now."

"Okay," Clay said. "We're heading back to Denver tomorrow."

"Call me the minute you get in. If any of this pans out, we might need to discuss some other options. That gun your wife bought won't solve anything if the Allejandro cartel is involved. It would be like throwing peanuts to try and stop a raging elephant."

"Yeah, right," Clay muttered as his hopes continued to drop. In the next room, he could hear water running. He got off the bed. "Hey, Dawson," he added.

"Yeah?"

"Hurry...okay?"

"I'm on it now," Dawson said.

The line went dead in Clay's ear. He laid the

pizza box on the table and headed for the bathroom.

Frankie was sitting on the side of the tub with her elbows on her knees and her hands over her face. There was a wet washcloth dripping water on the floor next to her feet.

"Baby…are you okay?"

She looked up. "I thought I was going to throw up."

"Are you okay now?"

She nodded.

"Come lie down," he urged, and helped her back to the bed, then stretched out beside her. She was trembling uncontrollably, but every time he tried to hold her, she kept pushing him away.

"Francesca, don't fight me," Clay begged. "I'm on your side, remember?"

Her face crumpled. "Oh, Clay…oh my God."

"Don't cry, honey. It's going to be all right."

"How can it be?" she wailed. "You heard him. The man is dangerous."

"But we don't know that the boy who was infatuated with you is the same man involved with Allejandro. And even if he is, that doesn't mean he's the one responsible for kidnapping you."

She laughed bitterly. "Please, Clay…just how many Pharaoh Carns do you think there are in the United States?"

He sighed. There was no denying that the uniqueness of the name certainly lessened the odds. And the fact that she had not been physically harmed during her two-year absence leaned toward the theory that, however twisted the reasoning, whoever had taken her had cared about her welfare. That fit the profile of the young man Addie Bell had described.

"I want to know the truth, don't you?" Clay asked.

Frankie stilled, her face streaked with tears, her eyes glittering with anger.

"Do you think you can face the truth?" she asked.

"What do you mean?" he said.

She rolled away from him and sat up in bed, unable to look him in the face. "What if I was his...what if he...?"

Clay's voice deepened with anger. "You mean, what if he had sex with you? Goddammit, Francesca, do you think I haven't thought about that a thousand times since your return?"

"I don't know," she whispered. "We haven't talked about it, and I just—"

"Do you think I'm so shallow that I'd judge you by circumstances beyond your control?"

She didn't answer.

"Look at me, dammit."

She did.

His voice softened. "If you'd been attacked on the street and raped, do you think I would not love you anymore?"

"No, but—"

"There are no buts," he whispered. "It's the same thing. Whatever happened to you was not by choice. We just need to make sure it doesn't happen again."

"I'm scared," she whispered.

"I'm scared, too," Clay said. "But as long as we have each other, we'll get through."

Her voice was still shaking. "If this criminal *is* the same man I knew as a child, and if he's the one who kidnapped me, then we're in a lot of trouble, aren't we?"

Clay sighed. "I won't lie to you, Frankie. If that's the case, it won't be easy to protect ourselves. But we'll do it. Remember, if it's him, we have an advantage this time that we didn't have before."

"What's that?"

"We know what he looks like."

"But, Clay, people like him hire thugs to get things done. He wouldn't come himself. We have no way of protecting ourselves against strangers. It could be anybody."

"Then we'll hide, Francesca. At least until your

memory comes back, or until the police get enough evidence to arrest him.''

She frowned. The idea of hiding didn't sit well with her. "I don't know," she muttered. "What if neither happens?''

"But it will, and in the meantime, trust me to take care of you.''

Frankie reached for him then, falling into his arms and burying her face against his chest.

"Make love to me, Clay. Make all of this ugliness go away.''

"Abracadabra," he whispered, and lowered his head for a kiss.

And it was magic indeed.

It went on and on and on, until Frankie's head was spinning and her heart was on fire. She was gasping for breath and begging him to take her, and still Clay wouldn't give in. His touch was tender, his skill at hitting all her pulse points maddening.

"Clay…"

"Not yet, Francesca.''

She sighed.

Then he moved away, and for a fraction of a second the abruptness of the motion left her stunned. Before she could object, he gently rolled her from her back to her stomach, leaving her face-down on the sheets.

"What are you—"

Suddenly, the question became moot. Clay was kissing the bottoms of her feet, then the backs of her legs. When he got to the bend of her knees, she moaned.

"Clay."

"Shh."

She closed her eyes and gave herself up to his demands.

Sometimes it was a nibble, sometimes a caress, once she felt the imprint of his teeth, and then it was gone. The weight of his body came next as he straddled her legs, then stretched out on top. He should have been heavy, but all she felt was the love. His hands slid beneath her rib cage, cupping her breasts, then stroking the nipples until they were hard, aching nubs. Her breath came in short, jerky gasps as she struggled to focus, but she was coming undone.

And then his hands were in her hair and he was moving it aside. She felt the warm, wet stroke of his tongue against her neck, then her cheek, and then he centered his mouth on that damnable tattoo.

She groaned, and heard him chuckle.

With one hand across her breasts and the other on the flat of her belly, he rolled onto his side, taking her with him. Before Frankie's world had stopped rocking, the hand on her belly slipped lower, stopping at the juncture of her thighs.

She jerked, and then gasped as his voice vibrated against her ear.

"Easy, baby, just follow the feeling, it'll take you where you want to go."

He started to move, stroking gently at first, and then harder and faster until Frankie was lost. Everything shattered, including her mind.

Duke Needham breathed a sigh of relief as he hung up the phone. Finding people who were not only willing, but able, to follow his orders had not been easy. But Duke had persevered. He had no intention of being the bearer of bad news and winding up like Stykowski, with a hole in the middle of his forehead. He headed for the exercise room, hoping the news he had just gotten would change Pharaoh's attitude for the better.

Pharaoh's hair was wet with perspiration, as were his T-shirt and sweats. The muscles in his legs were burning, weak from enforced inactivity. His heart was pounding as if he'd been running for miles, when in fact he had yet to walk two. He kept staring at the treadmill's digital readout, certain that it was not registering correctly, and getting more and more pissed by the minute. He did not tolerate weakness—not even in himself.

He'd been out of the hospital a little over a week. According to the doctors, his recovery was going well, even beyond expectations. But it was not going fast enough for him. In his business, it was dangerous to be weak.

He shifted his mind onto a different plane, refusing to focus on the shaking muscles and stabbing pains. Learning of Francesca's fate was all the incentive he needed to get well.

It was ironic that the L.A. cops he had on his payroll could not help him in a matter like this. Initiating a search, or acknowledging they knew anything about the woman's presence in Pharaoh's life, would directly involve them in her abduction. In normal circumstances, there would have been one or two who could have done some checking without raising any notice. But these weren't normal times. The earth had rocked and cracked, destroyed—and killed. And Pharaoh could hardly put out a missing-person report on a woman he had literally stolen.

He gritted his teeth and lengthened his stride as he thought back over the past two years. He'd envisioned their reunion as something out of a movie—that she would see him and fall into his arms, swearing her undying devotion. Instead, she had screamed with fright and tried to run. He'd grabbed her then, reminding her of his vow to take care of her, reminding her that she belonged to him. But she had argued, saying she didn't belong to anyone but Clay.

That was when he'd made his mistake. He'd slapped her. It didn't matter how many times he had tried to apologize later, she still flinched when he came close and fought his every touch. And while her sorrow was almost his undoing, it became a matter of pride not to weaken. The fact that she didn't want him was almost secondary to the fact that he couldn't let her go. Everything good had returned after she'd come back into his life. Francesca had gone from being not only his heart's desire but his luck, as well. And like the bird in the proverbial gilded cage, she had everything power and money could buy, except the thing she wanted most—her freedom.

"Son of a bitch," Pharaoh muttered as his legs suddenly gave way.

He grabbed at the treadmill, but missed. The floor was coming up to meet him when his momentum stopped abruptly. Dazed and disoriented, he reached toward a wall as Duke lifted him to his feet.

"Get me to a chair," he muttered.

"Yes, sir," Duke said, and slid an arm around

Pharaoh's waist, then all but carried him to the leather sofa nearby.

"Should I call the nurse?" he asked.

"Not unless you're tired of breathing," Pharaoh snapped.

Duke paled. As weak as Pharaoh was, he still feared the man.

"I'll get you some water."

Pharaoh sighed as Duke headed for the bar. He leaned back and closed his eyes, listening to the clink of ice cubes, then the sound of water being poured in a glass.

"Here you go, boss," Duke said.

Pharaoh took the water while coldly eyeing the bland expression on Duke Needham's face. If he'd seen pity... He grunted his thanks and lifted the glass to his lips.

Duke was waiting to deliver his news.

It occurred to Pharaoh, as he drained the glass, that Duke's arrival must have been more than fortuitous. His men knew better than to disturb him when he was on private time. He set the glass aside and looked up at Duke.

"What brings you down here?"

"Good news, boss. We've found her."

Pharaoh's expression stilled. "Where?"

Duke hesitated momentarily, but there was no getting around the truth.

"Where you suspected she might be...in Denver."

Pharaoh said nothing, but inside, he was screaming. She was alive...and she'd gone back to *him*.

And then it hit him. She'd gone back, but she hadn't told. If she had, the cops would have been all over him by now.

"What else?" Pharaoh asked.

"Details are sketchy, but word is she has some sort of amnesia."

Pharaoh leaned back on the sofa. That explained why he was still here and not battling a court proceeding.

"You want we should pick her up again, boss?"

"No," Pharaoh snapped. He didn't want her to see him like this—weak and helpless. "Not yet."

Duke shrugged. For a man who'd been out of his mind wondering what had happened to her, or if she was even still alive, Pharaoh showed little concern. But it wasn't for him to judge. As far as he was concerned, they were better off without her.

"Yes, sir," Duke said, and started to leave, when Pharaoh called him back. "Sir?"

"I want Law to stay on that house 24-7, do you get me?"

"Yes, sir. Round-the-clock surveillance."

Pharaoh waited until Duke was gone before he dragged himself off the sofa and headed for his living quarters in the west wing. By the time he reached his bedroom, he was perspiring profusely, mostly from pain. With a silent curse, he stripped off his clothes and headed to the shower.

The bathroom itself was a masterpiece of architectural design. Bottle-glass bricks in lieu of windows and floor-to-ceiling tiles of mirrored glass. Green plants hung from the ceiling; others grew in pots upon the floor. The towels were white, offset by the antique-gold fixtures and yellow-gold soaps in the shapes of pyramids.

As he walked inside, the reflection of his nudity was thrown back at him from every angle. Although his six-foot frame was slim and firm, healing scars still showed a dark, angry red, and there was a faint purpling on his ribs. In spite of the obvious trauma he had endured, it was the small tattoo in the center of his chest he saw first. He walked closer to the mirrors, and then closer still, until he could see the throb of his pulse at the base of his throat.

The tattoo was a mockery.

Eternity.

Francesca did not know the meaning of the word. He splayed his fingers across the center of his chest, while his heart beat a tattoo of its own against his palm.

He wanted her to love him as he loved her. He

wanted her undying devotion. But he wasn't going to get it. What he would get, though, was his way. He would have her back, even if he had to kill her husband to do it. But first, he had to get well.

"What do you mean, you don't know where he is?" Clay asked.

Detective Dawson shrugged. "Just what I said. You have to understand, there's a lot more going on out in L.A. besides running down a man for questioning. Everything is in turmoil. Emergency services are still not up and running full blast. There are areas of the city that people still can't go into. They're still uncovering the occasional victim. That earthquake was the worst in years. What did they say...7.6 on the Richter scale?"

"Something like that," Clay muttered, and then gave Frankie a worried look. Oddly enough, she seemed calmer than he felt.

"So what *do* you know?" Clay asked.

Dawson flipped open the file on his desk and leaned forward, making a mental note to get his eyes checked. For the past few months, words had begun to blur.

"Okay...Pharaoh Carn, of the Allejandro cartel, was raised in Albuquerque, New Mexico, at Gladys Kitteridge House. He was working as a groundskeeper on the premises when he was arrested for armed robbery. He did five years.''

''After that...where did he go after that?'' Frankie asked.

Dawson shuffled a couple of papers.

''Hmm, looks like the next thing we have on him, he was arrested for assault in Orange County.'' Dawson looked up. ''That's in California.'' Then he returned to the file. ''However, the charge didn't stick. After that, he began working his way into the cartel, doing a little muscle work here, a little legwork there. Within a few years, he was one of the men giving orders rather than taking him.''

Frankie shivered. ''It's weird to think I once knew someone like that.''

Dawson nodded. ''Yeah, I know what you mean. One day, about ten years ago, me and my partner were working narcotics when this bust went down. When we got inside the house, damned if I didn't wind up arresting a man who'd been one of my college professors.''

Clay wasn't interested in Dawson's past. It was Frankie's that was making them all lose sleep.

''So the young man who was obsessed with Frankie is the man who's part of a crime syndicate now.''

Dawson nodded, then gave Frankie a considering glance. "You haven't remembered anything else that could be pertinent to the case?"

Her shoulders slumped. "No."

Clay slipped his arm around her and gave her a hug. "It's okay, baby. You will." Then he looked back at Dawson. "Isn't there any way we can check out Carn's whereabouts during the time Frankie was missing?"

Dawson grimaced. "Mr. LeGrand, if it was that easy to keep up with scum like Carn, he'd probably be behind bars as we speak. Until and unless your wife remembers something specific that can tie him to the crime, we're stuck."

"But what about the earthquake...and the tattoo?" Frankie asked.

Dawson looked apologetic. "Look, Mrs. LeGrand. You just *think* you were in an earthquake. You can't remember. And you just *think* that the man who kidnapped you had a tattoo that matches the one on your neck. Maybe you're just remembering the man you knew as a child. Maybe he's all mixed up with the real man who snatched you. Do you see what I mean?"

Frankie wanted to scream. "It's not fair," she muttered.

"No, it's not," Dawson said. "But you give me something solid to go on and I'll be all over the bastard like flies on honey."

Frankie stood abruptly. "Clay, don't you think it's time we got out of Detective Dawson's way so he can do his job?"

Clay sighed. Frankie was mad, and he couldn't really blame her. Before he could say anything, Dawson stood, also.

"Mrs. LeGrand, I realize what I told you wasn't what you wanted to hear. Honestly, I think you may be on to something, but until Carn is located and questioned..." He shrugged.

Disgust colored her voice. "I know. All I have to do is wait around for the other shoe to drop."

"If you were my wife, I might be inclined to suggest that you and Clay take a trip—a long, long trip."

A dark flush spread across Frankie's cheeks. "I'm not running," she said slowly. "I will be damned if I'll let some maniac dictate my way of life. When he comes back—and I believe that he will—I'll be waiting."

"It's your call," Dawson said.

"And she's my wife," Clay said, then looked at Frankie, his fear for her overriding his better judgment. "Maybe we should—"

"No. I'm not budging. If he wants me that bad, I want to be sure he can find me."

Clay went pale. "Goddammit, Francesca. You are not using yourself as bait."

"It's my life," she muttered. "And I want it back."

Clay's belly was in a knot, but he knew better than to argue with her when she got like this.

"We'll talk more later," he promised.

She gave him a look that pretty much said he could talk all he wanted, but she wasn't changing her mind.

"I'll order a patrol car to check your house off and on during the day," Dawson said.

The look she gave Dawson in response wasn't much better. "Thank you for your patience," she said. "I doubt we'll be bothering you again."

Even after they were gone, Francesca LeGrand's words still rang in Dawson's ears. He tried to get back to his paperwork, but he kept thinking of the handgun she'd bought, instead.

He shook his head in frustration. Sometimes this job just plain sucked.

Thirteen

An entire week had come and gone since Frankie and Clay's return from Albuquerque, and every day that passed felt like the lull before the storm. No matter how ordinary their days or how quiet their nights, the stress of not knowing was wearing them down.

Clay was short-tempered at work, and Frankie fought a constant urge to dissolve into tears. Even though they had yet to locate him, the Denver police were still trying to pinpoint where Pharaoh Carn had been during the time Francesca had been kidnapped. And, unknown to Frankie, Harold Borden, the P.I. Clay had hired, was now monitoring everyone who she came in contact with. Everyone kept moving, but in place.

And then, a couple of days after Thanksgiving, it started to snow.

"Look, Clay, someone is moving into Mrs. Rafferty's garage apartment across the street."

Clay glanced up from his desk to the window.

where Frankie was watching it snow. Glad to have an excuse to abandon his paperwork, he got up.

"Hell of a day to move," he said as he came up behind her and peered over her shoulder into the storm.

Frankie nodded, then wrapped herself in his arms. "Selfishly, I'm glad it's snowing."

"I never thought I'd hear you say that," Clay said. "You hate the cold."

She frowned. "I still don't like it, but I like having you home."

Dependency wasn't part of Frankie's personality. Clay hated the stress she was under and worried constantly about how long she would be able to withstand it.

"Sweetheart, all you have to do is say the word and I'll hire a bodyguard to stay with you when I'm at work."

"Don't be silly," she muttered. "You installed a security system already. Besides, we can't afford bodyguards and—"

"No, baby. What I can't afford is to be without you."

Her chin suddenly quivered. "Sorry," she said, blinking back tears. "It seems that all I want to do these days is cry."

"If it makes you feel better, have at it. I know this isn't easy for you." Then he glanced back out the window and frowned. "Looks like Mrs. Rafferty's new renter is traveling light. A couple of suitcases and a box of books isn't much in the way of worldly goods."

Frankie squinted as she peered through the cloudy white swirls eddying off the edge of the roof. "I remember a time when I didn't own much more than that."

Clay tilted her chin. "How about some hot chocolate?"

She sighed, then forced a smile. "With lots of little colored marshmallows?"

He rolled his eyes in pretend dismay. "I don't know. I'm a marshmallow purist, myself. But I suppose if you have to have colors, then—"

She punched his arm with her fist. "Just stop it, mister. At least I don't put mustard on my scrambled eggs."

He grinned. "Hey, that's good stuff!"

"I try not to gag."

"Just for that, the little green marshmallows are mine."

"No way," Frankie said. "You know those are my favorites."

Clay's eyes twinkled as he lowered his voice in mock warning. "Okay, colored marshmallows it is, but you know it's going to cost you big time."

She grinned. "Exactly how much?"

He scooped her off her feet and into his arms.

"It's not *how much*, it's *what*."

Frankie tunneled her fingers through his hair, loving the spiky feel of the short dark strands against her palms.

"Exactly *what* are we talking about here?"

His answer was a grin as he started out of the room with her still in his arms.

"Hey, the kitchen is that way," she said, pointing over his shoulder.

"Sorry, lady, but you know the old saying. 'You get what you pay for.' You can't have the hot chocolate until you pay up."

She started to laugh. "Exactly what is this cup of hot chocolate going to cost me, anyway?"

He dumped her in the middle of the bed and started peeling off his shirt. "Kisses galore." Then he reached for her shoes.

She laughed. "And if I want those green marshmallows, too?"

He never cracked a smile. "That's going to up the ante."

"To what?"

He undid her slacks, then started to pull. "You'll see," he said softly. "I'll let you know when I've had enough."

Simon Law tossed the last suitcase on the bed and then pocketed the door key as he surveyed the two-room apartment. As far as apartments went, he'd had better. But it was clean, and it was warm, and considering the damned blizzard outside, it was better than the Ritz. He brushed at the snow still clinging to his hair and coat, reminding himself what he'd been sent here to do.

"What the hell did I do with my phone?" he muttered, digging through his pockets. They were empty.

He looked back out the window and groaned. The last time he'd used it was when he'd checked in with the boss this morning from the van, then he'd tossed it on the seat.

He eyed the deepening snow with disdain. Waiting wouldn't make this trip better. With a muffled curse, he pulled the collar of his coat back up around his neck and made a run to the van.

The phone was on the seat, right where he'd left it. Within seconds, he was making his way back up the apartment steps and cursing the snow. An Illinois farm boy, Law had left the family home years ago for the California sunshine. But now, here he was, back in the miserable cold and wishing someone else had answered Pharaoh Carn's call.

Within the time it took him to lock the door and shrug out of his coat, he'd already punched in the number to Pharaoh's private phone and dug a pair of binoculars from one of his bags.

"Hey, boss, it's me, Law. Yeah, I'm in." He stepped to the window, adjusting the binoculars to his vision. "Yeah, they're there. I saw them yesterday when I was looking at the place, then I saw them again this morning. Naw, they ain't goin' nowhere. Sure, I know what you said. Just watch 'em."

Pharaoh Carn rolled the rabbit's foot back and forth between his fingers as he listened to Law's report.

"I want to know where they go, what they do—everything! Get me?"

"Yeah, boss, sure thing. I'll be in touch."

Pharaoh hung up the phone. A thoughtful smile shifted the position of his lips—not much, but enough to register complete satisfaction. He hesitated briefly, then dropped the rabbit's foot in his pocket and reached for the intercom.

"Duke. Get the car. We're going to the Luxor. I'm feeling lucky."

"Yes, sir, Mr. Carn. I'll be right there."

Pharaoh's smile widened. This would be his first venture out since being released from the hospital, and of all the casinos on the strip, the Luxor, with its ancient-Egyptian theme, was his favorite. He was in the mood to throw a little money around on the tables, maybe drop in at the Isis for a late lunch. The fine gourmet dining in the Luxor's elegant restaurant was never a disappointment.

He rubbed his hands together as he strolled to a mirror. Maybe while he was out he would get a haircut, eat a good steak. He'd heard Jimmy the Shoe was in town. He hadn't seen Jimmy in a couple of years. It would be good to reconnect with some of the guys.

He thought of Francesca again, but this time there was no sense of urgency. He knew where she was. When he was ready, he would go get her. He'd made a mistake the first time by leaving her husband alive. It wouldn't happen again. This time, when he went after her, she would have no one left to run home to.

A few minutes later, he was on his way. The day was cold, but a long, cashmere coat over a three-piece Armani suit was more than sufficient protection against any chill. The men riding in the front seat with the limo driver were all the protection he needed today against other, less obvious, dangers.

The Franco brothers were out of Philadelphia and had been with him for a little over two years. Both men were long on brawn and short on brains, but that was the way he liked them. Second-guessing Pharaoh Carn could get a man killed. The Francos were in no danger.

"Mr. Carn."

Pharaoh looked up at Duke, who was sitting in the seat across from him. "What?"

"It's real good to see you getting out, sir."

Pharaoh gave his right-hand man a rare smile. "Thanks, Duke. It feels real good to me, too."

Duke nodded, then refocused his attention on the streets they passed. Part of his job was to make sure that Pharaoh Carn got no surprises. Duke was good at his job.

When they started south down Las Vegas Boulevard, Pharaoh's heart skipped a beat. Even from here, he could see the top of the thirty-story pyramid that was the Luxor. A few minutes later, the driver pulled up in front of the casino and stopped long enough for Pharaoh and his entourage to get out.

Duke exited first, along with the Franco brothers. The trio stood for a moment, surveying the crowd. Then Duke leaned in and nodded at Pharaoh.

Pharaoh winced slightly as he got out of the car, but he refused to let pain deter him. Not today. Today he felt vindicated in a way he couldn't explain. He took it as a sign that Francesca did not remember enough to have him arrested. He was untouchable, and he knew it.

He lifted his chin as the limo sped away, refusing to make eye contact with the Luxor's clients. It was something he'd learned on his first trip to prison. Staying aloof gave you a look of importance, and it often meant the difference between trouble and staying alive.

He took a deep breath, his pulse quickening as he moved toward the entrance. Immediately, his men surrounded him. One Franco brother led the way, Duke walked beside him, and the other brother brought up the rear. The swath they cut through the crowd was noticeable. A few feet inside the casino, a short, swarthy man in a tux stepped into their path.

"Mr. Carn! It's a pleasure to see you again, sir."

Pharaoh smiled. Jahar was the floor manager and capable of granting unusual requests at any hour of the day or night.

"Jahar, it's good to be here."

"How may we serve you, sir? Just ask. It will be my pleasure."

"I came to play," Pharaoh said, watching the intense smile break out on the little man's face. "But," he added, "I don't intend to lose."

Jahar almost giggled in response. "Well, sir, who knows? Lady Luck is a fickle bitch."

Pharaoh glanced at his watch. "I assume my regular table will be available in the Isis around three?"

Jahar nodded vehemently. "Yes, sir. I will see to it immediately."

Jahar disappeared into the crowd, leaving Pharaoh to amble about the floor at will. A few minutes later, he was at the baccarat tables, immersed in the game.

At a quarter past five, Pharaoh looked up from his dessert and coffee to see Jimmy the Shoe coming toward him from across the dining room. Duke saw him, too, and glanced at Pharaoh.

Pharaoh nodded. "Let him come."

Duke stood, moving aside as Jimmy the Shoe gave Pharaoh a hearty smile and slid into the chair Duke had vacated.

"I heard you was in town," Jimmy said. "Good to see you out and about. For a while there we didn't think you was gonna make it."

Pharaoh's smile froze, never reaching his eyes. "That's the trouble with gossip, Jimmy. Do I look like a corpse?"

"No, no, you sure don't, Pharaoh. Never seen you look better." And then he gave Pharaoh a quick, nervous smile. "Seriously, man, you come close, didn't you?"

Pharaoh considered his answer, then shrugged. "It doesn't matter how close a man comes to dying, or how many times it happens. What counts is that, when it's all over, he's still standing."

Jimmy nodded. "You got that right."

"So," Pharaoh said, "is this a social call? Can I get you a drink, or something to eat?"

Jimmy leaned forward. "Nah, but thanks. I just thought you would want to know that the cops are asking questions about you in L.A."

Pharaoh's good mood shifted. "What kinds of questions?"

"Real weird, actually. Nothing about the business. Just some stuff about a woman being kidnapped."

Pharaoh took a slow, calculated sip of coffee without revealing his shock.

"Kidnapping is for fools," he said slowly. "I'm not in the habit of indulging in pastimes that don't make me a profit, but, out of curiosity, who's asking? About the woman, I mean."

"The local cops and a private dick from out of state."

He sneered. "She must be some woman, to warrant that kind of interest. Who's she supposed to be?"

Jimmy shrugged. "I don't know. Just some woman."

"So…what are the cops asking?"

"They was flashing around her picture and asking stuff like, did you know her? Had anyone ever seen you with her? Stuff like that."

Pharaoh took another sip of coffee. "Well, thanks for the warning, Jimmy. I owe you."

Jimmy the Shoe shrugged. "Just thought you would want to know." He grinned. "But they ain't gettin' the answers they want. In fact, last I heard, no one knows where you're at. I remembered you had the place up in the hills here, and I just took a chance, you know."

Pharaoh nodded. "I appreciate your efforts, Jimmy. You will be rewarded."

Silence followed. When Duke suddenly moved a little closer to the chair, Jimmy started to fidget.

"It's been real good to see you, Pharaoh, but I'd better be goin'," Jimmy said. "You take care of yourself."

Pharaoh eyed the little man as he scurried off through the crowd. This could change everything. Whether he was ready or not, delaying his trip to Denver much longer could prove dangerous. This would take some serious thought.

"Duke, get the car. I'm ready to go home."

Duke whipped out a cell phone. Within moments, they were heading for the door. The Franco brothers were waiting at the entrance, and they fell into step with their boss, parting the casino crowds and ushering him into the waiting limo.

It had quit snowing around midnight. By dawn, the streets had been plowed free of snow and the sun was shining. Clay had gone to check on a project downtown and warned her that he wouldn't be home until late afternoon. After he left, Frankie snuggled a little deeper beneath the covers and drifted back off to sleep.

Consciousness hovered somewhere between reality and dreams, leaving her wrapped in a warmth of covers and memories. She sighed as she rolled over on her back, snuggling with Clay's pillow. She smiled to herself, remembering the green marshmallows he'd fed her. They never had gotten around to making that hot chocolate, but they'd made love. It had been hot enough and sweet enough all on its own. And so she drifted in and out of sleep, letting down her guard just long enough to let the fear back in...

"Don't fight me, Francesca. You've always been mine."

Frankie looked up at the man towering above her on the bed. His eyes were wild with frustrated lust, his nostrils flared. Rage painted a flush on his cheeks as he struggled to hold her in place. Pinned

*down by the weight of his body, it was all she could
do to breathe.*

"No, let me go...please let me go," she begged.

Fury was evident on his face. "You belong to
me, not him!"

"You're wrong! I belong to no one except myself," she screamed. "I give myself to whom I
choose, and I chose the man who is my husband!
You have no right to any part of me."

He tightened his hold on her wrists. As his face
came closer, Frankie gasped.

"What do you mean, I have no right? I have
every right," Pharaoh whispered. "Look at my
face. Look into my eyes. Remember the past? Remember everything that we shared? No matter how
long you try to forget, you have to remember me."

Slowly, Frankie quit struggling, facing the in-
evitability of the moment. Her heart was breaking
for Clay and for what was about to happen to her.
But she would die before she would give Pharaoh
the satisfaction of thinking he'd won.

The expression in her eyes went flat, as if her
soul had suddenly been sucked from her body.

"The fact that you can overpower me does not
change the fact that I despise the sight of your face.
You have stolen me away from my home. You can
take me, but know that it will be by force. You will

never have control of my heart. That belongs to Clay. He's who I remember. He's who I love.''

Pharaoh exploded in a white-hot rage. Frankie winced, preparing herself for the blow.

She woke up screaming Clay's name and for a moment was startled by the echo of her voice within the house.

"Oh God, oh God," she muttered, and crawled out of bed.

Staggering to the bathroom, she stripped off her gown and stepped into the shower. The water came out cold before it ran warm, but Frankie didn't care. Her hands were slick with soap as she scrubbed at her skin. She felt worthless and dirty. For weeks she'd been in denial, telling herself that while she'd been missing, she hadn't been used. But this changed everything. Unspent tears hung at the back of her throat, too painful to let go. How was she going to face Clay, knowing that the man who'd taken her had raped her, too?

And then it hit her so swiftly that she almost slipped and fell. She'd remembered something valid. She'd remembered begging for mercy—and she remembered his face. Surely this would be something the police could act on. Rinsing off the rest of the soap, she quickly dried and dressed, anxious to tell Detective Dawson about the dream

But when she called, his reaction wasn't quite what he'd expected it to be.

"Look, Mrs. LeGrand, you said it was a dream."

"Yes, but—"

"Then how can you be sure it isn't a manifestation of your fears? You told us earlier that while you had remembered some things about your abduction, you still couldn't remember your abductor's face."

Frankie felt sick. This was hopeless. No one was willing to believe her. She thought Dawson did, but obviously he'd been wrong. That was just wishful thinking. Clearly he thought she was as crazy as everyone else did.

"Yes, but—"

"And now, after being shown a picture of a man you grew up with, you've decided he's the man who took you."

Frankie wanted to scream. "I didn't just *decide* it," she muttered. "I just *remembered* it."

"No, ma'am," Dawson said quietly. "You dreamed it. There's a world of difference."

Frankie dropped into a nearby chair, her shoulders slumping, her expression as dejected as a woman could be.

"What's it going to take, Detective? Can't you see that I'm still in danger?"

His hesitation was her answer, and with it came anger.

"So, now we finally have the truth," Frankie said. "All of you think I just ran away...and then, for whatever reason, came back on my own."

"Now, Mrs. LeGrand, I didn't say that."

"You didn't have to." And then she continued. "Before we end this futile conversation, I want to ask you a hypothetical question."

"Yes, ma'am?"

"What if I'd turned up dead in another state? Would you have arrested Clay, or would you have assumed that I died while on a little journey of self-discovery?"

Dawson flinched. The sarcasm in her voice was impossible to miss.

"That's impossible to say without examining all the clues."

"Why?" she asked. "You haven't let any of the clues influence you thus far. Besides, you were willing to blame Clay the first time. You were wrong then. Why can't you admit that you might be wrong on this, too?"

Dawson was still struggling with an answer when she interrupted herself.

"Never mind. I think you've stated your position rather succinctly, and, I might add, without saying a word. You know something, Detective? If you ever decide to leave law enforcement, you should think about going into politics. You have the knack for it.''

The click in Dawson's ear left him with no illusions as to how much he'd failed Francesca LeGrand. Even after it was time to go home, he couldn't quit thinking of what she'd said. Were they wrong? It had happened before. Why *was* everyone dragging their feet about investigating Pharaoh Carn? This woman had all but declared war on the man and no one wanted to believe her—including himself.

Then he snorted beneath his breath as he dug his keys from his pocket. Why wouldn't they be dragging their feet? Pharaoh Carn was as dangerous as they came, and as elusive. Besides, it was impossible to interrogate a man you couldn't find.

Late that night, Frankie was still struggling with her conscience. She hadn't told Clay what she'd remembered. It wasn't a clue to where she'd been kept. Telling him would serve no earthly purpose except to give him more pain. Besides that, Frankie didn't think she could face him again if he knew. She felt guilty for surviving. Some women would have taken their own lives rather than submit to another man's touch.

Then she frowned. No. That kind of thinking

was just plain stupid. She owed it to herself, as well as to Clay, to survive by any means. She bit her lip to keep from crying and turned over in bed. Instinctively, Clay gathered her to him as he slept, and she made herself relax. Her decision had obviously served her well. She was back in Clay's arms, where she belonged.

Simon Law circled the house for the third time, each time taking careful note of the elaborate security system that was now in place. Angling his penlight toward a series of wires that fed into a box, he frowned. The boss wasn't going to like this. It would take a better man than him to bypass it without triggering an alarm.

A car suddenly turned the corner, its headlights illuminating the area with an indiscriminate sweep. Simon dived into some bushes only moments before the car sped past. Mentally cursing the snow that had gone down his neck, he crawled to his feet and headed toward the sidewalk. He'd gone several steps before he realized that his penlight was missing. He cursed again and started to turn back, when a light came on inside the house. Without thinking, he bolted for the street.

Within seconds he was in his van and speeding away. There was no danger of Francesca LeGrand escaping his watch tonight. Not when they were safely in bed. Besides, there was another little matter that he had to take care of—the removal of an obstacle from Pharaoh Carn's path.

Harold Borden parked at the curb, then killed the engine. For a moment he just sat, savoring the silence and mentally withdrawing from the work of the day. He glanced toward his house and the Christmas lights bordering the eaves. He frowned, making a mental note to change a couple of bulbs near the southwest corner and then reached for the sack on the seat. The scent of egg rolls had ridden with him all the way home, and he was more than ready for a midnight snack.

When he was on stakeout, he didn't often spend nights at home. But this business with the Le-Grands was different. When Clay came home, Harold went home, too. He grinned to himself, thinking he could get used to a job like this, and then rescinded the thought. The disappearance of Francesca LeGrand had driven him nuts. Not being able to help Clay had been worse. Now that he had a second shot at the problem, he was giving it his all. They were close, he could feel it. Things were starting to fall into place.

He reached for the handle and then opened the door. Immediately, the interior of the car was invaded by a cold swath of air. He gathered the sack a little closer to his chest and got out of the car in one quick motion. The scent of egg rolls dissipated some in the cold night air as he aimed his key ring at the car. The distinct click of the automatic locks sounded sharply in the silence of the street.

He inhaled deeply, then turned toward his house. Alice was probably asleep on the sofa, but she always waited up. He smiled. She was a fine woman and a wonderful wife. He considered himself a very fortunate man.

Suddenly a pair of headlights appeared to his right. A car had just turned the corner of the street. He dropped the keys toward his pocket as he began to circle the car, then cursed lightly as they clattered to the street. He bent over to pick them up.

The impact of flesh against metal was a loud, solid thud, accompanied by the squeal of tires and the sound of an engine swiftly accelerating. It woke Alice Borden from her nap on the sofa. She looked out into the darkness and saw her husband's car parked at the curb. And then she looked further and saw his body crumpled in the street.

She let out a wail, then started to scream.

Simon Law carried his pizza and beer up the steps, then paused at the door to his apartment, juggling his keys until he found the one that went to the door.

Moments later, he was inside. He peeled off his coat and wolfed down his first piece of pizza in only three bites. Night work always made him hungry.

He picked up a second piece, then strode to the window, peering through the binoculars. The LeGrand house was just as he'd left it. As he took another bite, his gaze suddenly slid to the circle of footsteps he'd left in the snow around the house. His heart started pounding as he traced the path with his gaze.

"Son of a holy bitch," he muttered. Damn the snow for stopping before it had covered up his tracks.

His thoughts scattered. Should he pack up and run, or should he hang tough? And if he ran, could he get far enough to escape Pharaoh's wrath? Everyone in the organization had heard about Stykowski. It wasn't healthy to bring Pharaoh bad news.

He lowered the binoculars, staring out into the darkness in shock. And then, the longer he looked, the more he realized he'd missed one obvious fact. Granted his footsteps were still there, but they stopped at the curb. The streets were clear. There was no way of tracing where he'd gone.

Breathing a slow sigh of relief, he finished his

pizza, then flopped down into an easy chair and laid the binoculars in his lap. He needed to rest, but just for a minute.

When he woke, it was morning.

Fourteen

Clay was swallowing his last bite of toast as Frankie came into the kitchen.

"Do you have everything you need?" she asked. "Even though the snow has stopped, it's bitter outside."

He grinned and swallowed. "Yes, Mother. My gloves are in the truck, and I'm wearing long johns under my jeans."

A slow smile spread across her face. "Okay, so I fuss." Then she took away his coffee cup and set it down on the counter. "Hug me," she said.

The poignancy in her voice tugged at his heart.

"It would be my pleasure," he said softly. "Come here, baby."

Frankie settled within his arms, cherishing the strength with which he held her and storing away the feel of his blue flannel shirt against her cheek.

"You going to be all right today?" Clay asked. "I can easily drop you off at Mom and Dad's, or

Mom would probably come over and stay here with you.''

Frankie sighed. The urge to hide was so strong, but she couldn't let this fear control the rest of their lives. Besides that, she didn't feel very well, and coping with someone else's presence wasn't very enticing.

"I'd rather not," she said, giving him an apologetic smile. She loved her in-laws but didn't feel like being the center of their attention. "Besides, I have my gun, and Harold the snoop should be lurking not very far away. I'll be fine."

Clay resisted the urge to frown. The fact that she had felt threatened enough to buy the damned gun still bothered him. They were ordinary people. This shouldn't be happening in their lives. And while her reference to the private investigator was a little sarcastic, after what she'd been through, he could hardly blame her. Then he glanced at his watch. As she'd said, Borden should be arriving almost any time.

"Okay, then, if you're sure."

She grabbed him by the collar and tugged him down for a kiss.

"Kiss me, Clay, and quit fussing."

He grinned. "Well, since you put it like that..."

And he dipped his head as she melted against him,

Moments later, they separated, although reluctantly.

"I'd better go now, while I can still focus," Clay said. He gave Frankie a considering look. "Do you feel okay? You look pale."

She didn't doubt it. Her tummy was beginning to roll. "I'll go back to bed as soon as you leave, okay?"

He touched her forehead, then the side of her face. "You don't have a fever."

"Clay..."

"Look, sweetheart, I can call Dad and—"

"Go to work," Frankie said.

He shrugged. "I'm out of here. Call me if you need me, okay?"

She nodded, then followed him to the door, locking it behind him as he dashed toward his truck. Seconds later, her stomach lurched and she made a dash toward the bathroom.

Clay sat in the truck with the engine running, waiting for it to warm up. As he sat, his thoughts were already in gear. Except for a trail of footprints, the snowfall on the yards and trees was pristine. He grinned, thinking that if he'd still been a kid, he would have found a good excuse to stay home from school and make snowmen all day.

Twice he looked around for a sign of Harold

Borden's car, then glanced at his watch and shrugged. It was still early, and there was always the possibility that some of the side streets were bad. But the snowplows would be out again soon, and he had to get to work. He put the truck in gear and began to back up.

Moments later, he was in the street. He shifted the truck into four-wheel drive and started forward, glancing one last time at his house in the rearview mirror. As he did, something in the reflection caught his attention. He slowed, then stopped in the middle of the street, staring intently into the rearview mirror and trying to figure out what was bothering him about his house.

Suddenly it dawned on him. The flesh crawled on the back of his neck as he slammed the truck in reverse, the tires spinning on the ice-packed street as he began backing up. Moments later, he slid to a stop at the curb. When he got out, his legs were shaking. The longer he stared, the more frightened he became.

There in the snow was a perfect set of footprints circling his house. Just thinking of someone watching their every move, listening to their every word, watching them sleep, was obscene.

He pivoted, his gaze sweeping the neighborhood, trying to spot something out of order. Nothing jumped out at him. In fact, since the snowfall, the houses on the street were picture-postcard perfect. Then he looked back at the tracks. There was a knot in his belly as he took out his key and started to run.

Warmth enveloped him as he bolted into the house. With shaking hands, he locked the door behind him and started through the rooms, looking out every window and tracing the path left in the snow. It wasn't until he was on his way out of the kitchen that he realized Frankie hadn't appeared. Surely she hadn't gone back to sleep this quickly.

"Francesca? Are you all right?"

As he started down the hall toward the bathroom, he heard water running.

"Frankie, where are you?"

She appeared suddenly, standing in the doorway and holding a wet cloth to her face. Her eyes were round with worry, her face pale and drawn.

"You scared me."

"Sorry, sweetheart."

"Did you forget something?"

"No." He hesitated, but only briefly. "Look, Frankie, we need to talk, but first I've got to make a couple of calls."

Before he could explain any further, she suddenly spun and darted back into the bathroom.

He was startled by her abrupt departure, but the

reason soon became clear as he heard the sound of her nausea. He went running after her.

"Sweetheart, you really are getting sick."

Frankie leaned against the sink, wanting the room to stay still.

"It just hit me," she said. "I think I need to lie down for a minute."

"Bless your heart," he said gently, and helped her into their room, and then into bed.

"I'm feeling a little better already," she said as Clay pulled the covers up to her chin.

"Good, and you'll feel even better if you stay where you're at," he added.

She gave him a weak, shaky smile, and then closed her eyes, willing that tilt in her belly to settle. She could hear Clay moving around in the room. When she looked, he had taken off his coat.

"Won't the truck start?" she asked.

He hesitated. Finally, he answered. "It's not the truck."

She frowned. Reticence was not one of Clay's normal traits. "Then what is it?"

He started out of the room. "Let me make the calls, then we'll talk."

There was something in the tone of his voice that was making her uneasy. And he wouldn't look at her when he talked. It occurred to her that this was more than dead batteries and snowpacked streets. She struggled to sit up.

"Why don't you make your calls in here?"

He stopped in the doorway and turned. When she saw the look on his face, her heart lurched.

"Talk to me, Clay."

"There's a trail of footprints circling our house."

"You belong to me—only me."

The memory screamed through her mind, leaving her weak and speechless. All she could do was moan as she covered her face with her hands.

Clay cursed beneath his breath and then sat down beside her. Moments later, Frankie crawled into his lap and wrapped her arms around his neck.

"It's him, isn't it, Clay? Oh God, oh God, he came back."

"We don't know that," Clay said, but he held her close just the same. "Sit tight, baby, I'm going to call Borden and then the police."

Another feeling of sickness swept over her, but it wasn't the same as before. It passed, leaving behind nothing but despair.

Clay shifted her to a more comfortable position in his lap, and dialed, waiting for the private investigator to answer his phone. When a woman answered instead, Clay hesitated, thinking he had dialed a wrong number.

"I'm sorry," Clay said. "I think I misdialed."

"No, I'm sorry," the woman said. "I didn't think to answer correctly. It's just that this morning has been so awful. This is Borden Investigations."

"So, Harold finally broke down and hired some help."

"Um, not really," she said.

"Look, ma'am. I need to talk to Harold. Is he in?"

The woman hesitated. "Sir, are you a client or a friend?"

Clay frowned. "A client, although we've known each other for the better part of two years."

Then Clay heard her sigh.

"I'm very sorry to have to tell you that Mr. Borden is dead. He was killed in a hit-and-run accident last night as he got out of his car in front of his house."

Clay's expression went flat. *Oh hell.* "Did anyone see how it happened?"

"I don't think so. His wife found him lying in the street." Then she added, "If you're a client, Mrs. Borden has asked me to refer his active cases to Rocky Mountain Investigations. They are a reputable group, and Harold held them in high regard."

"Thank you," Clay said. "And please give Mrs. Borden my condolences."

He hung up, then sat, staring at a small tear in the wallpaper near the corner of the bedpost.

Frankie had been silent until she'd heard Clay's last words. At that, her heart dropped. They could only mean one thing.

"Clay?"

"Harold Borden is dead. Hit-and-run last night, in front of his house."

"Oh no! How awful! Do they have *any* idea who did it?"

"I don't think so."

Frankie shuddered, holding on to Clay a little tighter.

"Poor Mrs. Borden. I can only imagine how she must feel."

"Yeah," Clay muttered, and then dialed another series of numbers, all the while telling himself that this was just a horrible coincidence, and that the trouble they were in had nothing to do with Borden's death. A few moments later, his second call was answered.

"This is Dawson."

"This is Clay LeGrand."

"Hey, boy, you're up and at 'em a little early this morning. What can I do for you?"

"Someone was outside our house last night."

Dawson laid a half-eaten bagel on a stack of files and sat up a little straighter.

"A peeping Tom?"

Clay thought of the houses all along the block. Not a yard had been walked in but theirs.

"You tell me," Clay said. "The yards of the other houses are untouched. Not even a dog track."

"Still, you know how kids are when it snows. They just have to stomp it all up."

"They didn't stomp anything," Clay said. "It's just a neat, single trail, circling the house and leading right back out to the street."

"Yeah?" Dawson said. "So don't you have a private dick on your payroll? Maybe it was just him checking to see if you were both okay?"

"Not unless it was his ghost," Clay said. "He was killed in a hit-and-run last night."

This time, Dawson took notice. "The hell you say." He started shuffling papers. "That's quite a set of coincidences you have going there."

"My thoughts exactly," Clay said.

"Okay. Sit tight. It'll take Ramsey and me about fifteen minutes to get there."

"I'm not going anywhere," Clay said, and then hung up the phone.

Frankie's eyes were wide, her expression almost shell-shocked.

"Francesca..."

She didn't answer.

Clay shook her slightly. "Frankie?"

Her head wobbled on her neck, like a broken doll's; then she looked at him and shuddered.

"He came in through the front door. I was smiling. I thought it was you. When he laughed, I started to run."

Anger hit Clay's gut first. "Son of a bitch."

She blinked, her gaze refocusing on Clay's face. "I knew him, Clay. It was Pharaoh. Pharaoh Carn."

Smoke from the burning incense drifted across Pharaoh's vision as he paused before the statue of Osiris. He'd lost track of how long he'd been in the cryptlike room, but he had to admit, his heart felt lighter, his purpose clear. He blamed his earlier lack of focus on the fact that he had not fully healed. But those days were over. Being among these relics had reminded him of a fact he'd almost let slide. Kings were omnipotent. They set the rules, they didn't follow them. Like his ancient namesakes, he would destroy his enemy and take back what was rightly his. It had been done before. It would be done again. He turned his back on the dim, sunless room and the effigies of ancient gods. There were things to be done and little time to do them.

A short while later, he exited the sauna to find

Duke waiting for him. Unconcerned with his nudity, he strode forward, thrusting his arms into the robe Duke was holding and wrapping it around his hot, sweaty body.

"Simon called," Duke said.

Pharaoh paused.

"That little matter of the hired snoop has been taken care of," Duke said.

"How?" Pharaoh asked.

"Hit-and-run."

A smile of satisfaction settled on Pharaoh's lips. "You know, it's too bad, but people should look both ways before crossing the street," he said softly.

Duke smiled. "Yeah, boss, you're right about that."

Pharaoh's stomach growled. "I'm starving," he said suddenly. "Tell cook to fix me a mushroom omelet. I have a few calls to make, so have it sent to the library."

"Yes, sir," Duke said. "Anything else?"

Pharaoh thought of the task ahead of him. "Yeah. Get me a barber." Then he added, "And a manicurist, too. My nails look like hell."

Duke hurried away as Pharaoh strolled toward the showers. For the first time since the earthquake, he felt good. Real good. He was back where he belonged—in total control.

* * *

Detective Ramsey was outside the LeGrand home with a man from forensics, taking pictures of the trail left behind in the snow. Inside, Avery Dawson sat nursing a cup of hot coffee and listening intently to what Francesca LeGrand had to say. Every so often, he put down his cup to make a note. At one point, he stopped her to ask, "So, what you're saying to me is that you're beginning to remember?"

She nodded, glanced at Clay, who was sitting beside her, and turned back to Dawson. "It's happening more and more with each passing day."

"And so you *are* naming Pharaoh Carn as the man who abducted you two years ago?"

She clenched her hands into fists and scooted a little closer to the edge of the chair. Her voice quivered, and she began to rock back and forth where she sat.

"The door was locked. Clay always locks it when he leaves. They must have picked the lock. I was in the kitchen. I heard it open. I thought it was Clay, coming back for something he forgot."

"What happened then?" Dawson asked.

"I was smiling when they came in the room."

Dawson interrupted. "They?"

Frankie looked startled at her own words, then started to frown as she pictured them in her mind.

"Yes, two others. They were shorter, but very muscular. They looked alike."

"As in dressed alike?" Dawson asked.

"No, like brothers."

Dawson nodded and kept on writing. "Then what happened?"

"He laughed...Pharoah, I mean. Said he'd been looking for me for a long time." She shuddered. "I screamed, then started to run." She shut her eyes, remembering the feeling of being yanked off her feet and slammed against the wall.

"And?"

She looked up, her face devoid of expression. "And he caught me."

"How did he get you out of the house unobserved?"

Frankie started to shake and reached for Clay's hand. Immediately, he had his arm around her, holding her tight. She swallowed around the lump in her throat, then took a deep breath.

"I don't know. The last thing I remember is being held down, and then a sharp pain in my arm. I suppose they drugged me."

"What do you remember next?" Dawson asked.

Her focus shifted as her gaze went blank.

"I'm not sure. There was a plane. I remember waking up in a plane." She sighed. "I'm sorry. My mind is just a jumble of images." Then she straightened, "But the few things I do remember, I know are true. Pharaoh Carn took me from my home. I think I was kept somewhere within the confines of a large estate. The grounds were vast but well kept. There were bars on the windows of my room, and I think if it wasn't for that earthquake, I would still be there."

"Okay," Dawson said. "If we press charges, are you going to be willing to testify against him?"

Just the thought of facing the man again made her sick. She clenched her jaw as she looked up at the man who was her husband, staring intently at the strength in his face and the love in his eyes.

He nodded.

It was a silent affirmation that whatever she decided, he was behind her all the way. When she looked back at Dawson, her fear had turned to resolve.

"Yes, I'll testify. I'll do whatever it takes."

"I'll start the ball rolling," Dawson said. Then he glanced at Clay. "I'll pass your theory on Borden's hit-and-run to homicide. It's a long shot, but it never hurts to cover all the bases."

"Thanks," Clay said.

Footsteps sounded on the porch, and they all turned toward the door as Paul Ramsey came inside.

"Did you get the pictures?" Dawson asked.

"Yes," Ramsey said. "Along with frostbite and a penlight someone dropped." He held up a plastic bag with the small flashlight inside. "Does this belong to either of you?"

"No," they said in unison.

"Didn't think so," he said, and dropped it into his pocket.

Frankie stood abruptly. "Would you care for some coffee?"

Ramsey smiled. "Yes, ma'am, if you can make it to go."

"Come with me," Frankie said. "I think I've got some disposable cups."

"Bring me one, too," Dawson said. "I'll have one more for the road."

As soon as they were gone, Clay stood. "What are our chances of making this stick?" he asked.

Dawson shook his head. "I won't lie to you. They're slim, damned slim. A man like Carn will have a dozen alibis and people who'll back him up. Unless we can come up with some physical evidence, it's going to be tough. And that's if we can find him to charge him."

Clay cursed beneath his breath and strode to the window. He stood for a moment, squinting against the glare of sun against snow. A couple was walking down the sidewalk, laughing and talking. Mrs. Rafferty was out in her front yard with a broom, searching for her morning paper in the snow. Their neighbor to the south was up on the roof, hanging Christmas lights. Everything looked so normal, and yet it was all so wrong. Somewhere out there a madman was hiding, watching their every move. But where had he gone? Even more frightening, when would he be back?

"This is a real nice neighborhood," Dawson said. "It's hard to imagine any suspicious characters lurking about here."

Clay stuffed his hands in his pockets as he turned away from the window.

"I know. I grew up in this house. When Frankie and I got married, my mom and dad bought a new house and moved, renting this one to us. I've known these people for the better part of my thirty-three years. Nothing changes. Everything stays the same."

Dawson nodded. "Yeah, I know what you mean. But familiarity is good, you know. Even if it gets a little monotonous, it still feels safe."

"What feels safe?" Frankie asked as she came back into the living room with Dawson's coffee to go.

"This street—this neighborhood," Clay said. "We were saying how nothing ever changes."

She shrugged. "It's true. Except for Mrs. Rafferty's renters, of course."

Clay froze, then spun toward the window again, staring intently at the small, gray van parked across the street.

"What?" Dawson asked.

"A new renter moved in only a couple of days ago."

"So?" Dawson prompted.

"So the only thing he moved in was a couple of small suitcases and a box."

Dawson frowned. "No furniture?"

"It's furnished," Frankie said.

"We'll check him out," Dawson said. "But it's not against the law to travel light."

"You're right," Clay said. "I guess I'm jumping to conclusions."

"No, son. I'd say you're just being careful," Dawson said. "And under the circumstances, I can't say as I blame you."

A few minutes later, they were gone.

Clay took one look at the wan expression on Frankie's face and frowned. "Back to bed with you, my love."

Her shoulders slumped. "I won't argue with you," she said. "But I don't feel sick. Just weird."

"So take your weird self to bed," Clay said, teasing a grin from her as he tucked her in. "Maybe you can sleep. I'm calling Mom and Dad.

There are some things I need to do, and I'm not leaving you alone.''

Frankie didn't argue. She couldn't. She was already drifting toward that place where thought ceased and limbo began.

Simon Law was pacing the floor. Ever since he'd awakened this morning to a clear sky, he'd been nervous. He cursed aloud and strode to the window, peering through a small gap in the curtains. The cops were still there.

"Shit, shit, shit," he muttered. Pharaoh wasn't going to like this. He'd told him to stay put. To remain unobtrusive. But Simon had wanted to get an idea of the layout of the house. Using the cover of darkness had seemed like a good idea. How could he have known that the damned snow would stop?

He peered into the street and made himself relax. The footsteps ended at the sidewalk in front of the LeGrand house. There was no way they should suspect him. His gaze shifted to his van. It was clean as a whistle. He'd made sure of that. The car he'd used for the hit-and-run last night was hot. He'd heisted it about a half hour before he'd done the deed, then dumped it across town, near an all-night bar. Everything had been going as scheduled.

If that damned snow hadn't stopped falling, none of this would be happening.

Then he sighed. There was no way Pharaoh could blame him for this. Who could predict the forces of nature? He tried to relax.

Yet when he saw the two cops hesitate at their car and point to his apartment, his heart skipped a beat.

Easy, he told himself, that means nothing. But when they started his way, he panicked. Without thinking things through, he grabbed his coat and cell phone and darted out a small door that led to a fire escape on the back side of the property. Seconds later, he was over the fence and in the alley, running for all he was worth as Dawson and Ramsey knocked on his door.

Dawson waited for an answer, then knocked a second time, only louder.

"I don't think he's home," Ramsey said.

Dawson looked back at the street. "His vehicle's still here, and it's a little cold for a stroll. Why don't you go talk to his landlady while I look around a bit?"

Ramsey nodded and headed down the stairs. Dawson followed, but instead of going across the driveway to Mrs. Rafferty's house, he circled the garage. When he saw the footprints in the snow leading away from the house, he thought little of it. But when he realized that the man had jumped a fence and gone down an alley, rather than take the sidewalk as a normal route, he began to frown. He'd been a cop too many years not to know when something didn't add up.

He went back around the front and down the drive to the van, jotted down the number of the license tag and headed for his car. He was calling it in when Ramsey joined him.

"What did she say?" Dawson asked.

Ramsey shrugged. "Nothing that will help. She ran an ad in the paper. The man answered and rented it on a month-to-month basis. She said he calls himself Peter Ross."

"Did she say what he does for a living?"

"He didn't say, she didn't ask. She said she needs the money to make ends meet, and as long as her renters are quiet and prompt with their payments, she has no quarrel with them."

Dawson nodded. "I called in the tag and vehicle description. The info will be on our desk by the time we get back to the office."

"What do you think?" Ramsey asked.

Dawson rested his elbows on the steering wheel as he looked from the LeGrand house to the apartment across the street and then back again.

"I think it would be almost too easy to assume

that the new man in the neighborhood is the one who spied on them."

"Yeah, that's what I was thinking," Ramsey said.

"But, I was also thinking," Dawson added, "that I assumed too much before and look what happened. I would have bet my retirement that Clay LeGrand killed his wife." He cocked an eyebrow at his partner as he started the car. "Thank goodness I never made that bet. I would be kissing my old-age pension goodbye."

A few blocks away, Simon Law paused for breath and took out his phone, made his call, then waited for the sound of his master's voice.

The manicurist was small and young. Her Oriental features were fragile, even beautiful. But Pharaoh wasn't interested in anything she could do for him except groom his nails. Allejandro always said that a man's intelligence could be measured by the dirt beneath his nails. Pharaoh didn't intend to give his boss a reason to doubt him.

He leaned back in his chair and closed his eyes, savoring the mindless pleasure of the gentle finger massage and the woman's quiet breathing. So when the phone rang, he announced his displeasure with a curse.

"Duke, take a message."

Needham's movements were fluid as he moved to do his boss's bidding. "This is Needham."

Simon shivered. "Duke, it's me, Simon. I got a little problem down here. I need to talk to Pharaoh."

Duke hesitated. "Boss..."

Pharaoh frowned. "Dammit, I told you to take a message."

"It's Law. He says he's got a problem."

Pharaoh jerked, causing the manicurist to miss the cuticle she was trimming and nip his finger instead.

"Dammit, woman, be careful!" he yelled.

The manicurist paled. "I'm so sorry, Mr. Carn. Please...I'll be careful."

"Just get out," he snapped, waving his hand toward the door. "Duke, get her the hell out. I've got business to discuss."

Moments later, she was gone and Pharaoh was all alone.

"This is Carn," he said.

Simon shuddered. His feet were freezing, and his nose was starting to run. And he was thinking of his father's dairy farm and how uncomplicated his life there had been.

"I ran into a little problem and had to leave the apartment," he said.

"Like what?" Pharaoh asked.

Simon shuddered again. He'd rather Pharaoh curse and yell than speak with such uncommon politeness.

"LeGrand called in the cops. They stayed in his house for a while, and when they came out, they started across the street toward my place."

"Why?" Pharaoh asked. "They wouldn't come for no reason."

He hesitated, then blurted everything out all at once.

"Last night, I was just checking the layout, you know. They've got a hell of a security system. It's going to be a bitch to get inside. But it was dark. Everyone was asleep. I didn't do anything but look in the windows. You told me to keep an eye on them, remember?"

Pharaoh took a deep breath and closed his eyes, willing himself to stay calm.

"I also told you to stay put."

"Yeah, but I thought—"

"I don't pay you to think. I pay you to follow orders."

"And I did, boss. I nailed that P.I. just like you told me."

"And you're about to get nailed in return," Pharaoh snapped.

"No way... At least, I don't think so," Simon said.

"Then why were the cops there?"

Simon took a deep breath. "The tracks. They could see where I walked around the house." He started to curse. "How the hell was I supposed to know it would stop snowing? It's been snowing ever since I got here." Then he added, "But they couldn't tell it was me. The tracks stopped at the street."

Rage spiked, leaving Pharaoh so angry he was shaking.

"And you, you stupid fool, being new in the neighborhood, would be the first person they question."

"What do you want me to do?" Simon asked.

Pharaoh glanced at his watch. "Do you know where the bus station is?"

"No, but I'll find it," he said.

"Be there in two hours. Someone will be waiting for you."

Simon breathed a sigh of relief. "Thanks, boss. I'm sorry, boss. It won't happen again." Then he disconnected.

The line went dead in Pharaoh's ear. "You're right about that," he said softly, and hung up the phone.

True to his word, Simon Law walked into the

bus station five minutes shy of the appointed time, his gaze raking the sparse crowd. He didn't recognize anyone there, but that was okay. He was a little bit early and needed to use the head.

His footsteps echoed within the confines of the large, empty room as he strolled toward the urinals on the wall. As he was in the act of unzipping his pants, the door behind him opened. He looked over his shoulder, smiling in recognition.

"Hey, Paulie, just give me a second and I'll be right with you," he said.

"Take your time," Paulie said, and then walked up behind him and slit his throat.

Simon slumped to the floor, dead before he could scream.

Fifteen

With a sense of déjà vu, Betty LeGrand tiptoed down the hall of their old house and peeked in at her daughter-in-law, just as she had done so many times when Clay was a child. Her heart tugged at the innocence with which Frankie slept, her dark hair all atumble on the pillows and the covers pulled up under her chin. She smiled to herself as she turned and went back up the hall. At least Frankie was getting some rest.

Her husband, Winston, came out of the kitchen carrying two cups of coffee and handed one to her.

"How's she doing?" he asked.

"Still sleeping," Betty said. "Which, in this instance, is probably for the best."

Winston frowned as he followed his wife into the living room, and sat down beside her. A few moments of silence passed between them as he blew on the surface of his coffee and Betty picked up a magazine.

"This is a hell of a mess, isn't it?"

Betty looked up. "*Mess* is hardly the word," she said softly. "I'm so worried about the kids' safety, I can hardly sleep at night."

Winston smiled, then brushed a bit of hair away from her face. "They're not kids anymore, honey."

She sighed. "I know, but you know what I mean. Our children are always our children, no matter how old they get."

"When did Clay say he'd be back?" Winston asked.

"Early this afternoon. He wanted to get the crew started and then talk to his foreman. They thought they could put up the insulation and maybe even start some Sheetrock in the west wing of the annex."

Winston nodded, then took a slow sip of coffee.

"Getting the contract for that hospital wing will pretty much set that boy on his feet," he said.

Betty smiled. "He is doing well, isn't he?" Then she laid her hand on his knee and squeezed gently. "But he had the best man training him from the start."

Winston grinned, a smile so like Clay's that, for a moment, Betty just stared, amazed that such a unique feature could be duplicated so perfectly.

"We're going to get through this, aren't we, Winston?"

The concern in her voice was obvious. He set down his coffee and put his arm around her shoulders, giving her a comforting squeeze.

"Sure we will, honey. Frankie's memory is returning more and more every day. And the more she remembers, the better off we'll all be. At least now we know the face of the enemy."

Betty shuddered and leaned her head against her husband's shoulder. "I won't rest until that horrible man is behind bars," she muttered.

Winston hugged her again. "The police are on the case. It's just a matter of time."

Silence followed. Betty picked up her magazine, and Winston returned to his coffee. Outside, a patrol car drove slowly past the house. It wasn't the first time, and, until this was over, it wouldn't be the last.

About a half hour later, Betty heard Frankie stirring.

"Sounds like she's awake," Betty said. "I think I'll go check on her. Maybe she'd like some hot soup, or something to drink."

She got up quickly and hurried into Frankie's room.

"Hi, honey, how are you feeling?" Betty asked.

Frankie was just coming out of the bathroom. "Better, I think."

"Would you like something to eat? Maybe some soup or a—"

At the mention of food, Frankie paled and groaned, then pivoted sharply, seconds ahead of another wave of nausea.

Betty followed her into the bathroom, moments later wiping Frankie's face and hands as if she were a child.

"Bless your heart," Betty said. "I'm sorry. I shouldn't have mentioned *f-o-o-d.*"

Frankie managed a wan smile. "At least spelling the word doesn't make me sick," she muttered.

Betty chuckled. "Nausea is a terrible feeling, I know. Why, when I was pregnant with Clay, I was sick every morning for weeks."

She turned to rinse out the washcloth and missed seeing the look of total shock spreading across Frankie's face. But when she heard her groan, she spun, fearing the worst.

"What is it, dear? Are you feeling ill again?"

Frankie grabbed Betty's hand, unable to speak.

The utter fear on her daughter-in-law's face was spreading to Betty, as well. "Francesca, tell me, darling. What's wrong? How can I help?"

Frankie started to shake. "My period. I don't remember when I had it last."

A slow smile of understanding spread across

Betty's face as her gaze automatically slid to Frankie's belly.

"Oh, my dear, that would be wonderful," she said softly.

But there was another image that kept overpowering Frankie's memories of making love with Clay. It was bearing the weight of Pharaoh's body and how hard it had been to catch her breath.

"Oh, Betty, you don't understand. All that time I was gone... What if...how will I know if...?"

Suddenly Betty understood, and she dropped onto the side of the tub beside Frankie and took her in her arms.

"Francesca...darling."

Frankie couldn't stop shaking. "Oh my God, oh my God...if I'm carrying a baby, it might not be Clay's."

"Stop it! Stop it right now!" Betty muttered. "No matter what, it will always be yours." Then she pulled Frankie to her feet and cupped Frankie's face with her hands. "And if my son's half the man I think he is, that will be enough. He loves you, Francesca, more than he loves his own life. For a while after you disappeared, I feared for his sanity. The countless trips he made to morgues all over the country, afraid each time that the body they asked him to view would be you—and, in a way, afraid that it wouldn't. The harassment by the press, the fear that he would be arrested for a murder he didn't commit."

Tears welled and spilled, rolling silently down Frankie's face as Betty continued.

"Can you understand? It was the not knowing that was eating him alive." Then Betty sighed. "If you *are* pregnant...and even if it's not Clay's child...it will still be part of you." She grabbed a handful of tissues and handed them to Frankie. "Here, wipe and blow. There's no need crying over a maybe. Let's find out for sure before we define a need to self-destruct."

Frankie almost smiled. "I won't self-destruct," she promised. "I fought too long and too hard to get home to quit on myself now."

"Good," Betty said. "That's the way I like to hear you talk. Do you feel like getting dressed?"

Frankie nodded.

"Okay, and while you're dressing, I'll make you some tea and dry toast. Trust me, whatever your ailment, it will help a queasy stomach. And I'll send Winston to the pharmacy to get a home pregnancy kit. Either way, we'll know something within the hour."

Frankie looked startled. "Oh, but—"

Betty shook her head. "No buts, my dear. Besides, if you *are* pregnant, everyone will know soon enough. Better to know now than to stew over it and maybe make yourself sicker.''

Frankie's lips trembled. ''Oh God, Betty, what if it's true? How will I tell Clay?''

Betty hesitated, torn between Frankie's needs and what she knew would be best for her son.

''Sweetheart, why don't you just take the test first? If it's negative, then you have nothing to dwell on. And if it's positive, then we'll make a new plan. What do you think?''

Frankie started to argue, but the longer she thought, the more she realized Betty was right.

''You're right,'' Frankie said. ''There's no need worrying Clay about something that might not be true.''

''You're not a worry to him, you're his love,'' Betty said, but inside, she was beginning to panic. What if she'd been wrong about Clay's reaction? What if she set Frankie up, only to find later that Clay let her down?

''You get dressed while I send Winston to the store. This will be a first for him. He's never been able to face a salesclerk with anything more personal for me than a tube of toothpaste.'' Then she grinned. ''Oh Lord, I wish I could be a fly on the wall to watch his face when he takes a home pregnancy kit to the checkout counter.''

Frankie looked startled. "Oh, I didn't think about that. Maybe we shouldn't—"

"You just get dressed," Betty said. "Winston will get over it. Besides, the lure of a possible grandchild will probably do the trick."

After a quick kiss on Frankie's cheek, Betty left. Frankie walked into the bedroom and slumped onto the side of the bed. The wheels of her future were in motion. There was nothing for her to do but hang on for the ride.

"Hey, Dawson, you've got a message on your desk."

Avery waved a thanks to the detective standing by the file cabinets and then headed for his desk, with his partner right behind him. Glad to be back in the office and out of the cold, he picked up the fax, then sat down in his chair with a solid thud. But his expression changed as he began to read.

"You don't look all that happy," Ramsey said as he hung up his coat on a nearby coatrack.

"The van at Mrs. Rafferty's apartment is registered to Carla Brewer, of Escondido, California. She reported it stolen about a week ago."

"Damn," Ramsey muttered. "What do you make of that?"

Dawson looked up. "It means that the man who lived across the street from Francesca LeGrand was a thief and a liar, but it still doesn't make him a peeping Tom, or connect him in any way with Francesca LeGrand's previous disappearance.''

''Anything come up on the name Mrs. Rafferty gave us?''

Dawson glanced back at the fax and then flipped it toward Ramsey.

''No. There were hundreds of Peter Rosses in the system. And considering the fact that he was driving a hot vehicle, I sincerely doubt he was using his real name.''

''What do you think about bringing Mrs. Rafferty in to look at some mug shots?'' Ramsey asked.

Dawson shrugged. ''May as well. We don't have much else to go on.'' When Ramsey turned toward his desk, Dawson added, ''Better notify the Escondido Police Department that we found the stolen van. I'm going to talk to the captain.''

Frankie paced the floor from window to sofa and back again, waiting for Winston to come back from the store.

''Sweetheart, sit down,'' Betty said. ''Relax. You may be just borrowing trouble. There *is* such a thing as an old-fashioned case of the flu, you know.''

''It doesn't feel like the flu,'' Frankie muttered.

Betty sighed and returned to her tatting. Before she was nine she had learned the lace-making skill from her grandmother and had kept in practice off and on through the years. She held up the piece of lace for inspection and thought that it would be perfect for the edging on a christening quilt.

"There goes a police cruiser," Frankie said.

"They've been going by off and on ever since the detectives left."

Frankie stared blindly about the peaceful little neighborhood, at the Christmas decorations adorning the porches and trees, at the children playing on the sidewalks at the end of the street. Once it had seemed so perfect—so safe. Now everything seemed threatening and ugly—and all because of her. She turned away from the window in sudden anger.

"Why don't you hate me?"

Startled by the question, Betty dropped a knot, then looked up. "Why, sweetheart, why on earth would we hate you?"

"Look what I've done to your son—even to you and Winston. I feel dirty and scared, like a child who knows they've done something bad but doesn't really understand why."

"That's absurd," Betty said, and patted the cushion on the seat beside her.

Frankie shook her head. "I can't sit." She

turned back to the window overlooking the drive, then, a few seconds later, shrank back in sudden fright. "Oh my Lord," she whispered. "Clay's home."

Betty dropped her tatting and started to get up, but she wasn't fast enough to stop Frankie from bolting out of the room. Heartsick, she watched her daughter-in-law go, then went to unlock the front door to let her son in.

"Hey, Mom, where's your car?" Clay asked as he entered the house.

"I sent your dad on an errand. He should be back soon."

Clay nodded, hung up his coat, then kissed his mother on her cheek.

"How's Frankie?" he asked.

Betty bit her lip, then managed a smile. "Why don't you ask her yourself?"

Clay paused. There was something in the tone of her voice that he didn't like. "What's wrong?"

Betty shrugged. "From my point of view, absolutely nothing. Now go talk to your wife. I've done all I know how to do."

Clay hurried out of the room and down the hall, wondering what the hell else could have happened while he'd been gone. Seconds later, he entered the bedroom to find Frankie standing at the window with her back to the door. Even though he knew she'd heard him coming, she didn't move, or acknowledge his presence in any way. His heart skipped a beat.

"Frankie?"

She turned, and the look on her face made his heart skip even faster.

"Baby, what's wrong? Are you feeling worse? Do you want me to take you to a doctor?"

Her chin quivered and then she took a step toward him. "Oh Clay, I—"

Clay crossed the floor and took her by the hand. "Come here." He led her to the side of the bed. "I like to touch you when we talk."

Her expression crumpled. "I need to ask you something."

He wanted to take her in his arms and kiss away all the bad things in her life, but he could sense her need for space. He settled for holding her hand.

"You know you can ask me anything and it will always be all right," he said.

Her mouth felt dry, her palms sweaty. There was a sick knot in the pit of her stomach, like the kind she used to get at the orphanage before visiting day, the kind she had gone to bed with each night, knowing that there was no one on earth who wanted her to be their little girl.

"I may just be borrowing trouble," she began.

"Then we'll owe it together," he said, and

brushed a stray lock of hair from the corner of her cheek.

She tried to smile, but it wouldn't come. Instead, it turned into a grimace that threatened to grow into something worse. Something that, once started, she wouldn't be able to stop.

"Your mother made a comment this morning that got me thinking."

Clay stiffened. He couldn't imagine his mother ever insulting Frankie, but if she had, he wouldn't stand for it.

"What did she say?" he asked.

The abruptness of his tone alerted Frankie that she'd given him the wrong impression.

"No, no, Clay, it wasn't anything bad. In fact, she was commiserating with me because I kept throwing up. She said she knew how I felt, because she'd done the same thing every morning for weeks after she got pregnant with you."

"And...?" he prompted.

She took a deep breath and looked him straight in the eye.

"And I can't remember when I had my last period."

A slow smile began to spread over Clay's face. Frankie groaned. Before he started handing out cigars, she needed to finish.

"But I do remember looking up into Pharaoh Carn's face and knowing I was going to be raped."

He grunted, as if someone had punched him in the gut. For the length of a heartbeat he saw fear and uncertainty in her eyes, a concern that, once again, she was going to become unwanted. He sighed and leaned forward until nothing but their lips were touching. She didn't move. He cupped the back of her head and tasted the fear on her lips, then pulled back.

"Francesca."

"What?"

"Look at me."

Her eyes were wide, her expression questioning.

"Do you remember our deal?"

She blinked. This wasn't the response she'd imagined. "What deal?" she mumbled.

"I get to name our first baby."

She took a deep shaky breath and tried to speak, but the words wouldn't come.

Our. He'd said *our.*

"Do you remember?" he asked.

Her eyes suddenly filled with tears. "Yes."

"So, if you're pregnant, I'd better get busy making my lists, because our baby's going to need a good name."

She threw her arms around his neck and started to cry.

"I am so scared. Ever since the day I saw you, I imagined giving you babies, but now... Oh God, oh, Clay, what if it's not your—"

He kissed her, hard and fast, swallowing the horror of her words before they were said. His breath was short and choppy; his emotions were barely in check. He wanted to laugh—and, dear God, he needed to cry. Instead, he made her a promise he knew he would keep.

"I swear to you, and to God, that I will love the baby as much as I love you."

Before Frankie could voice another fear, she heard a car pulling into the driveway of their house. She got up and ran to the window.

"It's Winston," she said. "He's back from the store."

Before he could stop her, she was out of the room and running up the hall. Curious as to what his dad could be bringing that was so all-fired important, he followed.

"Did you get it?" Frankie said as Winston came through the door.

He rolled his eyes and handed her the sack with the kit inside.

"Hell, yes," he muttered. "That smart-ass girl at the checkout counter took one look at the box, then at my gray hair and wrinkles, and grinned. If that wasn't bad enough, she winked at me, too."

The somberness of the moment was broken with an outburst of Betty's laughter, which added even more confusion to the moment as Clay entered the room.

"What's so funny?" he asked.

Betty couldn't do anything but point at her husband and laugh, while the tears ran down her face.

In spite of Frankie's fears, the image of Winston at odds with the world made her smile. She kissed him on the cheek. "Thank you very much," she said softly.

"Come on, everybody. Let me in on the joke," Clay said.

Frankie held up the sack. "Your mom sent Winston to the store for a home pregnancy kit."

The sight of the little brown sack hit Clay like a kick to the gut. That sack held the answer to the rest of their world. And yet, knowing his dad as well as he did, he could appreciate what it had taken for him to make the purchase.

A slight grin tilted the corner of his mouth. "So, Dad, I guess the answer is, when you've got it, flaunt it."

Winston gave his son a go-to-hell look, while his wife erupted into a new fit of giggles. He glared at Betty, as well as his son, and then gave Frankie a quick kiss.

"I'm taking that cackling old hen over there

home now, and I suppose that I'm going with her.''
Then he grinned. ''Besides, it's too damned cold—
and I'm too damned old—to be looking for another
roost.''

''Thank you,'' Frankie said.

Winston squeezed her arm. ''Just give us a call
later on—one way or the other.''

Frankie nodded.

Moments later, they were alone. She turned to
Clay, the sack clutched to her chest.

''Will you let me come with you?'' he asked.

She lifted her chin and held out her hand.

''I wouldn't have it any other way.''

Across town, another set of questions was about
to be answered, as well. Avery Dawson plunked
another mug book in front of Anna Rafferty and
opened it up.

''Mrs. Rafferty, we really appreciate you helping
us out like this.''

The old woman sighed. ''This is the seventh
book, I believe.''

Dawson winced. The old woman was already
giving out on them, and there were dozens still left
to view.

''Yes, ma'am.''

Mrs. Rafferty sighed again. ''Well, maybe a
couple more.''

She opened the book and began peering at the pages. Suddenly she pointed. "Oh look!"

Dawson jumped to his feet. "Is that him? Is that the man who rented your apartment?"

"Oh no," she said. "But he looks just like Papa did when he was young. Isn't that amazing? I always heard that everyone in the world has a double. My goodness, Papa would have had a fit, knowing that he and some common criminal shared a face."

Dawson dropped back into his chair and swallowed a curse.

"Yes, ma'am, I'll bet he would. Now, if you don't mind, just keep looking. It's very important that we get to talk to your renter."

She nodded and went back to her task, leaving Ramsey grinning and Dawson rolling his eyes.

A short while later, she had finished that book and started on number eight when she suddenly pointed.

"Him!" she cried.

"What about him?" Dawson asked, half expecting to hear that this one looked like her dear, departed husband, Edward, of whom much had already been said.

"That's the man! That's the man who rented my apartment!"

Dawson stood abruptly and looked over her shoulder. "Are you sure?" he asked.

"Oh yes," she said. "I never forget a face. Besides, see the way one eyebrow goes higher than the other? Of course, I never said anything to him, but it gives him such a confused expression."

Dawson looked, reading the name beneath.

"Simon Law." He looked up at Ramsey. "Run a make on this man. See what you turn up." Then he turned back to Mrs. Rafferty. "Ma'am, you've been a big help to us today. Detective Adler here will escort you down to the main lobby."

"Will someone please call a cab for me?" she asked.

"That won't be necessary. One of the officers will see you home in his patrol car."

She perked up at the news. "Oh my! A real police car! I do wish my Edward was alive to see this day." Then she giggled. "Papa always said I'd wind up in the arms of the law."

Dawson threw back his head and guffawed. After the day they'd had, the old lady was a welcome respite. He shook her hand as he helped her to her feet.

"You go easy on our boys, Anna Rafferty, or I'll have to arrest you myself. And don't worry about Ross. I've got men staked out at your house.

As soon as he comes home, we'll have him arrested."

The old woman was still smiling when she exited the room.

Dawson reached for his coffee cup. He'd missed lunch. His belly was growling. But it was going to have to settle for another jolt of caffeine.

Clay sat on their bed, using the headboard for a backrest. Frankie sat between his legs, reclining against his chest. His arms were close around her, his slow steady breaths warming her neck. The thump of his heartbeat was strong against her back, and the only other sound in the room was the tick of a clock on the opposite wall.

The test stick from the home pregnancy kit was upside down in her hand. She felt as if she were holding a time bomb, primed to go off.

"Is it time yet?" she asked.

"No, not for another minute."

She sighed.

"Don't, Frankie. Whatever the results, it will be all right."

"I know," she said quietly.

And they waited.

Even though she'd been staring at the minute hand on the clock, when Clay's voice suddenly rumbled near her ear, she jumped.

"It's time," he said.

Her fingers clenched around the stick, suddenly afraid to look. Then Clay's hands slowly splayed across her belly.

"I love you, Francesca."

Her vision blurred. Even after she lifted the stick and turned it over, she couldn't see for the tears. And then she heard Clay exhale softly, as if he'd been holding his breath, and she knew the test was positive. It was at once the most wonderful, and at the same time the most horrifying, moment of her life. She was going to have a baby. But whose?

And, God love him, it was Clay who came through for her once again.

"Let's call Mom and Dad," he said. "They've been waiting for years to be grandparents. This ought to put them over the moon."

Frankie pulled out of Clay's arms and turned to face him.

"What about you, Clay? Where does it put you?" she asked.

He smiled and shook his head, as if he couldn't believe that she'd asked. "So deep in your life you'll wonder where the hell your personal space went," he said gruffly. Then he grinned. "I'm going to be a father. After we call Mom and Dad, we need to celebrate."

Frankie's heartache lifted—not a lot, but enough to know that they would get through this after all.

"I don't much feel like going out in all this snow."

He grinned. "Then we'll order in. You pick. I'll call."

She hesitated. The thought of a meal was suddenly the best idea anyone had come up with all day.

"I think maybe Chinese, or would you rather have pizza?"

"I would rather have you," Clay said softly, and rolled her over onto her back and laid his head in the curve of her neck.

The knot in her chest loosened a little bit more. She wrapped her arms around his neck.

"You're in luck," she said softly. "Tonight, I'm the house special."

Clay grinned. "Oh no, Francesca. You're always the house special, and I'll never be full. Not of you. Never of you."

Then he looked away, moving his hand from her breast to her belly, shoving aside her sweater and sweats until his hand was palm down on the soft surface of her skin.

"Hey, in there. Grow strong and healthy, little baby. When you're ready, we will be waiting for you."

When he looked back at Frankie, there were tears in his eyes. And that was her undoing.

"I love you, Clay LeGrand."

He grinned. "I know."

She punched him lightly on the arm. "Here's where you're supposed to say, 'I love you, too.'"

His grin widened. "But, sweetheart, that would be so predictable."

A laugh bubbled up her throat. "And God knows we can't have that, can we?"

"My daddy always said that the first time a woman knows where you're going to be at any given time of the day, your goose is cooked."

Frankie grinned, then ran her finger lightly down the side of his cheek. "So...my dear gander, prepare yourself to be roasted, because for the next eight or so months, I predict you will be forever underfoot."

He chuckled and began pulling her sweater over her head.

"What's the deal with eight months? Try the rest of our lives," he said.

She sighed as he took her in his arms. "The rest of our lives? That would be my pleasure."

Sixteen

Morning dawned cold and gray. The wind from last night had drifted the snow, obliterating most of the trail of footprints. Clay didn't have to see them to know that the danger to Frankie still existed. With every passing day, he sensed her fear increasing.

Frankie was awake, but, at his mother's suggestion, was slowly nibbling on some saltine crackers before getting out of bed. He could hear the faint crunch as she took little bites. Hiding his worries, he forced a grin as he turned.

"Sounds like there's a little mouse in my house."

"I feel like one," she said, frowning as she brushed at a crumb. "Shoot, I'm going to have cracker crumbs all over the sheets."

"It could be worse," he said.

She rolled her eyes, remembering her bout of nausea yesterday morning.

Clay chuckled. "Are you ready for some tea?"

She thought about it for a moment, and when nothing threatened to come up, she nodded. ''I think so,'' she said.

''Good! I'll have some with you.''

Frankie started to get up, but Clay stopped her.

''Don't push it, sweetheart. Just lie there. Let me wait on you for a change.''

She dropped back onto the pillows with a frustrated thud. ''I hope this morning-sickness stuff doesn't last too long.''

''We'll make an appointment with your doctor. Maybe he can give you something that will help. Now, give me a couple of minutes. I'll be right back.''

She watched him leave, and closed her eyes, telling herself she was imagining the pain on his face. He'd told her he loved her. He'd sworn that he would love the baby no matter what. She had to believe he was telling her the truth or she would go mad. Then she sighed and turned over on her side, hugging his pillow against her.

The thump and bang of pots and pans was a comforting sound as she drifted in and out of sleep. The noise was her boundary of safety—her reassurance that she was not alone.

A short while later the phone began to ring. She rolled over to answer, but it stopped before she could pick up the receiver. A couple of minutes later Clay burst into the room with the portable phone in his hand.

"Frankie, pick up the phone. It's Addie Bell, from Kitteridge House. There's something you need to hear."

Frankie's heart skipped a beat as she rolled over in bed and grabbed the receiver. "Addie?"

"Francesca! I hear congratulations are in order!"

Frankie looked at Clay. He was grinning sheepishly. She sighed. Maybe her worries were all for nothing. If he was already bragging about their news, he must be okay with the rest.

"Took us both a bit by surprise," Frankie said.

"I'm sure," Addie said. "However, back to the reason I called. It may not amount to a hill of beans, but I've been trying to remember anything and everything about that boy, Pharaoh Carn, and last night, while I was watching a movie on cable, something I saw jarred my memory."

"What?" Frankie asked.

"Pharaoh has a tattoo. In fact, he snuck out after hours one night to get it done. He must have been around fifteen, maybe sixteen. I was furious, both at the fact that Pharaoh had snuck out and at the example the tattoo was setting for the other boys."

Instinctively, Frankie reached for the back of her

neck, rubbing at her own tattoo as she looked up at Clay. He nodded grimly as Addie continued.

"It was one of those Egyptian-looking things. Sort of a cross, but it's not. It had a funny loop at the top. And it was in color...yellow, I think." She paused. "I know it's not much, but considering what you've been through, I didn't want to hold back anything I'd remembered."

Frankie's heart was racing as she scooted to the edge of the bed. "Oh, Addie, you will never know how much this means to us. Look, I hate to rush you, but we have to call the detectives working on the case. Do you mind if we give them your number again, in case they want to corroborate what we tell them?"

"Of course not. I'll be glad to do anything to help."

"Okay," Frankie said. "And thanks again for calling."

"Keep in touch," Addie said. "I'll be wanting to know if it's a girl or a boy."

"Yes, we'll do that," Frankie said.

The line went dead in her ear. She looked at Clay again, her eyes wide with disbelief.

"Clay...this is what Detective Dawson was talking about, isn't it? Could this be the physical evidence he keeps saying he needs?"

Clay shrugged. "I don't know, but we'll soon find out. How do you feel?"

She looked down at herself, frowning at the cracker crumbs that fell from her nightshirt onto the floor.

"Like I've been eating crackers in bed."

Clay grinned. "I have the tea made. If you'll give me a minute or two, I'll bring it in."

"At the rate I'm going, I'd have that in my lap, as well. I think I'd rather have it in the kitchen."

He frowned. "If you're sure?"

She waved him away. "I'm going to get dressed. You make the call. I want Dawson to get on this as soon as possible."

Clay headed for his office to call Avery Dawson while Frankie began picking out clothes. Their lives were settling while Pharaoh Carn's was coming undone. He could feel it.

Avery Dawson weaved his way through the city traffic while Ramsey was trying to finish a sandwich.

"Dammit, Avery, slow down," Ramsey muttered as he steadied his coffee with one hand while trying to eat with the other.

Dawson eyed his partner's food with a wary eye.

"You might be wishing you'd saved that for later," he muttered. "You know what a weak stomach you have, and the captain said that the John Doe's throat had been cut.''

Ramsey shrugged. "I've seen worse," he said, stuffing the last bite of a meatball sub into his mouth.

"Don't say I didn't warn you," Dawson said.

"Consider me warned," Ramsey retorted, and washed down the bite with the last of his coffee.

A few minutes later, Dawson pulled up at the bus station. A cold, blustery wind whipped under their long coats as they got out of the car. They made a dash for the building, only to have their steps impeded by the gathering crowd.

"Police. Coming through," Ramsey said. The crowd parted to let them pass.

A few moments later, they were inside the men's rest room.

"Who found the body?" Dawson asked as a uniformed patrolman approached.

The patrolman pointed toward a pair of teenage boys sitting on a bench just outside the door. The defiance that had given them the courage to sport purple hair and silver nose rings was blatantly missing now. Their faces were pale, their eyes wide with shock. Dawson exhaled softly. Hell of a thing for a couple of kids to find. He started toward them.

"Boys, I'm Detective Dawson. This is my partner, Detective Ramsey. We want to ask you a couple of questions."

The boys nodded in unison.

"You two were the first to find the body?"

They nodded again.

"Did you see anyone...besides the victim, I mean?"

"No, sir," one of them said. "When we went in, the room was empty." Then his voice cracked. "Except for the dead guy."

"Did you touch anything—either of you?" Dawson asked.

"No, no, we didn't touch nothin', we swear. We just ran outside and told some guy to call the cops."

Dawson paused. There was no use proceeding with this line of questioning right now. Other than the fact that they'd been in the wrong place at the wrong time, he doubted if they knew anything that would help.

"Ramsey, get their names and addresses. Follow me inside when you're done."

Ramsey nodded and set to his task as Dawson went back into the bathroom.

Fred True, the medical examiner, was just finishing his examination as Dawson entered. But when Dawson looked at the body, he blanked on all the questions he'd been planning to ask

"Holy shit," he muttered.

True looked up. "Friend of yours?"

"We just ran a make on him."

"So did someone else," True said, then ripped off his surgical gloves and tossed them in a bag.

"How long before you're through here?" Dawson asked.

"I'm done," True said, turning to his assistant. "Bag him and tag him, Sonny. Dawson here just made our job a little easier. He's got an ID."

Dawson looked down at the body one last time. "Law. His name is Simon Law."

Ramsey walked up in time to hear what Dawson said. "You're kidding me," he muttered, looking over Dawson's shoulder to the man below.

Dawson turned. "Nope. Our missing renter— slash—thief seems to have a hard time making friends." He clapped Ramsey on the shoulder. "Let's go. I'm curious to see what comes up on his files."

A short while later, they were back at their desks.

"Anything come down from records yet?" Ramsey asked.

Dawson was still sifting through the papers on his desk.

"Nothing I can see... Oh, wait! Here it is."

He shed his topcoat and flopped down in his chair as Ramsey got up.

"You going after coffee?" Dawson asked.

Ramsey nodded.

Dawson handed him the mug from his desk. "Bring me a cup, too, will you?"

"Will you have a Danish with that?" Ramsey quipped.

Dawson didn't bother to look up. "Just shut up and do as you're told," he muttered.

Ramsey grinned as he walked away. He was all the way across the room when he heard Dawson curse.

"What?"

Dawson held up the paper.

"Law. His last arrest was for running numbers in L.A."

"So how much time did he do?" Ramsey asked as he set the coffee down on Dawson's desk.

"None," Dawson said.

Ramsey frowned. "Why not?"

"Frederick Mancusco was his lawyer, that's why."

Ramsey shrugged. "I don't get it."

"Mancusco is a mob lawyer. Allejandro's lawyer, to be exact. Pharaoh Carn works for Allejandro, and Simon Law had just taken up temporary residence across the street from the LeGrand home, and, according to Francesca, Pharaoh Carn is the man who snatched her and—''

"Okay, okay. I get the drift," Ramsey said. "So what are we going to do with this information?"

Before Dawson could answer, his phone rang. He answered absently, his mind still on the report in his hand. "This is Dawson."

"Detective, it's me, Clay. I have some information for you."

Dawson dropped the report, wrote Clay's name on a piece of paper and shoved it toward Ramsey.

Ramsey nodded, then picked up the report Dawson had been reading.

"What's up?" Dawson asked.

"We just got a call from Addie Bell. Remember her, the administrator at the orphanage where Frankie grew up?"

"Yes, I do. Nice woman," Dawson said. "Seemed real upset about what had happened to your wife."

"Yes, well, she just called with another little tidbit of information that Frankie and I thought was real interesting."

Dawson leaned forward. He could tell by the tone of Clay LeGrand's voice that he was excited about something. "I'm listening," he said.

"Addie Bell said that one of the times Pharaoh Carn got in trouble when he was still at the home was for slipping out one night and getting a tattoo.''

Dawson's pulse leaped. Even before Clay finished, he knew what he was going to say.

"I don't suppose she remembers what it looked like?" Dawson asked.

"Yes, actually, she did. Said it looked like a cross, except for the loop on top. She also said she thought it was in color. Maybe yellow."

Dawson started to grin. "Just like the one on the back of your wife's neck."

"Now do you have enough to go after Carn?"

Dawson's grin widened. "Oh yeah. I'd say that if that tattoo still exists anywhere on Carn's body, his vanity will be his undoing."

Clay sighed. "Thank God. Now maybe we will be able to put this thing behind us."

Dawson's grin faded. "Don't get too excited. We've got to find him first. Pharaoh Carn has resources beyond your everyday, run-of-the-mill thug."

"I don't care what he has," Clay growled. "As long as it's not my wife."

It took two more days for the wheels of justice to begin to turn, but when they did, they went downhill fast.

Duke Needham burst into Pharaoh's office on the run.

"Boss, I just got a call from a buddy in L.A. He said the L.A.P.D. has a warrant out for your arrest, and they're turning the city upside down."

Pharaoh dropped the pen in his hand and stood abruptly. Francesca! He'd waited too long.

"Son of a bitch."

"What do you want me to do?"

Pharaoh strode from behind his desk and headed for the window overlooking the front of the estate. The day was clear but cold. In the valley below, he could see the ribbon of traffic along the strip and the ever-flashing lights of the casinos. Everything looked normal, although he was the first to admit that looks could be deceiving. He thrust his hand in his pocket, worrying the rabbit's foot as his mind began to race. Suddenly he pivoted.

"Have one of the maids pack a bag. No more than a couple of changes, and all for the tropics. I can always buy more clothes when we get to where we're going."

"Where are we going?" Duke asked.

A muscle jerked in Pharaoh's jaw. "Allejandro has been trying to get me down in South America for months. I've just decided to take him up on the offer."

"Yes, sir," Duke said. "I'll have the chopper sent in."

"Tell the pilot to chart a course for Denver first."

Duke inhaled sharply. This obsession the boss had with that woman was going to be the ruin of them yet.

"Considering what we've just learned, do you think it's safe?" he asked.

Pharaoh took a sharp breath, then his voice lowered ominously. "Don't question my decisions. Don't question my authority. Get the hell out of my sight and do as you're told."

Duke had one moment of remembering Stykowski's blood splattering all over his face and jacket and bolted for the door.

As soon as he was gone, Pharaoh picked up the phone. This move would open the door on a whole new life for him, but there was another door he needed to close first. The door on Francesca's past. He punched in the numbers, then sat down on the edge of his desk, waiting for the call to go through. Moments later, the smooth, baritone voice of Pepe Allejandro vibrated in his ear. Pharaoh took a deep breath and tried for a positive approach.

"*Patrón!* This is Pharaoh."

"Pharaoh, my friend, I have been expecting your call. You are in serious trouble, I think."

Pharaoh winced. The tone of Allejandro's voice made him nervous.

"No, Pepe, I have the situation under control."

"What are you going to do about this?" Allejandro asked.

"I'm making plans accordingly. I've decided to take you up on the Colombia deal, but first, I have a favor to ask."

"I'm listening," Allejandro said.

"There's a thing I must do before I can go. I want to—"

"I know what you want," Allejandro snapped. "It is that woman again. She's the reason you are in this mess. I must tell you, Pharaoh, that I do not like my men bringing personal concerns into the business, so you listen to me! You get out of Nevada today. Head straight for the border. Miguel will have a plane waiting for you in Tijuana. From there, you will be flown to South America. We will have no further contact until you are at the estate."

"But, Pepe, you don't understand. This woman is my luck. Without her I—"

Pepe Allejandro's baritone deepened warningly. "No, Pharaoh. You are the one who does not understand. These are my orders." There was a moment of silence, then Allejandro added, "Do *you* understand?"

Pharaoh tensed. He knew all too well the consequences of disobeying Allejandro's orders, but he left his answer vague.

"When I get to Tijuana, I will call Miguel."

"That is what I wanted to hear," Allejandro said, then abruptly disconnected, leaving Pharaoh with no misconceptions as to how pissed the man was.

His belly rolled at the thought of what he was about to do. But he wasn't leaving the country without Francesca. When he had her again, he would find a way to make her come around to his way of thinking. He wouldn't accept that she hated him, as she'd so often claimed during the past two years.

When she was small, he'd been her best friend—the family she no longer had. All he needed to do was get rid of her husband and it would happen again.

He ignored his conscience as he hurried up to his room to oversee his packing. Allejandro would not like what he was about to do, but if he pulled it off, it would be okay. Pharaoh kept telling himself there was no way Francesca would be expecting him to come back. Not with a warrant out for his arrest. Surprise would be his ace in the hole.

Soup bubbled in a pot at the back of the stove. The homey scent of baking corn bread wafted throughout the house as Frankie carried a load of clothes toward the utility room to wash. As she passed a window, she glanced outside. Clay was still shoveling snow off the backyard path that led to the alley where their garbage was picked up. Her favorite CD was playing in the background. She hummed along with it, every now and then letting her voice rise in accompaniment to a familiar verse in the song. Just as she was putting soap in the machine, the phone rang. She slammed the lid and punched the control, taking absent note that the water had begun filling as she ran to answer.

''Hello?''

Silence.

''Hello? Hello?''

A dial tone suddenly clicked in her ear.

She hung up and shrugged. Some people certainly needed a good dose of telephone manners. The least they could do was say sorry, they'd dialed the wrong number.

She moved toward the stove, gave the soup a quick stir, making sure nothing was sticking to the pot, then checked the corn bread. A few more minutes and it would be done.

She looked out the window again. Clay was nowhere in sight. She shrugged. He'd probably moved to the front walk. Partly out of curiosity, and partly from a need to know where he was, she went to the living room to look out. He was there, at the corner of the house, knocking icicles off the roof. She grinned to herself and started to wave, when suddenly the lights flickered, then went out.

She waited a moment, hoping they would come right back on, but when she heard the washing machine suddenly stop filling, she groaned. The food would finish cooking with no problem. The oven was gas-powered, but there would be soap caked all over the clothes. She darted toward the kitchen to check the breaker box just as a gray sedan turned the corner and started down the street. And because she did, she missed seeing it slowing, and then seeing it stop.

Shoveling snow was not one of Clay's favorite tasks, but as a native of Denver, it was something he'd certainly done all his life. By the time he had finished the back walk and moved toward the front, he was sweating beneath the layers of his clothing. Every time he exhaled, the warmth of his breath created a small white cloud of condensation.

The front walk loomed, snowpacked and appearing longer than its thirty or so feet to the curb. He swung at some icicles hanging from the eaves of the house as he passed, then watched them shatter and fall, only to be swallowed silently by the snow.

He moved a step to the right and took another swing at a fresh set of icicles. They tinkled like broken glass as the shovel connected, then flew through the air. Like the others, they disappeared into the snow's depths. He couldn't quit thinking that this time next year, there would be a baby in the house. The notion tugged at his heart. My God. A baby. Would it be a girl or a boy? Did it matter? Hardly. Not when the name of the father was more in question.

Then he shook off the thought. He'd told Frankie the truth when he said it wouldn't matter. He'd spent two years praying for a miracle to happen. As far as he was concerned, it had. And whether she had brought this baby with her, or they'd made it after her return, nothing could alter the fact that she was his life. What came from her could be nothing but pure, no matter what the circumstances of the conception.

His focus shifted from the icicles hanging from the roof to his reflection in the window before him. Suddenly he became aware of something else—the reflection of a car pulling up to the curb behind him.

He turned as two men were getting out. One was tall, with broad shoulders and a graying ponytail hanging down the back of his coat. He'd never seen him before, but the other man looked familiar. Clay frowned. Where had he seen—*oh Jesus.*

He grunted, like a man who'd been kicked in the gut, and bolted for the house, yelling Frankie's name. The shot was little more than a pop, but it hit him in the back, shoulder high, spinning him around and dropping him in his tracks. He disappeared from sight, hidden by the snow, like the icicles he'd knocked from the roof.

Duke paused above Clay's inert body. "Do you want I should—"

"Leave him," Pharaoh snapped as they made their way up the walk through the unshoveled snow. "We're not going to be here long enough for it to matter."

Duke glanced nervously over his shoulder. The neighborhood looked deserted, just as it had before, but in a place like this, you could never tell for sure if they'd been unobserved. He kept thinking, damn Pharaoh to hell for pulling this off in broad daylight, but all he managed was a frown as he pulled his collar up around his ears and headed for the front door. He started to knock, when Pharaoh grabbed his hand.

"No," Pharaoh said.

"But, boss, they got a security system," Duke said, pointing at the sticker on a nearby window.

"It won't be on, and the door won't be locked. Not when Mr. Fix-It was outside shoveling snow."

Duke glanced at the man Pharaoh had just shot and then reached for the knob. As Pharaoh had predicted, it turned without a hitch.

The scent of baking bread hit him face first. Pharaoh took a deep breath, and then reality surfaced as his heart skipped an anticipatory beat. Within seconds, they would be together again. And this time, it would be forever.

"Got the stuff?" he asked.

Duke slipped his hand in his pocket, fingering the loaded syringe.

"Yes, sir."

"Then let's get this over with," Pharaoh muttered. "I've got a date with a chopper down in Tijuana, and I don't like to keep my dates waiting."

Frankie was halfway to the kitchen when she heard Clay shouting her name. She stopped and then turned, and in that moment, something skittered across her mind like a passing ghost. As she stood, a memory came flooding back—of being in this very place and hearing the click of the latch as the front door opened, then hearing footsteps coming across the living-room floor and thinking it was Clay.

Only it hadn't been Clay.

Her heart began to pound, and her hands began
to sweat.

"Clay?"

No one answered.

"Clay?"

The silence was deadly.

Panic hit with the force of a blow to the gut,
and it was all she could do to make herself move.
Without giving herself time to think, she darted out
of the kitchen and down the hall toward the bedroom, as fast as she could go.

Seconds later, she was yanking open the drawer
to the nightstand and pulling out her gun. One
quick look told her it was loaded. She moved to
the window. The front end of a dark gray sedan
was just visible. And then a bright bit of color in
the snow caught her eye. She looked closer, squinting to see between the shards of frost covering the
glass. A low moan slid out from between her lips
as she realized she was looking at Clay's coat—
and Clay's hand—in the snow.

Stifling a sob, she made a run for the phone.
With shaking fingers, she dialed 911. Just as the
dispatcher came on the line, she heard the front
door opening.

"Help, I need help," she whispered. "Tell Detective Dawson that this is Francesca LeGrand.

Tell him that I think they've come back for me again.''

"Ma'am. Ma'am. What is your emergency?" the dispatcher asked.

Frankie stifled a moan. "I think my husband has been shot and the people who did it are coming in my house. I've got to go. They're going to find me," Frankie whispered, and started to hang up the phone.

"Ma'am, don't hang up," the dispatcher said. "I've got help on the way."

"You don't understand," Frankie said. "I can't let them find me again. Tell Detective Avery Dawson. He'll know."

She laid the phone down and slipped to the door, all but holding her breath as she listened to the footsteps moving through the house. Suddenly the lights began to flicker as the power came on. The sudden whoosh of water as the washing machine began to fill sounded loud in the silence of the house. She heard something hit the floor with a crash, then the sound of muffled curses.

With one backward glance, she slipped out of the bedroom and into the hall. The last thing she wanted was to get trapped inside the house with the intruders. Clenching the gun with both hands, she began to move.

Seventeen

Clay opened his eyes to find himself staring straight up at the sky. There was a fire in his back that even the snow couldn't put out, and he struggled to remember why he would hurt.

Memory hit, like a fist to the gut. He had no way of knowing how long he'd been lying here, but the last thing he remembered was seeing Pharaoh's face and shouting Frankie's name. Had she heard? Did she have time to get away? Or, dear God, did he take her? Was she already gone?

A deep groan slid out from between his clenched teeth as he rolled onto his side, then up on hands and knees. It was only after he looked down at where he'd been lying that he saw all the blood.

That was when he knew he'd been shot. The thought of Frankie and their baby at the mercy of a man like Pharaoh Carn was enough to get him past the nausea that pushed up his throat.

God…help me. Gritting his teeth, he grabbed a clump of a nearby hedge and pulled himself up.

* * *

Frankie moved silently down the hall with her back against the wall. Her hands were steady, her focus clear. All the hours she'd spent at target practice came back to her in a rush. Breathe in. Breathe out. Don't panic. And don't jerk the trigger.

It never occurred to her that she would not be able to shoot. She'd felt the kick of the gun in her hands too many times to get squeamish now. Not when she knew Clay was stretched out in the snow only a few feet beyond these walls.

The low, urgent undertones of men's voice came from somewhere off to her left. They were in the utility room. Obviously, when they'd heard the washing machine come on, they'd thought that she was there.

She paused, her heart pounding. There was a sudden metallic taste in her mouth. Fear.

Her resolve deepened even further. There was no way she would let herself be taken again. The boy who'd been her friend had turned into a devil.

Then she heard a soft chuckle, and her heart skipped a beat. With the sound came a flood of childhood memories, coupled with two years of hell.

Of dark eyes and a smiling face.

Of gentle hands braiding her hair.

Of tying her shoes and pushing her high—so high—in the schoolyard swings.

Of hugs and toys and extra pieces of candy that the other kids didn't have.

Of locked doors and barred windows, of opulence and neglect.

Of knowing that there was no escape from a man with this kind of power.

Then of running without looking back.

"Francesca...I know you're in here."

She shuddered as the images faded. Panic shafted. The front door was too far away. All she could do was pray that the 911 dispatcher would send her some help before it was too late. Gathering her courage, she aimed her gun at the doorway leading into the kitchen.

Avery Dawson was at a stoplight when his cell phone rang. He answered, a bit surprised to hear the downtown dispatcher's voice.

"Detective Dawson, we have a message for you that we didn't want to broadcast. A woman called 911 a few minutes ago, identifying herself as Francesca LeGrand. She said to tell you that her husband had been shot and that the people had come back to get her."

Oh damn. "Have officers and an ambulance already been dispatched to the residence?" he asked.

"Yes, sir. About two minutes ago."

"Send backup, as well," he ordered. "And tell Emergency Services that we're on the way."

He ended the call, then tossed the phone on the seat.

"Francesca LeGrand just made a call to 911. Clay's been shot and, according to the dispatcher, at the time of the call, intruders were in the house."

Ramsey slapped the light on the dash and hit the strobe as Dawson hit the siren.

Dawson made a U-turn at the intersection and headed back the way they'd come. His gut was in knots at the thought of what was going on at that house. After all the city of Denver had put Clay LeGrand through, he couldn't be dead.

Ramsey checked his revolver, then slid it back in his shoulder holster as Dawson skidded around a corner.

"Careful, buddy," Ramsey said. "There are still some patches of ice on the streets."

But Dawson just kept on driving without slowing down. Ice be damned. The system had let this couple down once before. He wouldn't let it happen again.

The silhouettes of two men suddenly appeared, framing the arched doorway leading into Frankie's kitchen. She slid a few feet to her right and shifted her stance, taking care to stay between them and the front door. She took a deep breath, focusing first on the man with the gun. He was familiar, right down to his size 52 shoulders and the graying ponytail that hung down his back.

Duke Needham, Pharaoh's second in command.

After a moment of hesitation, she kept her gun aimed on him.

When Pharaoh saw her, his heart skipped a beat. So beautiful. But then his gaze slid from her face to the gun in her hand. He frowned. This was something he hadn't expected. He took a step forward, and she instantly shifted her stance, aiming the gun at him instead. He paused in shock. The look on her face seemed so...

He shuddered. For lack of another word, all he could think was that her expression was deadly. He tried smiling, speaking to her in a soft, chiding voice, as a father would to a child.

"Francesca...what are you doing? Put down that gun."

Her gaze never wavered, but she didn't respond.

A skitter of nerves momentarily shook his concentration.

"Come on, Francesca, you can't shoot me. Remember me? I'm the one who held you when you cried. I taught you to tie your shoelaces. I braided your hair and read stories to you when you were sick. I love you, Francesca. You belong to me.''

Frankie's eyes began to tear. ''I trusted you... once. But look what you did. You took me from my home...from my husband. You stole two years of my life and my innocence. That's not love. That's obsession.''

She inhaled a shaky breath as Duke suddenly separated himself from Pharaoh.

''Don't move!'' she screamed, and took deadly aim at Duke Needham's head again.

Duke froze. With less than twenty feet between them, being a good shot was immaterial to the fact that, at this range, she could hardly miss.

Pharaoh took a deep breath. This was more complicated than he'd imagined. He held out his hand and took a step forward. At the motion, Frankie's aim once again shifted to him. As it did, Duke made a lunge toward her.

Before Pharaoh could blink, Frankie squeezed off two shots in rapid succession. Duke's legs buckled, first his right, then his left, as the bullets entered and exited his knees, shattering bone and muscle. The gun he was holding went sliding across the floor. Frankie kicked it out of the way as she held her aim.

Duke's agonized screams suddenly filled the room, making coherent speech impossible. Stunned,

Pharaoh could only stare in disbelief at what Francesca had done to his man. There was no fear on her face, only fury. He thought of her husband, lying dead in the snow, and it occurred to him then that his own life might be at stake.

"Francesca, don't," he said, holding his hands out to his sides to show he held no weapons. "I would never hurt you," he said.

Duke's screams had shut down to low moans. In the far distance, Frankie thought she could hear the faint sound of sirens, but she couldn't be sure.

The blood...it was everywhere.

No one had warned her about blood when she'd bought the damned gun.

"Francesca...listen to me," Pharaoh said as he took a step toward her.

She tightened her grip and took a couple of steps backward toward the door.

"You raped me, you son of a bitch!"

Pharaoh froze, horrified by what she'd just said. "Never."

"You did! You did! I remember the weight of your body, holding me down. I saw the look in your eyes. I knew, Pharaoh, I knew!"

Pharaoh groaned. "No, Francesca, no. I never touched you that way. Only once did I...did we...but you cried." He drew a deep, shaky breath. "I stopped when you cried."

"I don't believe you," she muttered. Frankie swayed. Her endurance was waning. "Two years you kept me locked in that cage of a room."

"I gave you everything," he argued "The best clothes, the best food, the best of everything."

"Without free will, there is nothing," Frankie said.

Pharaoh's expression began to crumble. He, too, could hear the approaching sirens. He was torn between wanting to make things right and the need to escape while he still had time.

His life flashed before his eyes. As a child, always being the last one picked in a game. Of never belonging, never knowing the feel of being loved—always fighting to stay alive.

And then Francesca.

He shuddered, cursing himself for the weakness that loving someone could bring. He thought of Allejandro and of Colombia, and of the wealth and power that awaited him there. With a heartfelt sigh, he swiftly reached into his pocket and pulled out a gun, aiming it straight at Francesca's chest.

Frankie gasped and took a quick step back. But the bore of the barrel followed her movements.

"You can shoot," she said, "but so will I. At worst, we'll both die. At best, we'll both be wounded. Either way, you won't get away. You're caught, Pharaoh. It's over. Let it go. Let *me* go."

He shook his head, like a wounded animal trying to stay on four legs.

"But you don't understand. You are my love... and my luck. Without you, it's over anyway."

"Then so be it," Frankie said, and took aim.

Suddenly the front door crashed inward, slamming against the inside wall. Clay's voice was faint and breathless as he stumbled between Frankie and the barrel of Pharaoh's gun.

"Don't!" Clay groaned. "For God's sake, don't shoot her. She's going to have a baby."

Frankie screamed. The back of Clay's coat was covered in blood.

The gun in Pharaoh's hands wavered, as did his voice. "Baby?"

Clay slid to his knees, then onto all fours. "Please," he begged. "Just don't hurt her."

Frankie dropped the gun as she went down beside him. Her hands were on his face, then his back, then his face again, trying to stanch the flow of blood.

"Don't you die on me, Clay LeGrand. Dear God in heaven, don't die."

Clay groaned as he slumped on his side. From where he was lying, he could see the shock on Pharaoh Carn's face.

Frankie bolted to her feet and started out of the

room to get something to stem the flow of Clay's blood.

"Stop!" Pharaoh shouted, and instinctively tracked her movements with his gun.

Frankie paused, her expression set with determination.

"Either shoot me or get the hell out of my life," she shouted. Then she pointed to the man on the floor. "He's who I love. When I lost my memory, I didn't forget him. I forgot you."

Sirens were louder. Pharaoh knew it was only a matter of moments now. His finger twitched on the trigger. He had everything he'd ever wanted in life.

Power.

Money.

Respect.

And then he sighed.

Everything except her.

He looked at her belly. Within months, it would be round with child. Another man's child. He tried to feel rage. It wouldn't come.

His voice was sharp, even bitter with recrimination. "You're giving him a child."

It was at that moment that Frankie realized Pharaoh's indignation was real. If he felt cheated—if he felt anger—then that meant the baby she was carrying could not be his. So he'd been telling the truth all along. He hadn't raped her. Relief flooded her.

"I would always have stayed your friend," she whispered.

Pharaoh's arms suddenly went limp. "You mean...if I—"

"Remember that day...two years ago...when you came into my house?"

Pharaoh blinked.

"All you had to do was just say hello."

Pharaoh groaned. For the first time in as long as he could remember, he felt a need to cry.

He shuddered. "I didn't rape you."

In that moment, Francesca's heart broke—for the boy that he'd been and for the man that he'd become, for the friendship she'd lost, and for the horror she'd endured at his hands.

She looked down at Clay and then back at Pharaoh. There were tears in her eyes as she pleaded for his life.

"Please...let me help my husband. I couldn't bear life without him."

A bitter smile twisted the corners of Pharaoh's lips.

"Yeah, I know what you mean," he said softly, and then made a run for the door.

Avery Dawson knew a shortcut. He was half a block ahead of the ambulance when he came to a skidding halt in front of the LeGrand house. An unfamiliar dark gray sedan was still parked at the curb. He pulled his revolver as he exited the car.

"Take the back," he told Ramsey. "I'll take the front."

"Hadn't we better wait for backup?" Ramsey asked.

"Hell no," Dawson muttered. "It may already be too late."

He ran toward the side of the house, taking cover behind a bush, then a tree, moving ever closer to the blood-smeared door standing ajar. His heart was racing, his mind sorting through scenarios he didn't want to accept. All he could think was, please, God, don't let these people be dead.

Moving in a crouched position, he stepped out from behind the tree just as a man burst out the front door. He took one look at the face, and then the gun in his hand, and took aim and shouted.

"Police! Drop your gun. We have you surrounded."

Pharaoh Carn spun. He knew before he pulled the trigger that it was going to be a case of too little, too late. The first bullet hit him shoulder high. His shot went off in the air, and he felt numb before he felt pain. The gun he was holding dropped out of his hand and into the snow. He looked down in disbelief. Not realizing what his actions would imply, he reached inside his coat toward the warm, wet stream running down his chest.

Dawson saw him reach into his coat and reacted accordingly.

The second bullet plowed through Pharaoh, ripping everything vital and leaving him with only seconds of thought. Behind him, he heard Francesca's scream. He turned, his arm outflung toward the sound of her voice. And then everything changed to slow motion.

The cop was coming toward him, shouting something he couldn't hear.

Sunshine began to dim.

The rhythm of his heartbeat thundered in his ears as the earth began to shift.

He felt himself falling...falling.

Heard his heart beating slower and slower.

Images flashed through his mind.

Francesca at four, holding that blanket and sucking her thumb.

Francesca at eight, laughing as he pushed her high in the swing.

Francesca at ten, handing him a ribbon to tie in her hair.

Francesca...

Francesca.

The snow enveloped him like a blanket as the cold arms of death softened his fall.

As the gunshots erupted, Frankie had screamed, then thrown herself over Clay's unconscious body. Afterward, the silence was worse than the noise. The sound of running footsteps coming up on the front porch sent her into a panic. She grabbed the gun she'd dropped earlier and took aim, putting herself between Clay and the noise.

And that was the way Dawson and Ramsey saw her, blood-smeared and tensed, with her gun aimed waist high at the first person to come into her sights.

"Police! Police!" they both shouted at once.

Dawson rushed to her side as Ramsey yelled, gun still drawn.

"Frankie, are there any more of them inside the house?"

She pointed at Duke Needham's unconscious body on the floor near the opposite wall.

"Only him." Then she started to shake.

Ramsey spun, took one look at Duke Needham's wounds and eyed Frankie with newfound respect.

"Whoa...you got him where it counted, didn't you?"

She laid the gun on the floor and took Clay's head in her lap. Her clothes were smeared, her hands covered in blood—his blood.

"Help him. He's been shot."

Dawson waved to Ramsey. "Tell EMS the location is secure." He glanced at Needham. "And if another ambulance hasn't already been dispatched, get one rolling."

Ramsey bolted for the front door as Dawson searched for a pulse in Clay's neck.

"He's still with us." He gave Frankie's arm a quick squeeze. "You did good, but you have to hang in there a little while longer. With a woman like you to live for, you can bet your last dollar this man will pull through."

Then he moved to Needham, checking his condition and retrieving the gun that he'd dropped when he fell. Seconds later, paramedics came through the door and Frankie was moved aside. Dawson took her by the elbow and helped her to a nearby chair.

"Is there someone we can call?"

Her teeth were chattering, and she couldn't stop shaking.

"Clay's parents. They need to know." Suddenly she covered her face with her hands. "Oh, God. If anything happens to Clay because of me..."

Dawson made her face him.

"Whatever happens to your husband is Pharaoh Carn's fault, not yours. We are not responsible for the actions of others, only our own."

She shuddered, then reached for the phone, frowning as she held it to her ear. The lack of a dial tone puzzled her, until she remembered.

"I left the phone off the hook in my bedroom."

"Just sit," he ordered. "I'll hang it up."

Before he got back, they were already loading Clay onto a stretcher and readying him for transport to a trauma center. Frankie stood, and moved to Clay's side, touching his cheek, then his hair.

"Don't you die, Clay LeGrand. It took me two years to get home, so don't you dare die."

Dawson moved her aside as the paramedics rolled him from the room.

"Your phone is working now," he said gently. "Why don't you call Clay's parents? After that, maybe you'd like to clean up a bit before I take you to the hospital?"

Frankie looked down at her clothes and at the blood drying on her hands. She stared at him in disbelief.

"It's over...isn't it, Detective?"

He started to nod, and then something made him hug her instead.

She hesitated at first, and as his arms enfolded her, she began to go limp. If he hadn't been holding her, she would have gone to her knees. She laid her cheek against the wool of his coat.

"Help me."

Empathy twisted a knot in Dawson's belly. "I won't leave you alone. I promise. I won't leave you alone."

Ramsey came running back into the house.

"The other ambulance is on its way." He sniffed the air. "Hey, do I smell something burning?"

Frankie shrugged away from the detective's grasp.

"Our supper. I think I've just burned our supper."

Epilogue

Spring had been a long time coming to Denver. The winter had been a test of Frankie's endurance. The week Clay had spent in the hospital, hovering between life and death, and then the ensuing month of his recovery, had been the longest of her life. Only the fact that she was carrying new life had kept her sane and focused on taking care of herself, trusting the doctors to take care of Clay.

Christmas came and went before Clay was released, and on the day he came home from the hospital, it had been all she could do to walk back into their house. Old memories—bad memories—hung heavy in the air, like the scent of a sickly-sweet perfume. Clay had seen it almost immediately.

As the days passed, Frankie's mood didn't ease. She moved through each day like a robot, jumping at sudden noises, waking in the middle of the night screaming out Clay's name.

He held her and loved her and reassured her all

that he could. But the fact still remained that one man had died on the steps of their house and Clay's blood wouldn't come out of the rug on their floor.

Then, one morning, he woke with a plan. Frankie's morning sickness had thankfully passed, and she was in the kitchen preparing breakfast when Clay entered.

"Good morning, sweetheart." He slipped a kiss behind Frankie's right ear near the ankh tattoo.

She paused, then turned. "Good morning," she said, and returned the kiss on his lips.

After trading a groan and a sigh, Clay tore himself free, grinning at the blush on her cheeks.

"You better be careful," he warned, patting the flat of her tummy. "That kind of greeting will get you in trouble."

Frankie caught her hand and pressed it tighter against her belly. "I'm already in trouble," she said. "It just doesn't show."

He laughed. "But it will, and soon."

She sighed and tucked a strand of hair behind her ear, then absently rubbed at the spot that he'd kissed.

"Does this bother you?" she asked.

Clay was pouring himself a cup of coffee. He turned the pot in one hand, his cup in the other. "Does what bother me, Frankie?"

"The tattoo."

He frowned. How could he help her let go of bad memories when she was constantly reminded of her ordeal?

"Hell no," he muttered. "Why should it?"

She shrugged, then looked away. "I don't know. I just thought that maybe...I mean, sometimes you might feel..."

"You know, Francesca, over the months, I've come to consider it sort of sexy."

It was the last thing she would have expected him to say.

"But—"

"No, hear me out," he said, setting down the coffee and his cup. He lifted her hair, twirling it around his fingers until the small ankh was bared to his sight. "There it is, hiding beneath all this thick hair, tucked in behind this pretty little ear, just waiting for me to taste it. Sometimes, when I'm at work, I think about that little tattoo and smile, knowing that it marks a spot I particularly love to kiss."

Frankie's mouth dropped. "Why, Clay, I never knew you were such a poet!"

He wiggled his eyebrows in mock dismay. "Francesca, my love, there are many things you don't know about me, not the least of which are the hidden talents I possess."

She snorted beneath her breath. "What hidden talents?"

He wiggled a finger beneath her nose, then leered. "I'll teach you to make fun of me. You just wait until tonight, pretty lady. I'll show you hidden."

Frankie's morose mood lifted, as Clay had known that it would. And even after he was on his way to work, he kept thinking about what he'd said. It was true. That tattoo no longer represented a mark another man had put on his wife. Like the baby growing inside her, it was just something added to a woman he already loved. But it wasn't until the men were on their first break that he had time to act upon his idea. He glanced at his watch, calculating the time it would take to act on his plan against how much of the day was left. Before he could change his mind, he put the foreman in charge and headed to a little place he knew on the far side of the city.

It was just after six in the evening when he pulled into the driveway and parked. A small package lay on the seat beside him, along with a dozen red roses and a six-pack of Coke. Since the onset of her pregnancy, anything alcoholic was strictly forbidden, but a toast tonight would be in order.

He slid out of the seat, wincing slightly as he

gathered up the flowers, package and Coke. He hurried toward the front of the house with a smile on his face. It widened considerably when Frankie met him at the door.

"Welcome home. I missed you," she said.

Clay handed her the flowers.

"For me? What's the occasion?"

"You'll see," he growled, then leaned down for the kiss she offered.

"Mmm...what do I taste?"

"Me," she said.

"Yeah, you and something orange."

She grinned. "That's for me to know and you to find out."

She eyed the package he was holding. "What's that?"

He returned the grin. "That's for me to know and you to find out."

She laughed and waved the roses under his nose. "I'm going to put these in water. When you're through playing games, come to dinner. It's done."

He handed her the six-pack of Coke. "I'll be right there. Just give me a couple of minutes to wash up and change."

She was putting out the last of the food when he came to the table. He set the package on her plate, then took the bowl she was carrying and set it on the table for her.

"Can I help?" he asked.

"With the dishes," she quipped.

He groaned, but both of them knew he would do them, just as he did every night after they ate.

Clay pulled her chair out from the table, then waited for her to sit down.

"My, but we're being awfully formal tonight," Frankie said, smiling as he scooted her, chair and all, toward the table.

He arched an eyebrow but refrained from speech, waiting instead for her reaction to what he'd put on her plate.

"I take it I'm to open this before we eat?" Frankie said, tearing into the paper before he could answer.

Clay held his breath, watching her expressions changing from curiosity to recognition, then understanding. When she looked up, there were tears in her eyes.

"Oh, Clay, does this mean what I think it means?"

"Look on page 154. It's my favorite, although there are a couple of others that run a close second. Of course, the final decision is going to be yours. After all, once it's built, I plan on living in that house for the rest of our lives."

She set the book of house plans aside, got up from her seat and sat down in his lap.

"Aren't you even going to look at it?" he asked. "There might be other floor plans you like better."

"We'll look later, together," she said softly, and locked her fingers behind his neck. "But right now, I need to do this."

She leaned forward, capturing his smile with her lips and taking pure delight when he groaned.

"You are the best husband a woman could ever have," she said softly.

Clay cupped her face with his hands, tracing the shape of her lips with his thumbs.

"And you, Francesca, are one hell of a wife. You not only saved my life and yours, you saved the life of our child. This is a time of starting over for us, and I want it to be from the ground up. Barring any delays, we should be able to move into our new house by early summer. A new home for a new baby and a new life. What do you say?"

"That I love you?"

He pulled her close, nuzzling the curve of her neck and taking joy from the steady pulse he could feel beating there.

"That'll do for starters."

Frankie was lying in bed, reading the last pages of a book, when she heard Clay turn off the shower. Anxious to finish before they turned out the lights, she returned to the story, focusing intently on the mystery about to be revealed.

Just as she got to the next to the last page, Clay sauntered out of the bathroom stark naked. To say her attention wavered would not be a lie. But she bravely focused and turned the page, reading line after line as the last knots of the plot were tied.

He laid out a change of clothes for tomorrow, then sauntered back into the bathroom, again passing her line of vision.

Suddenly she gasped.

This time, regaining concentration was impossible. Half a page from the end, she tossed the book aside and bolted out of bed.

"Clay LeGrand! What have you done?"

He turned in the doorway, looking over his shoulder at the shock on her face. Innocence dripped as he spoke.

"I don't know what you're talking about," he asked.

She shoved him all the way inside the bathroom, where the light was brightest.

"Like hell you don't," she gasped, and turned his backside to the light.

There on his right side of his butt was a gold ankh tattoo, identical to the one behind her ear.

"What have you done?" she said, tracing it with the tip of her finger.

He winced. "Careful," he muttered. "The damned thing's still sore." He moved toward the full-length mirror on the bathroom door, turning first one way and then another for a better view of his rear. "But it's sort of sexy, don't you think?"

Frankie dropped onto the side of the tub and stared up at him in disbelief.

"Why?"

He wrapped a towel around his waist, then sat down on the closed lid of the commode until they were facing each other.

"Because every time I see you touch your tattoo, I see pain on your face. So...I thought giving you a different connection to the damned thing might be a good idea. From now on, every time you see your tattoo, you'll remember me...only me."

Then he stood and turned, yanking off his towel to give her another clear view of his decorated behind.

"So, what do you think?"

For a moment, she couldn't think what to say. Finally she looked up. The uncertainty on his face nearly broke her heart. She shook her head in dismay.

"I think that you're crazy," she muttered.

He grinned. "Hell, Frankie, you knew that when

you married me. What do you think about my tattoo?''

He clenched and unclenched his butt muscles, making the tattoo move.

She arched an eyebrow. ''You think you're quite a stud, don't you?''

His grin widened as he began to strut back and forth, giving her the benefit of the way it moved with his body.

''You tell me,'' he said, and suddenly swooped, lifting her off the tub and into his arms.

''I'll let you know in the morning,'' she said softly as he laid her on the bed.

In the midst of their passion, her book fell to the floor. It would be another day before she learned how it ended, but she didn't have to wait to know how her own story went.

With Clay, it would be happily ever after.

If you enjoyed what you just read,
then we've got an offer you can't resist!

Take 2 bestselling love stories FREE!

Plus get a FREE surprise gift!

Clip this page and mail it to The Best of the Best™

IN U.S.A.	IN CANADA
3010 Walden Ave.	P.O. Box 609
P.O. Box 1867	Fort Erie, Ontario
Buffalo, N.Y. 14240-1867	L2A 5X3

YES! Please send me 2 free Best of the Best™ novels and my free surprise gift. Then send me 3 brand-new novels every month, which I will receive months before they're available in stores. In the U.S.A., bill me at the bargain price of $4.24 plus 25¢ delivery per book and applicable sales tax, if any*. In Canada, bill me at the bargain price of $4.74 plus 25¢ delivery per book and applicable taxes**. That's the complete price and a savings of over 10% off the cover prices—what a great deal! I understand that accepting the 2 free books and gift places me under no obligation ever to buy any books. I can always return a shipment and cancel at any time. Even if I never buy another book from The Best of the Best™, the 2 free books and gift are mine to keep forever. So why not take us up on our invitation. You'll be glad you did!

183 MEN CNFK
383 MEN CNFL

Name	(PLEASE PRINT)	
Address	Apt.#	
City	State/Prov.	Zip/Postal Code

* Terms and prices subject to change without notice. Sales tax applicable in N.Y.
** Canadian residents will be charged applicable provincial taxes and GST.
All orders subject to approval. Offer limited to one per household.
® are registered trademarks of Harlequin Enterprises Limited.

BOB99   ©1998 Harlequin Enterprises Limited

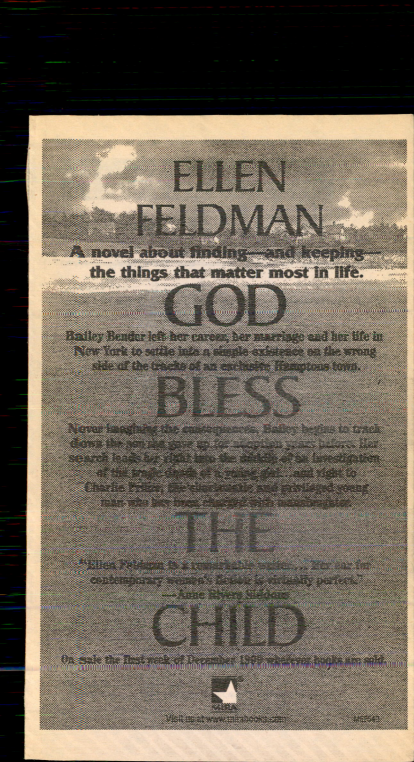

SHARON SALA

66487	REUNION	___ $5.99 U.S.	___ $6.99 CAN.
66416	SWEET BABY	___ $5.99 U.S.	___ $6.99 CAN.

(limited quantities available)

TOTAL AMOUNT	$_____
POSTAGE & HANDLING	$_____
($1.00 for one book; 50¢ for each additional)	
APPLICABLE TAXES*	$_____
TOTAL PAYABLE	$_____

(check or money order—please do not send cash)

To order, complete this form and send it, along with a check or money order for the total above, payable to MIRA Books®, to: **In the U.S.:** 3010 Walden Avenue, P.O. Box 9077, Buffalo, NY 14269-9077; **In Canada:** P.O. Box 636, Fort Erie, Ontario, L2A 5X3.

Name:_____

Address:_____ City:_____

State/Prov.:_____ Zip/Postal Code:_____

Account Number (if applicable):_____
075 CSAS

*New York residents remit applicable sales taxes.
  Canadian residents remit applicable GST and provincial taxes.

MIRA